Oh Great, Now I Can Hear Dead People

Oh Great, Now I Can Hear Dead People

Deborah Durbin

Winchester, UK
Washington, USA

First published by Soul Rocks Books, 2012
Soul Rocks Books is an imprint of John Hunt Publishing Ltd., Laurel House, Station Approach,
Alresford, Hants, SO24 9JH, UK
office1@jhpbooks.net
www.johnhuntpublishing.com
www.soulrocks-books.com

For distributor details and how to order please visit the 'Ordering' section on our website.

Text copyright: Deborah Durbin 2011

ISBN: 978 1 78099 482 6

This novel is entirely a work of fiction. The names, characters and incidents portrayed in it are
the work of the author's imagination. Any resemblance to actual persons, living or dead, events
or locations is entirely coincidental.

A CIP catalogue record for this book is available from the British Library.

Design: Stuart Davies

Printed in the USA by Edwards Brothers Malloy

This book is dedicated to my three beautiful and talented daughters, Becky, Georgia and Holly.

Acknowledgements

I would like to thank (and in no particular order) my three beautiful daughters for their patience while writing this book – we won't be living off microwavable meals for much longer, girls! To my wonderful husband who listens to me go on and on about publishing statistics. To my lovely mum who is a constant support and always there whenever I need her. To my sister and brothers who give me oodles of support. To all my friends for encouraging me and telling me I'm fabulous and finally to my dad: although you're not here in person, I know you're always around me and your catch phrase, 'You don't ask, you don't get' is my daily mantra.

Thank you to everyone at Soul Rocks and John Hunt Publishing for all your hard work and making this dream come true.

CHAPTER ONE

They say everyone has a sixth sense. Maybe they do. This is something I occasionally contemplate when I'm lying awake at night, contemplating things, as you do. They also say that if you work hard and get a good education you will go far in life. So naturally you would think, that when you had dedicated three years of your life to studying cognitive functioning and bipolar disorders, you would be able to walk straight into a fantastic job as a psychologist, wouldn't you? Not so. Well not in my case anyway, which is why I am spending my days sitting in my pyjamas, watching day-time TV and considering the prospect that I might actually be unemployable. What do they know, anyway?

Allow me to introduce myself: Samantha Ball, 26 years of age, psychology graduate, unemployed, currently £22,262 in debt, and if I'm not careful quite possibly soon to be homeless if I don't scrape together this month's rent.

Having spent my first two years at university learning all about abnormal and, quite frankly, rather disturbing human behaviour, I decided for my third year to specialise in lachanophobia (that's the fear of vegetables to you and me). The reason for this was that, despite the fact that statistically fewer than 3 percent of the world's population suffer from this bizarre phobia, I really did think it was an interesting subject. I had also developed a bit of a crush on Professor John Summers, the course tutor, and my head was bypassed by my heart, despite the fact that it turned out he had a Greek boyfriend called Darius.

Anyway, result being I came out of college with a degree in psychology, specialising in lachanophobia and for a while I actually believed that the world was my Savoy cabbage. I soon realised, however, that there isn't actually much of a market for terrified veggie-phobics and that wherever they were they were well and truly staying in their closets. Still, it could be worse, I could have chosen to specialise in consecotaleophophobia (that's the fear of chop-sticks to you and me).

Had I realised that a year on I would be unemployed and trying to explain to people that I was a qualified shrink for veg-fearing folk, I would have done what my best friend Amy did and dropped out of college in the first year in favour of a job at a fast-food restaurant. Amy did just this, and three years on she is now an area manager, earning £50,000 a year and eating as many French fries as a girl could possibly wish for.

It seemed Amy got it right; she never attended lectures, and would think nothing of spending her entire student grant on a pair of pretty Jimmy Choos and hang the fact that she had nothing left over to last the rest of the year. I kept a study plan, for God's sake, which I hasten to add, I followed religiously for three years. I gave up my weekends so that I could cram in another 16 hours of neuroanatomy and studied the peripheral nervous system like no other. And what did I come out with? A degree, a mountain of debt, and an apartment that comes complete with its own mushroom farm. Amy on the other hand is currently sunning it up on her third holiday this year in the Maldives!

So, here I am, sitting in my dressing gown, with my cat Missy on my lap, watching repeats of the *Big Brother* eviction and wondering whether I am eccentric enough to apply for next year's auditions. Or maybe I could apply to be one of their psychologists. I could be the one who makes sure the housemates don't have a problem with cabbages, or if they do, then who better to cure them than me?

The phone rings: it's my mother.

'Hi, Mum,' I say, trying to sound cheerful.

'No luck then, love?' she says, referring to my latest attempt to secure employment, pay my rent and maintain my dignity.

My mother knows only too well what the answer is going to

be. She rings me at least once a day in anticipation that I will suddenly say, 'You'll never guess what, Mum. I found this support group hidden away in the middle of the Forest of Dean for people with serious anxieties relating to organically grown produce, and they need a psychologist right away!' But I don't, because as she well knows there are no such groups, or if there are they are hidden deep, deep in the forest, afraid to come out and shout, loud and proud, 'We hate veg!'

'Nope, not yet,' I reply, trying to sound jolly and as if I couldn't care less that I really am unemployable.

'Ah, love. You know you could always re-train... extend your skills?' my mother ventures. She is a great believer in retraining, is my mother. In fact, you could call her an authority on re-training. Having originally trained as a nurse, my mother re-trained as an aromatherapist in a bid to demonstrate her disgust at the state of the NHS. She then re-trained as a yoga teacher when she realised that people thought she was running a dodgy massage parlour in her home, and finally re-trained (again) as a gardener/writer – Kim Wilde has nothing on my mum. Ironic really, while I am trying to find a job that helps people get over a relatively unknown phobia, my own mother is busy writing a book on how to grow juicier vegetables. I can imagine my clients (if I had any, that is) discovering this connection and saying, 'Are you taking the piss?'

'Mum, I've just spent three years at university. I don't particu-larly want to re-train,' I hiss, trying not to sound as though I'm hissing.

'Well, it has been over a year, love,' my mother kindly points out. 'Do you need any money?' This is like asking a fish if it needs water. Yes, I do need some money. I am totally skint. Instead I say, 'No, I do not,' in my most indignant how-could-you-ask-that kind of voice. I know, I know, it's a generation thing. Unfortunately I was born during the 80s when power-suited women, with big shoulder-pads brainwashed us into believing that we should, and could, earn our own money and that to accept handouts – especially from your mother – was one of the deadlier sins. The generation of independent women, eh?

No, I will not accept handouts from my mother or anyone else for that matter. I *will* get a job. I *will* get a job. I repeat the mantra silently to myself.

'Sammy? Are you still there?'

'Yes, sorry, Mum. Look I'll be fine. I'm sure something will turn up soon.' I know she's only trying to help, and for that I love her.

'So… have you seen anything of Jack recently? Ooh and I hear that Amy is in the Maldives!' she shrieks. Hmmm, rub it in a bit more why don't you, Mum?

'Yes, she is,' I say, trying to sound as though I'm not the slightest bit jealous of the fact that my best friend is, at this very moment, lying on her back in the baking hot sun while I'm using a king-size 12-tog to keep me warm.

'And Jack?' my mum enquires.

Aside from Amy, Jack is my oldest and dearest friend and I love him to bits. He is taller than me, he has stunning good looks, he's intelligent, funny, caring and… well, everything you could possibly wish for in a man really. So why, I hear you ask, am I not nicely settled down with him in cosy-coupledom? Jack is my best friend and has been for a very long time. If we became a couple, as in boyfriend and girlfriend, and consequently broke up – which, given my track record with men, would inevitably happen – we wouldn't be friends ever again, and I don't want that.

My mum, on the other hand, cannot understand this theory. It's all right for her. She got lucky. She's from the school of 'a husband is for life, not just for Christmas'. She married her childhood sweetheart and they were together for 30 years, right up until my wonderful dad died, two years ago.

'Jack's fine,' I say tersely.

'And?' my mother digs.

'And nothing, Mum! We are just good friends and that is all we will ever be,' I say, despite being somewhat annoyed that Jack really does tick all the right boxes in the *Cosmo* quiz for the ideal man. For starters I know everything there is to know about him. I know what music he is into – indie rock. I know his favourite food – baked bean sandwiches. I know his biggest fear – that a moth will fly into his ear and not come out again. I know, I know, I keep telling him that it is highly unlikely that a moth would want to invade his ear, but he insists that he once saw a documentary about it and the man went deaf as a result of the 'old moth in the ear' business.

I know what Jack would and wouldn't wear – ripped jeans and slogan t-shirt, yes. Dinner jacket and bow-tie, no. And because he has no family to call his own – he was fostered at the tender age of three, and brought up in a time when anyone could become a foster parent and children's social welfare checks were something the foster parents looked forward to cashing at the end of the month – he's become attached to my family and treats my mum and brothers like his own. And to have a relationship with someone who thinks he's your evil twin brother would be just plain weird in my book.

'Gosh, Samantha, you are trying sometimes,' my mother says despairingly.

'Mum!'

'Well, I'm sorry, love, but you've got to live life to the full. You never know when it will be snatched away from you.'

She tugs at my heartstrings every time she says this, which is almost every day, and I can't bring myself to be cross with her. I know she misses Dad terribly and ever since his death, her way of coping is to do just that: live life to the full. I, on the other hand, feel confused by the whole situation and full of unanswered questions, mostly starting with 'why?'

'I love you, Mum,' I say.

'And I love you too, Sammy. Now if you need some money...'

I smile and put down the receiver.

My mum's right, of course. I do have to sort myself out. If I don't do something soon, I will end up with ten cats running riot in the flat, and we'll all be eating nothing but cat food. Children will poke fun at me and call me the Mad Old Cat Lady.

CHAPTER TWO

The two presenters on the TV are debating whether mobile phones really frazzle your brain – hmmm, good question. I ponder this to myself, but pondering is not going to get me a job, is it?

Don't get me wrong, despite the fact that I am currently both unemployed, broke and relying on day-time TV for entertainment, I am proud of the fact that I went to university. As my mother keeps reminding me, I am the only member of our family who ever did. My brothers shared my dad's philosophy that higher education was for losers and there was no way that they were going to waste three years on some cruddy campus.

My older brother Paul gave up school early on, claiming to be allergic to fluorescent lighting or something and instead bummed around the world, settling for being a surfer in Australia instead and running some sort of part-time dodgy detective agency. I know, go figure.

You can't rely on Paul for anything and that's just how he likes it. My darling brother doesn't like anyone to be too dependent on him, which is probably why he has never had a long-term girlfriend and, at the age of 29, is happy to bum around and behave like a teenager for ever more. He's even got a pony-tail, for God's sake! I'm sure he's going to end up like one of those weirdos that you see at summer festivals pretending to be young and trendy, but in reality, look like your grandfather with a bandana tied round his head.

On the other hand, Matt, my younger brother, is a completely different kettle of fish. He discovered at an early age how lucrative it was to create websites for small businesses, long before anyone and everyone had the ability to design a website for free, and quickly cashed in on the opportunity.

I look through the job section of the paper for the umpteenth time. Most of the vacancies consist of advertisements for call centres needing people to advise their customers that their windows are far superior to those of their competitors, or nursing homes in desperate need of people willing to wipe bottoms for £5.60 an hour. Hmm, I don't think either is suitable, do you? If I were to apply for the call centre job, I think I would probably spend most of my time analysing the customers and talking their problems through with them. As for wiping wrinkled bottoms, I can't even empty Missy's cat-litter tray without retching.

Something catches my eye as I flick through the remaining pages of the paper and I flick back again.

Don't know where you are heading? Want to know what your future holds? Call Mystic Answers for all your questions on 0871 123 45678 and speak to one of our psychic mediums.

Well, it's worth a try, I suppose. I'm not getting anywhere by doing nothing and maybe, just maybe, someone else might have the answer. Not that I'm into all this psychic stuff, you understand, just as I don't believe a word of the horoscopes that I read on a daily basis, but desperate times call for desperate measures.

I pull the phone onto my lap and tap out the premium-rate number, trying to ignore the fact that this is about to cost me £1.50 per minute. Perhaps if I talk quickly I won't add a huge phone bill to my growing list of outstanding bills. An automated machine answers.

'Thank you for calling Mystic Answers. Whilst we try to connect you, please be aware that you must be 18 years of age or over to use our service, and that you ask permission of the person that pays the telephone bill. All calls are monitored for the protection of yourself and your reader. We are obliged to state that opinions differ in relation to clairvoyance and mediumship and all readings are for entertainment only. Thank you for your patience. Please hold the line while we try to connect you to one of our readers.'

I do as I am told and listen to a mystical melody of pan-pipe/dolphin music (I'm not quite sure which – it could be a pan-pipe-playing dolphin for all I know) while I wait. A minute or so goes by before a low voice speaks to me – it's cost me £1.50 just to get through.

'Hello, I am Miracle. (Yeah, like that's your real name.) How may I help you?' the husky-voiced lady enquires, and I wonder if her voice really is that low or whether it's all part of the act.

'Oh, um hello,' I stutter, not sure what to say next. 'I... um... well...' 'You would like a reading?' she asks. Damn she's good. 'Um... yes, please. Thank you,' I reply hesitantly.

The phone goes quiet for a moment and I wonder if she thinks I'm a lunatic and has hung up on me.

'Hello?' I ask.

'Please bear with me, dear. I am making a connection. Yes, OK, I will tell her,' she whispers. I, on the other hand, look quizzically at Missy. 'OK my love, I have someone here. An older man by the name of John.'

My stomach does a flip as I think of my dad – no, it couldn't be. Miracle continues.

'He's saying you're not very happy at the moment and can't seem to settle down to anything.'

No shit, Sherlock. I mean how many Pollyannas phone a psychic phone line in the middle of the day? Still, I'm not going to give anything away.

Miracle continues, 'He says you have to stop worrying and take things one step at a time, my love. I'm being told that in the near future you are going to be doing something completely different. You will change so much in your outlook, which will, in turn, change the way you see other people.'

Well, she got my dad's name right, but it's all a little bit vague, don't you think? No one phones these lines unless they have a problem, do they? I let her continue.

'You're very psychic, my dear,' she says, and I laugh out loud.

'If I were that psychic, then I wouldn't be phoning you, would I?'

'Ah, but you are not yet aware of your potential,' the husky-voiced lady councils. 'I'm being told that you are going to be a huge success in this area of work, you just don't realise that you have the ability yet. John is telling me that you do, and that you should look into this because he knows you feel as though you might have chosen the wrong path. In fact, you're not working at the moment, are you, dear?'

I'm not giving this woman any clues so I simply say, 'You're the psychic; you tell me.'

'Well, I am telling you, dear. I know that you're not working and that you are desperate to find your vocation in life, but what you once thought was right for you is most definitely wrong, and you know this, don't you?'

I feel justifiably put in my place by Miracle. Although to be fair, it is the middle of the day and day-time TV is on in the background, so it's pretty obvious that I am not currently at a place of work, but crashed out on my sofa dressed in my pyjamas.

'In fact, I'm going to make a suggestion to you, dear,' Miracle whispers into the phone. 'I'm not really allowed to do this, but have you ever thought of doing psychic readings for a living?'

'Me?' I laugh. 'Let me think – er… no. I can honestly say it's not something that has ever crossed my mind.' I laugh again. Miracle doesn't.

'Well, I think that if you give this a go, you will soon see that I am right. This is the way that your life is supposed to be,' she says. 'Of course, you could always go back to your original plan and keep disappointing yourself. At the end of the day, the decision is yours. But I really do feel that you have a gift. I am being told so by my guides and yours.'

Ooh, so I have guides now! Wow, if there were marks for self-promotion, this lady would get ten out of ten! It really is a novel way of recruiting potential employees.

'I'm not psychic, I'm skint,' I say.

'Then you will be killing two birds with one stone, won't you?' Miracle replies. 'It's not often that I feel so strongly about something, but my guides and your father are all confirming that you have The Gift. I feel it's only right to let you know that you can put it to good use – and the money's not too bad either.' This time it's Miracle who chuckles.

'Think about it dear, and if you are interested, call this number back. Press the star key when you're connected and ask to speak to me. In the meantime, I can see that although you are currently single, you won't be for long if you just retrace your steps and look in the right place.'

OK, so how did she know I was single? Perhaps because us singletons have a desperate tone in our voices that other people can pick up on.

'There is a man who is very fond of you, though you don't know it and neither does he,' Miracle adds. 'He is the one for you.'

'Well, can you give me a clue because right now, I don't know anyone who is fond of me?' I say as I think of my disastrous love life, but that's a whole different story.

'You will,' she replies – don't you hate it when people are cryptic like that?

'Right,' I say, 'is there anything else?' realising that I have been on the phone for 12 minutes now and oh, bum, that's £18 I've just blown.

'Not at the moment, my dear, but please think about what I said. If you want to know more about this kind of work, call back and press the star key and ask for Miracle.'

'OK, I'll think about it, and thank you,' I whisper back. Lord knows why I'm whispering, but it seems like an appropriate occasion.

I put the phone down and look at Missy who is diligently licking her bottom.

'Well? What did you make of that then?' Missy looks up at me as if I've totally lost the plot and continues to clean her bum. She's right, though. A year ago I wouldn't have dreamed of phoning up a hot-line-to-the-heavens and now look at me. I'm even beginning to believe there might be something in all of this. And that's a point; how did she know my father was dead? Did I give anything away?

I tap my fingers rhythmically on the phone, wondering what to do next. No, I couldn't, could I? I mean, I know nothing about how a psychic works. OK, so I've seen Gordon Smith on telly scaring the wits out of Yvette Fielding, and that Derek Acorah bloke going into one of his trances and talking to his dead side-kick, but as for hearing voices in my head, if I started doing that I think I'd admit myself to the nearest loony house. I am a qualified psychologist, you know. However, Miracle did get my dad's name right *and* she did know that I was single and in a bit of a desperate situation. I still can't fathom out how she knew that. And if she was right on that score, then what's to say she isn't right about me being able to make money doing the same thing as her? I mean, surely she wouldn't want someone coming in and taking all her work away, would she?

I must admit I'm a bit miffed that everyone seems to think that I'm on totally the wrong path and that they also all think that I wasted three years at uni – even Mystic Miracle said as much. I humph and tap the phone again.

'What do you think, Missy?' I ask

Missy meows, which I take to mean, go for it, what's the worst that can happen? You make a total fool of yourself – again. Now leave me alone, I want to sleep. Trust me, when you've lived as long as I have with only a cat for company, you tend to get the gist of what a cat is saying.

I take a deep breath and re-dial the number, remembering to hit the star key as soon as the welcome message kicks in. I wonder if by hitting the star key I am transported, Harry Potter style, into a special members-only psychic club. I wonder if the star key is like one of those keys that unlock a totally new mysterious world. I've obviously been watching too much *Witches of Waverly Place* and had too much time on my hands lately.

'Hello, who would you like to speak to?' a female voice asks.

'Um Miracle, please?' I ask, still unsure whether this is a wind up or not.

'OK, hold on and I'll see if she's free.'

The line goes quiet for a moment.

'Hello?' the familiar husky voice says.

'Miracle? It's Samantha. I phoned you for a reading a few minutes ago and you said to call you…'

'Ah, Samantha. Hello again.' Miracle sounds pleased to hear from me. I wonder if she gets commission for this sort of thing? A kind of psychic referral bonus, like Avon ladies get. I tried being an Avon lady once, but ended up buying so many cosmetics that I really didn't need that I ended up owing them money.

'So…' Miracle says. 'I take it you're interested in what I suggested earlier?'

'Well, I think so,' I say, wondering what on earth I'm letting myself in for.

'Well, first and foremost, let me tell you a bit about how we work. Then, if you still like the sound of it, I will give you a test and see how you get on, OK?'

'Er, OK,' I say. A test? No one said anything about a test.

'Right, do you have a pack of tarot cards by any chance?' Miracle asks.

'Well, I do somewhere, but you'll have to hang on while I dig them out.' My mother bought me a pack when she and Dad went travelling to India. It was about the same time that she was on her alternative spiritual/yoga quest and wanted me to under-stand where she was coming from and find herself, or something like that. I have to say, I wasn't really paying attention at the

13

time. Apart from me, Amy and Jack having a play around with them one night, they have never been used and, as far as I know, are still in the kitchen drawer.

'Most of our callers like a tarot reading followed by a psychic reading,' Miracle continues.

'Hang on, I didn't say I was psychic!' I protest.

'Don't panic, dear,' she assures me. 'You will soon find that you tune into people and it will come naturally to you. Anything, runes, tarot cards, crystal ball, they are all just divination tools to help us tap into our psychic energies. You don't have to believe that you are psychic to be a psychic, you know.'

'Oh, right.' That's OK then. I breathe a sigh of relief. Miracle continues to tell me how the process works: You say when you are available for work; the company call you whenever they have a caller needing a reading; you do the reading – keeping the caller on the line generates a bonus for the reader – and that's basically it. You get 60p per minute, plus extra if the reading takes longer than 15 minutes. I quickly tot it up in my head – that works out at £9.00 for every 15-minute reading. That's £36 an hour, I tell myself – yippee!

I don't remember what else Miracle tells me. All I can think of is, wow! £36 an hour! That's more than I would get as a therapist.

'Samantha?' Miracle asks.

'Sorry, um, yes, that's fine.'

'Good, so we will call you Mystic Crystal...'

Mystic Crystal? Hang on, where did that come from? Oh, well, as good as anything, I guess. At least I'm not going to be called something daft like Silver Moonbeam and it does have a certain ring to it. Oh, dear, I've just realised something; with my surname being Ball my stage name is Mystic Crystal Ball!

'So, would you like to give it a go and do a test reading for me?' Miracle asks.

'Umm, OK. Oh, hang on, let me find my tarot cards.' I put the phone to one side and hurry into the kitchen, digging about in various drawers until I locate the rather battered box of tarot cards my mum bought me.

'OK, I'm back,' I wheeze, out of breath – mental note, must get fit, Samantha.

'Right, now imagine I'm a first-time caller and I've been put through to you,' Miracle says. I try to imagine doing this live. OK Sam, now just copy what Miracle did when you phoned her, I think to myself, wondering whether I should put on a husky voice or whether she might think I'm taking the piss.

'Hello,' I say, wondering what I'm meant to say next. 'Umm... welcome to Mystic Answers. I am Mystic umm Crystal and I will be your reader for today.'

'Good,' I hear Miracle say.

'Please bear with me while I make a connection,' I add for effect and take the tarot cards out of the box, drop several, and put them back into some kind of order.

'I want to know what my future holds,' Miracle says.

'Yes, of course you do, please bear with me...' I feel rather hot and flustered. The stupid bloody cards are falling all over the place as I try to get them into one neat pile. Why do they have to be too bloody big for your hands?

'Right,' I say, still out of breath, 'I am going to draw three cards for you and I will tell you what the meaning of each card is, if that is all right with you?'

'That's fine,' Miracle says.

I look for the book that came with the cards only to find that it is not in the box. Damn Jack! He was the last one to play with these and he's gone and lost the bloody book – the very book that gives me all the meanings of the cards. Oh bugger!

'Are you still there, Mystic Crystal?'

'Yes!' I snap. 'Sorry, please bear with me.'

'Just take your time,' Miracle says. I'm sure she's smiling when she says it.

'Now, Sam, just concentrate and try to remember what the

cards mean, I tell myself. God, this is worse than taking exams! I pick out three cards. The first has a big heart with a bolt of lighting running through it. Well, that's pretty obvious.

'You have recently suffered from a broken heart?' I guess. 'But don't worry because love will find a way. I feel it in my...' I'm about to say fingers and then realise that I'm quoting the opening lyrics to Love is All Around from the *Love Actually* movie – '...heart,' I add. I wait for a response but Miracle doesn't give anything away.

'OK, your second card is a money card.' No, I'm not psychic, I can tell this because it has ten shiny coins spilling out from a golden bucket and a woman with a huge smile on her face, looking very pleased with herself. 'This means that some money is soon going to come your way. It could be a settlement or something?' Again, Miracle says nothing and I silently pray that I'm saying the right thing.

'Now, your third card shows me that you are going to move house soon and live by the sea.' I make this assumption because the next card I look at has a lovely rose-covered cottage on it, which is oddly enough, beside the sea. There are roses and happy faces all around, so I'm guessing this is a good card. 'Your heartbreak will soon end and you will face a future of happiness, loveliness and... sand. Oh, and you will have everything you ever wished for,' I add for good measure.

I wait for a moment.

'Hello? Are you still there?' I ask.

'Yes dear, I am,' Miracle replies.

'And?' I'm somewhat frustrated now at our one-way conversation. I feel like I'm waiting to hear whether I've passed my driving test or not – and this is costing me money!

'That was wonderful,' Miracle says with glee in her gravelly voice. 'Amazing. So accurate, Samantha! Let me tell you something. My husband and I were married for 25 years before he decided to trade me in for a newer model. We recently divorced and I have just found out that I am entitled to a lot of money from him, and I *am* planning to move nearer to the sea.'

Wow! How chuffed am I feeling right now? Quite a lot actually!

'So, does that mean I've got the job?' I ask nervously – it's one thing getting it right purely by fluke, but quite another thing being let loose on the unsuspecting public.

'Yes, you've got the job.' Miracle laughs her throaty laugh.

Yippee! I want to shout. Instead I kick my legs in the air, waking Missy up and sending her flying off my lap in fright.

'Now, how many days would you like to work?' Miracle asks.

With three credit cards to pay by the end of the month and the rent for the next two weeks to find, I'm very tempted to say seven, but I don't want to appear greedy, so cut it down to five instead.

'Days or nights?'

'Oh, can I do a bit of both, please?'

'Sure, but just be aware that at night time we get a lot of drunks calling that stay on the phone for ages. Mind you, that's a good thing because the longer you keep the caller on the phone, the more money you get, and if you work after midnight, your rates are doubled,' Miracle informs me. Double yippee!

'Right, I'll book you in for tonight from seven until three in the morning and I'll see how you get on with that, yes?' she asks.

'That's great! Yes. Thank you,' I say, really meaning it. At this precise moment, all I can think about is that in one night I could earn myself nearly £300 – that's almost one credit card paid off!

Miracle makes me aware that I am effectively self-employed and so have to sort out my own tax and National Insurance, but then what's the point of having a clever brother if he can't sort out your accounts for you?

Putting down the phone, I take a deep contented sigh. I've just got myself a job!

CHAPTER THREE

'What, you? A psychic?'

This was Jack's response when I phoned him to tell him my good news, rapidly followed by the sound of him wetting himself with laughter. I wait patiently for him to stop laughing. And I wait, and I wait…

'Jack!' I scream into the phone. I do wish he would take me seriously sometimes! He coughs and splutters for a moment.

'Sorry hun, but…'

And then it all starts again. A girly giggle, quickly followed by a huge snort, and then more hilarity.

'Jack! Stop it!' I shout. 'I'm being serious!' And I am. I want to share my good news with my best friend and all he can do is behave like a child who has heard the word bum for the first time.

'I'm sorry, it's just…' He desperately tries to compose himself, but there really is no hope for him.

Jack is one of those people who, once something sets him off, cannot stop himself from giggling. And he does giggle too, like a little schoolgirl. It's always the same, it starts off with a kind of Benny Hill, hand-over-the-mouth-titter, and then, in no time at all, he is rolling on the floor, clutching his stomach and crying real tears.

'Have you quite finished?' I ask, somewhat annoyed at this one-way conversation. I hear Jack take a deep breath, and although I can't see him, I know for a fact that he's straightening himself up in a bid to prevent himself from collapsing in a heap again.

'Right. OK. I'm OK,' Jack says slowly. 'Right, sorry about that. It just… it just took me by surprise, that's all.'

I can sense that he is trying not to smile as he speaks.

'Right. I'm fine now. So, um, what are you called?' he says, desperately trying to sound composed.

'Mystic Crystal.' I snap.

Oh, no, here we go again. No sooner have I said the word Mystic, Jack starts making snorting noises all over again. The snorting soon becomes a high-pitched giggle, followed by howls of laughter. I can see him now, rolling around on the floor in hysterics.

As I've already mentioned, I love Jack to bits, and his sense of humour is part of the reason why we get on so well. To be honest, I would probably be rolling around in hysterics myself too if he had just told me that he'd landed a job as a phone psychic. However, a little support wouldn't go amiss right now.

Jack has been in my life for a long time, since we were in sixth form, to be precise. We were both fresh out of 'big school' and had both decided to stay on at school, rather than go to the local college. We started at the same time and were equally confused as to where we were supposed to be going on the campus. As we were both working towards an A level in economics, we kind of latched on to each other and have rarely left each other's side since – well, apart from the fact that he went to Cardiff University and I opted for Bristol because it was closer to home.

Every weekend, Jack and I would meet up and plan what we were going to do. And every weekend, he would turn up in some outrageous costume that he had hired from his Uncle Dave's fancy dress shop and stand outside in the street shouting my name until I promised to stop studying and come out to play.

Jack was blessed with the ability to do no work whatsoever and still come out with a degree in law. I don't know how he did it, but he did. I personally suspect that he used his boyish good looks in some way to charm the examining board. However, he didn't go into law. In fact, he actually despises lawyers, calling them the scum of the earth, but admits that a law degree does look good on paper.

Jack now divides his time between playing in a band and

working in HMV. Actually his band, *Otherwise*, is very good. Jack plays lead guitar and occasionally sings, if the song warrants it. I wouldn't say they were a patch on Oasis, but they do sometimes get paid for their music if they do a gig at the local pub, and he has two ready-made roadies in the form of me and Amy, should he ever require us.

'So, have you finished laughing at me?' I ask. Jack still hasn't managed to get a word out without bursting into fits of laughter.

'Sorry, Sam, but… I mean…' and off he goes again. Occasionally muttering that his stomach hurts and he needs to pee.

'Oh, I've had enough of this,' I huff. 'I'll call you back when you've finished wetting yourself laughing.'

With that I put the phone down. Ahh! The one person I wanted to share my good news with and he can't talk for bloody laughing! I can't even phone Amy to tell her my news as her mobile seems to be permanently switched off.

My jubilant mood has turned to one of dismay. Stupid Jack! Well, he'll be sorry when I'm raking it in from telling people's fortunes for a living. And anyway, it's only a temporary thing. Eventually, I will track down all those people in hiding who have an aversion to vegetables, and cure the bloody lot of them, so there!

I realise that Missy has departed to the kitchen and I am actually talking to myself and had better stop it. The last thing I need is for people to have an excuse to call me a crackpot. Right, I really should prepare myself for this evening. I wonder, as I make my way to the bathroom, what sort of people call a psychic line. There's your answer, I think, looking at my reflection in the bathroom mirror – desperate, unemployed people who watch too much day-time TV. Anyway, I'm trained to deal with desperate people, and not only will I be doing a very good public service, but I will also get lots of experience with dealing with different people, I tell myself, in order to justify the reason as to why I was so desperate that I had to call the psychic hotline in the first place.

I run a shower and contemplate what I should wear tonight. I know the callers aren't going to be able to see me, and I could be wearing my Betty Boop pyjamas and my dad's old gardening cardi for all they know. Nevertheless, I feel I should at least get into the spirit of things – no pun intended – and at least look as though I know what I'm doing, even if I don't. Perhaps I should dress in a headscarf and put a big hoopy pair of earrings in my ears? Or maybe I should go the whole hog and hire a fortune-teller's costume from Jack's uncle? That would get me in the right frame of mind.

Instead, I decide to wear my black jumper dress over a pair of black leggings and knee-length boots – black seems appropriate, don't you think? And I ought to be comfy if I'm going to sit for the next eight hours listening to people's problems and trying to fix them. I gulp at the thought. Am I really qualified to advise people on what they should be doing with their lives when I don't even know what I should be doing with my own?

Looking appropriately mystical – well, I think so anyway – I sit and look through the tarot cards my mum bought me. Thankfully, most of the 78 cards have pictures on them giving me some idea of what they mean; although the one with a man in Indian attire, holding in his hands a head belonging to someone else could be a tricky one to interpret. Hmm, perhaps I'll just take that one out of the pack altogether. And that one showing a picture of an animal with a cat's head on a goat's body – that's just plain weird. Oh, and that one depicting a man tied to a tree and a woman pointing a crossbow at him… I'm just guessing, but a woman scorned maybe?

As I'm working my way through each card the door buzzer rings, breaking my concentration. Missy heads towards the door and meows. She is such a nosey cat and I'm sure she thinks it's for her. I silently pray it's not my landlady again.

My landlady, Ms Morris, is one of the most unpleasant women I have ever had the misfortune to meet. No, really, she is. Obviously gnarled from life's experiences, she could easily give Cruella de Vil a run for her money. She hates noise, she hates cats and she hates me and is always looking for an excuse to pop downstairs and tell me off for something. Last week it was because Missy had accidentally knocked over a milk bottle on the front step. I wouldn't have minded if it had actually broken, but it hadn't. Her grievance was that it made the place look untidy – says she who mooches around all day in a grey anorak and a bad hairstyle.

I would guess that Ms Morris is probably in her late sixties. She lives in the flat two floors above, but in fact, owns the whole house we live in and rents out five or six of the converted rooms to students, or ex-students like me. I've never seen a man about, but then she is so bitter and twisted that nobody would put up with her for long. God, I hope I don't end up like her, with nothing better to do with my time than annoy the hell out of young people.

'Taddaaa!'

My caller isn't Ms Morris on the warpath, it's Jack, sporting a full mystical fortune-teller costume, complete with bright orange headscarf, red lipstick, a plastic goldfish bowl turned upside down, and the biggest pair of gold hoop earrings to come out of Claire's Accessories. Half of me wants to punch his lights out. The other half wants to laugh out loud.

'I see you are going on a long trip... to the kitchen to make your best friend a cup of tea,' Jack says in his most Mystic Meg voice.

'Oh, very funny indeed,' I say sarcastically in return. He does look very funny though. He's even gone to the trouble of wearing a multicoloured gypsy-style skirt over his black jeans. 'Come on in before someone sees you.' I feel embarrassed for him. 'You didn't seriously walk down the street dressed like that, did you?'

'No, not seriously. I did a little dance like this as I went.' Jack laughs as he demonstrates his impression of Beyonce. 'So how are you feeling, my little mystical one?'

I pull a face.

'Nervous, if you must know.'

'Well, never fear because Mystic Jack is here and my crystal ball tells me that...' he stares intently into his plastic fish-bowl '...you are completely and utterly bonkers and should book yourself into The Priory right away. You need help, girl. Ouch! What was that for?'

He's just earned himself a punch on the arm.

'For laughing at me down the phone, dressing up like a pantomime dame, and for taking the piss out of me,' I reply and throw in another punch for good measure. 'It's all right for you, you've got the job of your dreams,' I mutter as we make our way back to the lounge.

'Well, I did warn you not to get involved with vegetables. They're nothing but trouble. I told you that right from the start, but did you listen?'

'You sound like my mother. In fact, dressed like that, you look a bit like her too.' I shudder.

'And how is the beautiful Mrs Ball these days?'

'Well, she thinks very highly of you, though Lord knows why. She's still hinting that you would make the perfect boyfriend,' I say, packing all the cards together in a nice neat pile next to the phone.

'No, it would never work. She's a lovely woman and all that, but I've got a thing about women being older than me. It's probably some childhood psychological scarring or something, but thank her for the offer anyway,' Jack says with a sly smile. This time he's the target of a scatter cushion.

'You know, I'll have you for assault one of these days, Samantha Ball!'

Jack lifts up his skirts, tucks them into the waist of his jeans and grabs hold of two cushions from the sofa.

'Aim and FIRE!' he shouts as he throws the cushions grenade-style at me. I duck behind the sofa and prepare to arm myself with more ammunition – that's the handy thing about being a girl, we love cushions and so have plenty to throw around. I bundle as many behind the sofa as I can and throw and dive as I hit my target every time. Jack quickly runs out of ammunition and looks around to see what else he can use.

'Don't even think about it!' I shout as I see him picking Missy up from her slumber on the sofa.

'Take aim and FIRE!' Jack shouts as Missy flies through the air towards me. I drop my cushions in a bid to catch her and she lands straight in my open arms.

'You are in so much trouble now,' I say to Jack and grab as many cushions as I can hold, imagining that I am loading one of those guns that spit out bullets one after the other. As I hit Jack time and time again, he backs into a corner, steps back on the plastic fish-bowl, trips over his skirt and bangs his head against the wall.

'Man down! Man down! Medic required!' he groans.

Ouch! That thump on the wall didn't sound too good, in fact it sounded rather painful. Thinking he really has hurt himself, I rush over to find him eyes closed and apparently lifeless.

'Jack? Are you all right?'

No answer. Uh-oh.

'Jack?' I shake his arm. Oh my God, I hope he's not dead! That would be a hard one to explain – well, officer, he threw the cat at me so I grenade-ed him and he tripped over his skirt. No, that doesn't sound good, does it? I put my ear to his chest to make sure he's still breathing.

'Boo!' Jack sits up and grins at me. I give him another thump. 'Ouch! What was that for?'

'For pretending to be dead. Oh, and for chucking the cat at me. Don't you know you could have frightened her for life?' I scold.

'Nah, Missy knows she's an invincible cat. And besides, she says you deserved it for taking a mad job and just generally being mad.'

'Well,' I say, 'mad as it may be, it is a job and I'll do anything for money right now.'

'Anything?' Jack smiles and twitches his ruby red lips. 'Ouch! I'm going to end up black and blue at this rate,' he whines.

'Then don't be so annoying and bugger off, I've got to mentally prepare myself. I'm on in just under an hour and I haven't had anything to eat yet.'

Jack struggles to his feet and straightens his skirt.

'You're not going back out looking like that, are you?'

'Huh! At least I'm dressed for the part. You look like you're going to a frigging funeral.' He flounces dramatically out of the room.

'It will be your funeral if you don't bugger off and leave me alone. And don't go upstairs and upset Ms Morris!' I yell after him, this being one of Jack's favourite pastimes – to knock on her door and persuade her to let him in and offer him a ginger nut and a cup of tea. He then settles himself on her sofa and tells her all his problems – not that Jack has any, he just makes some up. What Ms Morris makes of him, goodness only knows.

'Yes, Mum. Break a leg tonight and text me. Loves ya!' he sings as he lets himself out.

'Loves me too!' I yell back.

After sharing a tuna sandwich with Missy – is that odd, sharing your food with your cat? – I check again to make sure there is still a dial tone on my phone, and that I haven't been disconnected in the past fourteen minutes. Within moments of me replacing the receiver, the phone rings, making me jump – why does it always do that? I let it ring twice so as not to appear too eager and then answer it.

'Hello?'

'Samantha, it's Miracle here. I have your first caller, sweetie. I'll just put her through.'

Oh crikey, I'm on!

CHAPTER FOUR

'Hello?' I listen for a moment and wonder what I should say next. For all I know, it could be someone trying to get through to a sex line. It's not. It's a young woman on the other end of the line.

'Hello, I'm Mystic Crystal, and I'm your reader for tonight. How may I help you?' I say, that sounded good, didn't it?

'Hi,' a small voice says, and then she snorts as though she is blowing her nose into a tissue.

'How may I help you? Would you like a reading?' I ask.

'Yes... please,' the young woman answers. Oh, bugger, I thought she was going to give me a little more information to work on than that.

'OK, well I'm going to shuffle the cards for you and see what comes out. I can't make any promises...' I hesitate, wondering if I sound authentic. After all, this woman is paying premium rates to listen to me waffle on. I feel like a fraud and desperately want to say, hang on, I'll phone you back and we'll have a little chat. I don't though. I shuffle my set of cards – well, I say shuffle, it's more of a toss than a shuffle and they all land in an untidy pile on the carpet.

The girl sniffs again. OK, so that's a clue that she's sad about something, but what? Boyfriend? Quite possibly. She sounds too young to be married. Maybe she's pregnant and he's dumped her? Or maybe she's been fired from her job... because she's been sleeping with the boss and his wife has found out.

Yes, that's it! Blimey, where did that come from? Don't ask me how but I'm sure this is what the girl is upset about. Not only has she lost her man, but she's also lost her job. What am I doing? This is ridiculous. I haven't got a bloody clue what I am doing or why she has called. As I pick out several cards, which actually mean nothing to me, I try to search the pictures for clues to back up my out-of-the-blue theory. There's the broken heart for starters and then there's a card with a king type of figure on it, looking very smug with himself. Finally there's a picture of a big bright sun, with lots of children playing with old-fashioned hoop toys.

'Hello? Are you still there?' the girl asks.

'Yes, sorry. I'm just trying to... um... sorry, I'm trying to work out something. Can you just answer 'yes' or 'no' to this question for me?'

'OK,' she replies quietly.

Before I start getting carried away with myself, I need to know if I'm on the right track here, otherwise I am going to make myself look like a total fool.

'I don't want to upset you, but does this have anything to do with your boss?' I ask cautiously – please say yes, please say yes.

'Yes, it has,' she replies.

Yes! Thank God! I want to punch the air. How's that for woman's intuition? I've always been good at guessing what's wrong with someone. Whenever my friend Ali phones, I know instinctively if she's had a fight with her boyfriend, James. Mind you, Ali and James fight more often than they don't, so that's probably not a good example to give you. However, take it from me, I can usually tell when something is up. I venture a little further.

'Was your boss also your boyfriend?' I bite my lip, praying that I'm not wrong.

'Um...' is all she replies.

'Well? Look, I don't know you, and you don't know me, and all calls are completely confidential,' I say, hoping that they are indeed confidential and that this poor girl's phone isn't being tapped as we speak.

'Yes,' she replies again.

'You were having an affair with him and it's all ended in tears, hasn't it?'

I'm feeling a bit more confident now that she has confirmed

what I first suspected. Maybe it was the tone of her voice, I don't know, but all I do know is that she is upset and her boss has got off lightly. As she bursts into tears I feel quite angry with him.

'Oh, please don't cry. Listen – it's going to be OK. It really is.' I try to assure her, but who am I to tell her that everything is going to be rosy in the garden again? I can't see into her future, can I?

'He said he loved me,' she wails down the phone. 'He said his wife hated him and they were going to get a divorce and…' The tears start again. Oh help, what do I do now? Do I cut her off for being an emotional wreck?

'Listen to me,' I say, genuinely feeling sorry for this girl. It doesn't take a psychic to see that her boss fancied a bit on the side, got caught with his trousers down and yet he got off scot free – bastard! 'This is not your fault. You are not to blame for this and I know that you still feel as though you love him, and that he will rethink and will dump his wife and come running back to you with a job offer in hand. He won't, darling. This man is a coward. He got caught with you and right now, is desperately trying to convince his wife that you were the one who did all the running.' I hear her sniff loudly again. Oh I do hope I'm not upsetting her even more. I continue. 'Can you not see what he's done to you? You've lost a good job over this bastard – excuse my French – and he's deceived you. If he can do such a thing to his wife, the one he took vows with, what makes you think that he wouldn't do the same to you? Did you really think that he would leave his wife?'

'Yes, I did,' she whispers. 'He promised.'

'Like he promised his wife to love, honour and obey?' I ask. OK, I know I'm being a little dramatic, but someone had to say it.

Silence.

'Listen. I know for a fact just what type of man this is, and even though you really want me to tell you that he will realise that he's made a big mistake, and that you mean the world to him, he is not going to do that. He's going to employ another young, naïve girl to be his PA and will start all over again, until the next time he gets caught,' I say. I mean it's hardly rocket science, is it? The only reason he got rid of her is because he got caught out.

'But...' I suddenly say as I look at the sun card and a flash goes through my mind, 'within six months time, things are going to be so different for you and so much better. I can see lots of children around you. Now I don't think they are your children, but there are a lot of children here. I think you might go into teaching.' I try to sound confident. I haven't really got a clue what I'm waffling on about, but anyway.

'Wow!' the girl sniffs, 'I've just been accepted on a teacher training course. When Martin dumped me I didn't want to go back into secretarial work and I've always loved children. My mum suggested I try to get on a teacher training course and I've just found out I've been accepted.'

'There you go then,' I say, feeling rather smug with my guesswork. 'Things will get better, sweetheart. I know it feels raw at the moment and so unfair, but I do feel that this is a whole new start for you and I have a sneaky feeling that your Mr Right is just round the corner – well not literally, but you know what I mean.' I laugh. Actually this is quite good fun and I've been on the phone for 32 minutes – that's £19.20 already. Yippee!

'Thank you so much, Crystal. You have been spot on and I don't know what I would have done without you. It was a toss up between phoning the Samaritans or Mystic Answers. I'm glad I chose you now,' the young girl says, and I'm sure she is smiling. Well, at least she isn't calling me names and crying down the phone. 'I knew deep down that he was never going to leave his wife and kids for me,' she sighs.

I knew too, but without having to consult a psychic. Experience, pre my uni days, taught me that if nothing else. Older, married men will never, ever leave their wives, despite all the promises, threats and tears. I know because this is exactly what Tim promised me five years ago.

I was taking a year out prior to going to university and decided to apply for a job working at the local hospital in the mental health department so that I could get some work experience. Tim was one of the hospital's consultants and a handsome one at that. At first I didn't consider the fact that he might be married. At just 19 years old, I was just very flattered by all the attention he gave me.

It was only when we were out for dinner one evening and Tim had gone to the bathroom, leaving his mobile phone on the table that I discovered Tim was indeed blissfully wedded. Not only was he married, he had at least one child. His phone vibrated into life to signal that he had a text message and I know I shouldn't have, but I couldn't help but take a peek.

Dad, mum says cn u bring a pint of milk home with you when u finish wk? Lv Nat.

Despite telling myself that it must be the wrong number, I knew, deep down, that Tim was married and having a bit on the side. I was the side portion. So no, he was never going to leave her for you, my love. It didn't need a psychic to work that one out, but I certainly wasn't going to inform a total stranger of just how I knew.

'Well, I hope your prince charming arrives soon for you,' I say with a smile.

'Oh, I'm sure he will. In the meantime, I will put all my energies into my studies,' the girl says, sounding much brighter than when she first spoke.

I look at the travel alarm clock in front of me and realise that I have been on the phone to this girl for 45 minutes. Wow! £27 for little old me!

'Is there anything else?' I ask feeling a little more confident at having handled my first call so well.

'No, but thank you so much. I will recommend you to all my

friends,' the girl says. I resist the urge to shout yippee!

Replacing the receiver I take a deep breath. My palms are wet, my head throbs, but the feeling of elation is like nothing I have ever felt before. Even when I passed my exams, I didn't feel like I do right now. I manage a quick sip of water and a wee before the phone starts ringing again.

'Sam, it's Miracle. Well done on your first call. I was listening in and you were very good.'

'Thank you,' I say, feeling very proud of myself.

'You want another one then?' Miracle asks.

Oh, God. Do I? I don't know.

'Umm, ok,' I stutter.

'That's good because I have your next caller here for you,' Miracle laughs.

I wait to hear who the next poor desperate soul is, worrying that it might be someone who does this all the time and will immediately know that I'm a fraud.

'Hello?' A man's voice comes through. He sounds as though he's middle-aged, but I guess you can never tell on the phone. He might be a young man with an old voice, or an old man with a young voice.

I thought it was only women who phoned these lines. Unless of course, he misdialled?

'Um, hello,' I say. 'How can I help you?'

'I want you to tell me if my wife is having an affair,' the man asks.

CHAPTER FIVE

Blimey, you'd think we were on the *Jeremy Kyle Show*.

'What makes you think she is?' I ask.

The man goes into a tirade of reasons as to why his wife must be cheating on him, including the fact that she has had her hair and nails done today, is wearing perfume again and she wants to have sex with him. All the time. I listen to him as I shuffle the cards.

'I mean since the kids have left home, she is constantly dolling herself up and going out with her so-called friends,' he continues.

So your wife is making herself look nice *and* demanding sex from you – are you bloody mad? I want to shout down the phone. This woman has obviously realised that she is no longer just a mother, she is a woman and is trying very hard to recapture what they both once had and this idiot is suspecting her of having an affair! I shuffle the cards again and place four down on the carpet.

The four cards I place down tell a different story though. There is a man running away with a bag of gold in his hands and laughing at some people who are standing behind him. The next card shows another man surrounded by beautiful goddess-like women. The third card shows a woman sitting on a rock, crying, and the forth shows the broken heart card that I drew for the last caller and for Miracle.

As I look at the cards, I'm suddenly overwhelmed with anger at this man and I'm not quite sure why.

'Well, the cards you have are all about deceit and dishonesty,' I venture.

'I bloody knew it!' he shouts, 'I knew she was having an affair. Who is he?' he demands to know.

I shake my head as I suddenly realise what's been going on. I don't know how I know, but I just have this feeling. Call it that good old women's intuition if you like.

'Hang on one minute,' I say cautiously, wondering whether I should just placate this chap and tell him that he's right in his suspicions. But I can't bring myself to do it. 'As I said, there is a lot of deceit showing up here... but I don't feel that it's your wife who is deceiving you...'

'What are you trying to say? Are you saying that I'm the one having an affair? Are you? Is that what you're suggesting?' The man's voice becomes louder as he shouts into the phone. That is exactly what I am saying. I don't think for a moment that this man's wife is having an affair. What I do feel is that he is in fact the one who has been playing away from home. Don't ask me how I know. I just feel that this chap is playing the old game of blaming his wife for his own misdemeanours. God, I'm good. I should be in marriage counselling.

'No, I'm not suggesting that at all. All I am saying is that your wife isn't the one who is having an affair,' I confirm. I don't care whether I'm right or wrong now. This bloke is seriously pissing me off with his attitude.

'Where is your wife at the moment?' I ask, momentarily wondering if she's out on the town as we speak.

'She's at home. I'm... I'm in a hotel, if you must know... It's for work...' he stutters.

Yeah, and I'm a psychic. Of course it is, mate.

'And do you spend a lot of time away from home?'

'Well, I have to. I have a very high-pressured job in the city. It's part of my contract. I have no choice but to stay away,' he says.

'You don't have to justify anything to me,' I say. The man doth protest too much methinks.

'No, you don't understand. It's hard work. The constant pressure to reach targets at the end of the month. You have no idea how hard it is, and sometimes...'

'Sometimes you need a bit of company?' I venture.

The line is silent for a minute. That silence confirms what I suspected all along. This man's wife isn't the one who is cheating. It's him. Damn I am good!

'I'm sorry,' is all he whispers. The line is quiet again.

'I don't think I'm the one you should be apologising to, do you?'

The man sniffs. Is he crying? I think he is.

'I do love my wife. It's just that I don't see her as my wife. I see her as...'

'Your children's mother.' I answer for him.

'Yes,' he confirms.

'And she knows this. This is the reason why she is trying so hard to make herself look attractive to you again. This is the reason why she is wearing perfume and make-up and dressing up nicely *and* wanting you to... um, make love to her...' – ewww, just saying this to a total stranger makes me feel slightly queasy – 'and this is the reason she is going out with her friends more often. Your wife has realised that she is no longer just a mum. She is a woman who has needs, and wants to feel like a woman again and not just someone's mother. If you're never around to pay her compliments, or to take her out, if you're always away in hotels in the company of other women, then what is she supposed to do? Sit at home and do your ironing?' I ask. 'In fact, I wouldn't blame her one bit if she did have an affair, but she isn't. She loves you too much to do that and what do you think she will do when she finds out about what you've been up to when you're supposed to be working?' I ask.

'Oh, my God, you're not going to tell her are you?' The bloke sounds genuinely worried at the prospect.

'All calls are completely confidential, Sir,' I assure him, 'and besides, I don't even know who you are. You could be one of a million men out there who are cheating on their wives.' I know, but I couldn't help having a little dig on behalf of sisterhood.

'I won't do it anymore. I promise you. I know she loves me

and I will try to be a decent husband,' he promises.

'It's not me you should be making these promises to.'

'I know. I'm sorry I deceived you though.'

I shrug. 'Well, it's not me you were deceiving. It was yourself... and your wife,' I say like a wise sage. I'm still a little miffed at the way he made out that he was the one being wronged. But then, that's typical of men. They know they have done something wrong and yet they try to turn it round to be the woman's fault. And when they get caught out, they try to justify their behaviour! Not that I'm a bitter and twisted spinster or anything, but grrr to men in general.

The night goes pretty quickly after that. Most of the callers I have want to know when they are going to meet Mr Right – hmmm, good question – and of course I can't tell them, I mean even with a pack of cards in my hands I can't say precisely when they are going to fall in love with Prince Charming and quit running after ungrateful toads, so I tell them what they want to hear. If the woman on the other end of the phone sounded furious at being a jilted lover, I told her that her scum-bag of an ex wasn't worth the tears and the sleepless nights and that fate would soon bring someone wonderful rushing into her life. If it was a woman questioning her partner's fidelity, I would tell her that despite all the evidence stacked up against him, I went with what the cards said, and focussed on her and her future – with or without a cheating man in her life.

It is almost three in the morning and I breathe a sigh of relief that my shift is almost over when the phone rings again. My throat is sore, my eyes are tired and Missy has abandoned me in favour of my bed hours ago.

'Hello?' I croak into the phone.

'Sam, it's Miracle here. Do you mind just taking just one more call?'

Oh, bum. I was so longing to unplug the phone and collapse into bed.

'No I don't mind,' I say. Why I can't just say what I want to say, I'll never know.

'OK, I'm just putting you through,' Miracle says. I bet she's off to bed in a minute, I grump.

'Hello, I'm Mystic Crystal. I will be your reader for tonight, this morning, I mean,' I say, trying to sound as though I haven't been on the phone for the past eight hours and am in serious need of forty winks, while also trying not to snigger every time I say the words Mystic and Crystal in the same sentence.

'Oh, hello,' an elderly sounding woman says. 'I... um...'

The woman sounds obviously upset. I mean who phones a psychic hotline at three o'clock in the morning if they're as happy as Larry?

'Take your time,' I say. I suddenly feel overwhelmed with sadness.

'I... um... my... well, you see my husband passed away four years ago and... I'm sorry I ...'

'You still miss him terribly?'

'Yes. I do,' she whispers.

I start to panic a bit. What if she wants me to contact her dead husband? What will I say?

'I thought I was doing fine, but I'm not. I can't sleep at night – that's obvious seeing as I'm ringing you at this hour of the morning. I can't think straight during the day time...'

I know exactly how she feels. I think constantly about my dad and how everything around me reminds me of him. The photograph on the fridge door of our last family holiday; the pair of boots he bought for me because I was so skint and couldn't afford them myself; the silver pen he bought me to take to university with me.

It's probably not a cool thing to say at the age of 26, but I really did love my dad. He was the coolest dad in the world and I can't remember a time when we ever argued. I suppose being the only girl in the family, my dad treated me like a little princess whatever my age and I admit I could twist him round my little finger so easily. It was funny to see how far I could push him before he said no, which was invariably never.

'Dad, can I have a lift to London at the weekend? Dad, Sarah's been kicked out, can she live with us? Dad can you get me a loan for a car? Dad...' It didn't matter what my request was, my dad would always say yes, much to my mum's annoyance.

He had kept the news that he had prostate cancer quiet from the family until it could be silenced no longer. Dad never wanted any medical intervention, and by the time we knew about it, it had spread so far that any radiotherapy treatment would never have worked anyway. It broke my heart to see the tall, strong man I knew and loved turn into a helpless patient that I hardly recognised. He was only 65 when he died in a hospital bed. So, yes, I know exactly how this lady is feeling right now.

I turn three cards over as I think about how this woman must be feeling right now. Lonely, confused, angry...

'It doesn't get better with time does it? I know they say it will, but it doesn't and I do know what you are going through right now. Believe me,' I whisper. The cards I've drawn mean nothing to me and I doubt they will bring light relief to this woman either. Nothing will bring her husband back, just like nothing will bring my dad back. I suddenly get a sharp pain in the left side of my head and put my hand up to stop it hurting.

'My head hurts,' I whisper.

'He died of a brain tumour,' the woman says. Oh no, I hope I'm not about to go the same way. I close my eyes and see flashes of bright light zooming past my eyelids. I feel sick and dizzy all at the same time. All I want to say is, 'Valerie, I'm all right. It's all right to cry, love. It's truly amazing here.' I must have said it out loud because the woman on the other end of the phone line has broken down in tears.

'Oh my God, I'm so sorry. I didn't mean to upset you.' I suddenly realise that I've made this woman cry.

'No, no it's not you, my love. It's Frank. He was the only one who ever called me Valerie.' Oh, boy, this is beginning to scare me a little now. I remember when we had to do a study on the effects on telepathy. This professor from Arizona proved that people who are sensitive and tired could effectively pick up mind matter from another person – empathic, I think he called it. This is what I must have been doing. This woman's need was so strong that I must have somehow tuned into her mind and read her thoughts. Scary nevertheless. 'I'm sorry I have to go,' she says. Then the line abruptly goes dead.

CHAPTER SIX

It's five o'clock in the morning and I still can't sleep. I am so annoyed with myself for not being able to switch off, but the conversation with the last woman caller I had just keeps going round and round in my head and I can't forget her, or her husband Frank for that matter. The other callers were just in need of some common sense really, but that last one was, well, freaky to say the least.

Missy has curled up in a ball on my pillow. I swear she thinks she owns my bed. I really do. Oh well, I'll give it another ten minutes and if I can't sleep I'll get up and clean the flat or something. If that doesn't make me go to sleep, I don't know what will.

The next thing I know it is eleven o'clock in the morning and my mobile is meowing loudly in my ear. I unintentionally fumble under Missy's bottom area mistaking it for a cushion. Missy looks at me with utter contempt.

'Sorry, Miss,' I whisper. Where's the bloody phone. Ah ha, of course, in my boot, why didn't I think of that first? My vision is far too blurred to focus on what name comes up on the screen.

'Hello?' I croak.

'I see a short, ugly, stalker entering your life,' Amy does her best impression of a fortune-teller, although it sounds more like she's pissed.

'Oh great, not you as well,' I groan. 'I take it you're back from your holiday then, sweetie?' I say throwing myself back on to the bed, narrowly missing squashing Missy.

'I am, sweetheart,' Amy says in a suspiciously happy tone, 'and I hear that you have finally got yourself a job!' she shrieks. 'Although I have to say, you're not much of a fortune-teller, Samantha Ball, otherwise you would have predicted that I would have met the man of my dreams in the Maldives!' Amy shrieks again. She's a bit of a shriek-er is our Amy. At any given opportunity, she will shriek. Whether she is excited or sad for you, it doesn't seem to matter, she will shriek.

I've known Amy since we were eight years old and we were both forced to have home-made crowns strapped to our heads. We were the two wise men in our school Nativity Play. The third had not been as wise as he should have been; having eaten the semolina for lunch (silly boy) he consequently had an unfortunate attack of diarrhoea at the last minute, so he couldn't participate in being made to look like someone wearing their dad's best white shirt with a home-made crown strapped to their head.

I liked Amy because even at a young age she was very competitive and liked to win, no matter what. Show her a game of dominoes and that winning spirit would surge through her like electricity. In PE she was her fellow students' nightmare. Amy was aggressively competitive and from the first day she started at our school, I knew that she would stop at nothing to win whatever she had set her heart on.

Amy was faster at rope climbing than me, and she was better than me at beating our tutor at chess, so it was good to have someone like that on my side rather than against me. In the saga of the missing wise man, Amy naturally took charge.

'We'll show them,' she said with a reassuring, toothy smile and gave me a bear hug to show she meant it. And we did show them. We were the best bloody wise men a Nativity Play has ever seen and our improvised dance routine got a standing ovation, much to the head-teacher's annoyance. We have been there for each other ever since – break-ups, make-ups, you name it, we have always been together.

In fact, it didn't really surprise me that Amy had done so well since leaving college. I always knew she would. Amy wouldn't just take up a hobby such as karate; she would make it her mission to become the youngest person ever to get a black belt.

Amy wouldn't be satisfied with any old spotty oik; she would make sure that she got the school super-stud and then dump him, just because she could.

Being the best at everything wasn't my ambition. I preferred to concentrate on one thing at a time. Whereas at 13, Amy was already plotting and planning as to how she was going to master world domination. Today McDonalds, tomorrow the world.

'You've been talking to Jack then,' I guess.

'I certainly have!' Amy shrieks. 'So fill me in on all the details. I mean Sammy, hun, really! I leave you alone for a fortnight and you decide you no longer want to cure people of their veggie problems, you decide to become a professional psychic instead!'

Here we go again. If it's not bad enough that Jack thinks I'm a sandwich short of a picnic, now Amy won't let it drop either.

'Well, seeing as I couldn't find any carrot-fearing clients and I have to pay the rent, unlike some of us...' – Amy has already bought her own house thanks to a little help from one of her mother's property developer boyfriends – 'and a job is a job. I mean it's not going to be forever and I did earn myself £337 last night. Not bad for listening to people bang on about their problems,' I retort.

'I think it's brilliant, hun! So how do you do the psychic bit then?' Amy asks.

'What psychic bit?'

'You know, the bit where you contact the dead,' Amy says in a spooky voice.

'Oh, I can't contact the dead. I just make it up. You forget my dear that I spent three years in college learning how to read people. I'm trained to listen to people with problems and tell them what they want to hear. This way I earn enough money to pay all my bills without even leaving the house!'

'Well, psychic Samantha, let me tell you something your crystal ball won't tell you. I met this gorgeous guy out there called Kenzie. He's tall, dark, and as if it couldn't get any better, very, very handsome. And, you are not going to believe this Sam... he's also a Scottish lord! Can you believe that? He's bloody loaded, Sam! Just think, I could become a lordess!'

'You mean a lady. Ooh, Lady Amy – has a nice ring to it, don't you think?'

'Lady Amy,' Amy muses to herself, 'of course he doesn't boast about his money and his title. He's much too cool for that. Oh, Sam, he is just perfect.'

Amy proceeds to spend the next 45 minutes informing me of her new beau who apparently has two houses, one in London and the other in the middle of nowhere in the Scottish highlands and, according to Amy, her new fella is also sex on legs. Way too much information before I've even thought about breakfast and it only stands to remind me that I am still bloody single!

By the time I've made arrangements to meet Amy later and eventually get off the phone, it's midday and I decide to combine breakfast and lunch by offering to take my mum out for both at a little café in town. I know that at some point soon Mum will bump into Amy or Jack, and it will only be a matter of time before she finds out what I'm currently doing for money and how I am actually able to pay for her chicken and pineapple Panini, with side salad. I'm going to have to tell her. I mean it's not as though I'm a topless lap-dancer, is it?

'You're a what?' My mum splutters out a pineapple chunk on her plate – how come people are always mid-munch when you tell them something shocking and you end up covered in second-hand food?

'What do you mean you're a phone psychic? I didn't bring you up to be a psychic, Samantha!' Mum says a bit too loudly for my liking.

'Mum, shhhh will you?' I whisper. 'It's only a temporary thing, until I find a proper job.' I justify the reason why I'm about to send my mother into an epileptic fit. 'And it does pay the rent,' I add.

'I told you I would give you money, Sammy. People are going to think you're a right fruit-loop! I mean it's all right for old Doris Stokes...'

'She's been dead for years, Mum.'

'Exactly!' my mum replies. No, I don't fathom it either but I'm sure she thinks there's some method in her madness. 'And how is this...' – Mum can't seem to get the words out of her mouth – '...occupation going to affect your future career as a psychologist? I mean if people think you're already nuts, they're hardly going to think you're capable of making them better, are they? Do you think it's because of your dad, sweetie?'

'Eh?' What planet is my mother on today?

'Look Sammy, grief affects us all in different ways. Perhaps you're just trying to get closer to your father?'

'Mum, I'm not trying to get closer to Dad; I'm not putting my future at risk; I'm simply doing something that will earn me money and quickly. You keep asking me if I have a job and besides it was you who brought me back a set of bloody tarot cards! You were the one who was into all of that mystical stuff.'

'Yes, well I was just educating myself about different cultures and the cards I brought you back from India were only a memento. I didn't think you would be taking up fortune-telling as a career!'

'It is not my career, Mum. Like I said, it pays the rent until I can find a more suitable job and besides it's not that far removed from psychology. I mean the people who phone up these lines have real problems and I'm trained to deal with people who have problems. So it's not that far off what I eventually want to do,' I say. I'm getting a bit peed-off with all this negativity from all and sundry. I mean, they all keep on at me to get a job. I get a job which is not only interesting, but pays well, and all they can do is mock me or tell me it's not good enough.

'Well, I can't say I'm over the moon about it, Sammy love.'

Really?

'But if it's only going to be temporary, then I guess it will be OK. It will tide you over for a bit but don't you dare go playing around with any of those wiggly boards. They're nothing but trouble.'

'It's a Ouija board, Mum, not a wiggly board.'

'Oh, and how do you know that? Oh Samantha, you're not telling me...'

'No Mum! God, you can be impossible sometimes,' I huff again. What was supposed to be a nice brunch is turning out to be a big fat pain-in-the-butt brunch.

'Well, I don't know what your father would make of all this. Not to mention Paul and Matt. The next thing you'll be telling me that you're one of those wicker people.'

'Wiccan, Mum, not wicker!'

I daren't tell her that Miracle contacted Dad when I first phoned her. She would probably have choked to death on that pineapple chunk. Mum picks up a lettuce leaf and waves it dramatically in the air.

'Do you know how many food miles this piece of lettuce has probably travelled?'

'Eh?' I look up from my jacket potato at Mum's lifeless garnish.

'Hundreds if not thousands,' Mum adds in an authoritative manner. 'I'm writing all about it in my new book – *How Many Miles Has Your Food Travelled To Get To Your Plate?*'

'Oh right,' I say, quite thankful that we are now off the subject of me, Doris Stokes, Ouija boards and what appears to be my dire career decision making and on to something Mum wants to talk about, meaning her attempts to become the female version of Alan Titchmarsh.

'Did you also know that the tomatoes that you buy in the supermarket have probably been picked and packed by low-paid workers in Spain or somewhere as long as up to a month ago,' Mum looks aghast, 'and they have the cheek to call them fresh!'

'Hmmm,' I say and nod as though I care. Quite frankly, I've had just about enough of vegetables – I know strictly speaking a tomato is a fruit, but you know what I mean. I studied vegetables for three years; I don't want to know any more about them, thank you very much.

'That's what you should be doing, Sammy, writing a book, not messing around with all that silly fortune-telling stuff. You could write one about people who *don't* like vegetables. I'm sure there would be a market for it.' Mum brightens up.

'And who do you think is going to buy it, Mum? There are less than 3 percent of people who suffer from lachanophobia. I hardly think they are going to make it a bestseller do you?'

'Well, we've all got to start somewhere and it would make you more credible in the medical field,' she adds.

I'm tired from lack of sleep and my mother is just making things worse. I thought at the very least she would be pleased that I was earning my own money regardless of what I was doing to earn it.

My mum has a good heart and I know she's only worried about me, but she is also a bit of a traditionalist and anything that is slightly 'out of the box' is too much for her to cope with, which is rather ironic sometimes given the fact that she has travelled the world, seen different cultures and regards Margaret Thatcher as one of the most pioneering women to ever grace the planet.

Oh, well. I finish my cold jacket potato and make up an excuse that I have an application form to fill out for a psychiatric unit at the local hospital, which seems to make my mum happier. We kiss goodbye and I head for home.

CHAPTER SEVEN

Feeling as though I'd just told my mother that I am working as a prostitute, I decide to walk across town and see if Jack is taking one of his three-hour lunch breaks today. Fortunately for me he is, and I find him in the park playing air-guitar to his iPhone. He looks a complete loon. I chuckle as people – important looking people, in important looking suits – stare at Jack as if he must be someone who has just been let out in the community. Jack doesn't care though. That's what I like about him. Jack is just Jack and always will be. He won't change for anyone.

'I'm designed for life!' Jack suddenly shouts out, obviously unaware of the fact that he is not actually at Wembley Arena, playing alongside the Manic Street Preachers, but in the middle of Bath's Royal Victoria Park. Thankfully, today he is not wearing a dress and full pantomime dame make-up. Jack is in his favourite old blue jeans, which have more holes in them than a slice of Edam. To complete his carefully chosen outfit, he sets it off with a black T-shirt with the slogan *If you were a shoe, what shoe would you be?* I know, I don't understand it either. But if I were a shoe, I guess I would be a pink fluffy slipper – fun, snuggly and utterly dependable. Jack has his black Oakley shades on and if you didn't know any better, you would be forgiven for thinking he was in U2.

'I'm designed for life!' Jack shouts again and then suddenly smiles. I know he's seen me beneath those shades. 'Hey honeybee! How you doing? You stalking me again?' Jack shouts a little too loudly.

'Take your earphones out!' I yell back at him.

'What? Can't hear you? I've got me phones in! Oh right!' Jack yells back and pops his earphones out. The tinny base thumps out in rhythmic beats. I thump Jack in the arm.

'Ow! What's that for?' he protests.

'One, for shouting out that I'm stalking you, and two, for scaring all the tourists away with your singing,' I reply as I link my arm into his. We sit down on a park bench.

'Don't you realise that our wonderful historical city relies on the tourists? It only survives on selling over-priced tat like miniature Roman soldiers to them, you know.'

'Humm, so to what do I owe this pleasure?' Jack asks, peering at me from beneath his shades.

'I was in town meeting my mother – please don't ask how it went – and thought you might just be skiving off from work again, so I thought I would drop by and find you.'

'Skiving? Moi?' Jack feigns hurt. 'Actually I was just...'

'Practising your routine for when you're asked to play at Wembley, I know.'

'What's up then?' Jack asks.

'Why should there be anything up?' I ask, 'I just wanted to see you, that's all.'

'Samantha,' Jack looks over his shades again, 'I know when there's something wrong. You get that sullen look about you.' He's right of course. I do get a sullen look about me when something is up.

'Me? No, I'm fine. Really I am,' I say, very unconvincingly, I might add.

Jack looks at me again.

'It's my mother, and Amy.'

'Ahh, yes, I forgot to tell you I'd spoken to Amy. Sorry. I didn't think she would ring you up and go on about it.'

'Oh it's not your fault. They haven't said as much, but I know they both think I'm completely bonkers doing this fortune-telling job. My mother was mortified. You'd think I'd told her I was selling my body-parts on eBay to pay the rent.'

'Now there's an idea. Can you survive with just one kidney?'

'Yes you can, and no, I'm not that desperate. I just...'

'Wanted a bit of respect? Just a little bit, ooo just a little bit!'

47

Jack says in his best Aretha Franklin impression.

'Yes. Just for someone to say, well done, Sam. What with a year of being on the dole and the year before that losing my dad... All I wanted was someone to say...'

'Well done, Sam,' Jack whispers in my ear and smiles.

'Yes. See, that's all I wanted to hear from someone. I don't mind people taking the piss out of me, but at the end of the day, all I'm trying to do is earn a living just like anyone else. I bet you don't get the piss taken out of you from your mates at work,' I add.

'Ah well, that's actually because I have a really cool job,' Jack smiles. 'Ouch! Will you stop hitting me?'

'No, because you deserve it and because you laughed at me. I'll have you know that *my* job is a very cool job: I speak to dead people. On a level of coolness, I think you'll find that comes high on the cool-o-meter. Well, I don't actually speak to dead people, but I did speak to loads of very cool alive people last night,' I add.

'Oh yes, and who were these very cool people phoning you at two o'clock in the morning? Masturbators Anonymous by any chance?'

'No! Well I don't think they were masturbating when they were talking to me.' Oh crap, I hope they weren't. 'There were a few women who had been dumped by boyfriends, oh and a man who was having an affair but tried to convince me that it was his wife who was cheating! Can you believe it?' I look shocked. 'Oh, and my last call... well that *was* a bit strange. I had this elderly woman whose husband had died. You know I'm sure I recognised her voice...'

'Maybe it was your mum?' Jack smiles.

'Yeah right. The woman who thinks that I'm making a living impersonating Doris Stokes.'

'She's dead, isn't she?'

'Yes she is. Anyway, on the cool-job-factor scale I think I have the coolest job out of all of us.'

'Ahh, but Amy does get as many free fries as she wants. That's pretty cool.'

'Good point, but they make you fat and spotty.'

'And I do get you as many free CD's as you want. That's pretty cool.'

'Yes, but I can download them for free anyway. And I earned myself £337 in one night.'

'Well in that case, I think you must have the coolest job then.' Jack smiles and hugs me tight. 'Take no notice of what other people think, kid. You keep at it and one of these days you'll have your own hotline to old Doris. Oh shit!' He jumps up, 'I told Jerry I would be back to cover for him – he's got a root canal this afternoon – I've got to go. I'll text you later. Loves ya!'

'Loves me too!' I shout as Jack jumps over a park bench and heads off back into the town centre with his air guitar.

Missy and me spend the afternoon cleaning the flat. Well, I say Missy and me, in fact it's just me who cleans the flat. Missy spends most of the afternoon chasing a spider around the living room and cleaning her bum – you know that cat must have the cleanest bum in the world. Stupid spider. It should know by now not to come out of the bookcase when Missy is around. She likes nothing more than to hunt them down. And she does. One swipe with her paw and Incy Wincy will no longer be running up any drainpipes. Missy then spends her afternoon playing with its remains. I did warn that spider not to get too close.

With the flat gleaming like a Flash advert, I decide to have a quick bath before checking in for work. I think back to last night and the mysterious female caller who called so late. I'm sure I know her voice from somewhere, but can't think where.

Seven o'clock soon comes round and I log in with Miracle to say that I am now available for work.

'You did really well last night, Samantha. Did you enjoy it?' Miracle asks.

Enjoy it? Well, I don't know if I would use that word exactly.

I mean, to me, enjoyable means pigging out on a family bucket of Kentucky Fried Chicken while immersed in a romantic comedy, not listening to other people's problems and thinking of an answer to make them happy. However, it wasn't altogether an unpleasant experience.

'Yes, lovely,' I say.

'Good, because we've got a busy night ahead of us. We always find that Wednesdays are the busiest nights. I guess people get depressed that it's not quite the weekend, and decide to ring us,' Miracle muses.

'Really? I would have thought the weekends would be more busy,' I say. I have a bit of a theory about weekends. Psychology experts all agree that more people commit suicide on the weekends than any other time of the week. The reason being is that weekends give them time to think about things more deeply. They're not rushing around at work or trying to beat the rush-hour traffic. They're at home, often on their own, with time to think. I wonder if the Samaritans are busier at weekends.

'At weekends we tend to get a lot of drunken people phoning up. They go out for the night, get drunk, get depressed because they didn't get a date and phone us,' Miracle laughs her throaty laugh. 'It's also the time when there are a lot of break-ups, so we get a lot of dumped callers phoning to see if they will get back with their boyfriend or girlfriend,' she adds.

I like Miracle and in the little time that I've known her, we've become quite chatty with one another. I even look forward to ringing her up now.

'Oh hang on; I've got your first caller. I'll just tell her the rules and put her through to you.'

'Oh, OK. Thank you.' I was enjoying talking to Miracle and forgot why I was actually here. I wait patiently to hear the familiar bleep that tells me that my caller is connected.

'Hello, I'm Sa... Mystic Crystal,' I say, almost forgetting my stage name. 'How can I help you?'

'Well,' the girl starts. She has a Welsh accent and sounds about 12 years old. 'I'm not sure what I should do. I've got myself into trouble and I'm not sure how to get out of it.'

I'm tempted to tell her to phone the Samaritans, but continue to listen to her, hoping that she will give me a better clue as to what this trouble is. I mean, is she pregnant? On the run? Or what?

'This trouble you're in, is it something to do with a guy?' I guess.

'Mmmm.'

Good, I'm on the right track. She sounds young and doesn't sound as upset as she should sound if she were pregnant and the common reason why young women ring up is usually something to do with a man. I don't even bother to shuffle my cards and I know I'm taking a bit of a risk with my guess work, but I have a feeling that this man is a lot older than this girl is.

'Is this man older than you?' I ask.

'Yes. But you can't say anything,' she begs.

'All calls are completely confidential,' I assure her. I suddenly feel as though I'm dealing with an illicit affair, but I'm not sure whether to tell her this. Oh well, in for a penny, in for a pound.

'This man in your life, is he someone you're not supposed to be with? A teacher for example?'

The girl doesn't respond, but I have a feeling I'm right here.

'You don't sound very old,' I add.

'I'm over 16,' the girl insists.

'You do realise that you have to be 18 to call this line,' I say. I could be in serious trouble here if I advise her of anything and discover that she's under age. I pray that Miracle or someone from the company is listening in or recording this call.

'I am 18 and you're right; he's my teacher. Well, college lecturer actually. I didn't mean it to get so involved, but now someone's found out and said they are going to tell the Principal of the college and then he'll get the sack,' she wails.

'Calm down a minute. Now this person who knows about the two of you, do you really think he or she will tell your Principal?'

'It's a she, and yes I do,' the girl says.

'And what does this lecturer think about it all?'

'He's cool with it. He said it doesn't matter if he loses his job and that all he wants is for me – for us – to be happy.'

'He sounds nice,' I say. I can't help but think how romantic this all sounds. It's like something out of a Jill Mansell novel.

'But I don't know whether to finish it with him, otherwise he will lose his job.'

'No, don't finish it with him,' I say, suddenly. I know I'm taking a bit of a chance here, but in my experience, people who threaten to tell on other people rarely carry out their threats.

'Oh, really?' the girl sounds relieved. 'Do you think we will get married eventually?'

'It's a possibility. If he is happy to put his job on the line for you then I think you have a good chance of staying together and being very happy together.' Oh God, I do hope I'm right and she doesn't turn up at college tomorrow and discover that this person has told the Principal and he loses his job because of it. It's all very romantic in my mind, but what if I'm saying the wrong thing?

'And will I pass my exams?' the girl suddenly asks. Oh crikey, I'm really being put on the spot here! I think about this girl for a moment and feel nothing but happiness whenever I hear her speak. Maybe it's the accent – I love the Welsh. Surely that counts for something?

'Umm...' I try not to sound as though I haven't got a clue what to say next. 'I think you will pass your exams,' I venture, 'but you will have to work hard at them,' I add as a disclaimer. I mean obviously you have to study if you are going to pass your exams – unless your name is Jack or Amy that is.

'Brilliant!' the girl says. 'That is such good news and you have been brilliant! Thank you ever so much.'

A smile spreads across my face. Well, even if I have just made it all up and it all turns out to be wrong and her boyfriend loses his job and she fails all her exams, it was worth it just to make her happy again.

'You're very welcome.'

The rest of the evening consists of a few hoax callers, a mad woman who thinks I'm the Arch Angel Gabriel and insists that I fix her car by the morning because she has a very important meeting to go to; a pervert who gets off on telling me that he doesn't have any clothes on and likes to smother himself in tomato ketchup – maybe he thinks he's a chip? – and several women who are desperate to know when their prince charming on a white horse is going to appear.

By three o'clock I'm shattered. Missy has decided to take herself off to bed again and I decide that after the next caller I am going to call it a night. I would have told Miracle earlier, but no sooner than I am about to call her, she calls me and tells me I have another caller who insists she wants to speak to me. Bugger!

'It's Valerie,' the caller says before I have a chance to say anything. Oh no, it's the woman who phoned late last night. What if she's phoning to tell me that she knows I'm a fraud and that her name isn't Valerie and her husband is quite well and alive, thank you very much and she's going to report me to... well, whoever you report fraudulent psychic people to.

'Oh, Valerie. Umm... hello,' I say nervously.

'I'm sorry I hung up on you last night,' she whispers. 'I... I'm not very good at this kind of thing.'

You and me both love, I want to say.

'That's no problem. Are you OK now?' I ask.

Valerie sighs.

'I don't want to become one of those daft old women that make a habit of calling you, dear. I just didn't want you to think that I was being rude by cutting you off last night.'

'No, I don't think that at all,' I say. I wince and hold my hand to my head. The headache that I got the last time I was talking to Valerie comes back. It must be a sign that I am overtired.

'I just don't know where else to go... to find the answers I need,' she says.

'Like, why him?' I ask.

I know just how Valerie feels. I ask the same thing myself over and over again about my dad. Why did he have to go when he did? Why couldn't he have stayed around to see me graduate? Or get married? Why wasn't he allowed to be able to enjoy his grandchildren, if I ever have any? Why? Why? Why?

When I was growing up, whenever I asked about where we went when we died, my dad used to tell me about angels. He would always say that when the big white feather comes down and touches us on the head, then it's our time to go, Sammy Puddleduck. Despite being a bank manager, my dad was quite a philosophical guy and would always have an answer to any question I threw at him, and no matter how mad it sounded, I always believed and trusted him.

I remember when I was about six or seven, I was always fascinated by the way the streetlights would come on in our street one after the other. 'Wow!' I would say, staring at them in awe from my bedroom window. My dad told me that a little man called Fred used to run through a tunnel underneath the road and would switch on all the lights. That's why they came on one after the other. 'There he goes,' he would say, as we watched each one flicker on, one after the other. 'He must be very fit to be able to switch on all those lights before it gets dark,' I would say. 'Oh yes, Fred is very fit; he used to be an Olympic athlete, you know,' my dad would explain straight-faced.

'Yes,' Valerie eventually says. 'Why him?'

'Because when the white feather comes down and touches us on the head, it is then our time to go,' I whisper back to her. 'When it's our time, it's our time and we can't do anything to prevent that. It's like there is an invisible golden thread attached to each of us. For some of us the thread is long, for others it is shorter,' I feel as though this is what my dad would be saying to me if I asked the question 'why?'

'But why aren't we forewarned?' Valerie asks angrily, and rightly so. 'Why aren't we given any clues as to when it is our time? I would have appreciated Frank more. We would have done more things together. I wouldn't have kept on at him to unblock the sink or made him eat broccoli – he never liked broccoli.'

'Because if we knew, we wouldn't live our lives as we should,' I hear myself telling her. 'If we were told we are only going to live to such and such an age, then would we really enjoy the time we had?'

'I guess we wouldn't,' she admits, 'but it's still so hard.'

'I know it is, Valerie. I know how hard it is.' And I do.

'But he says he's fine and happy and his head doesn't hurt anymore. He's with you all the time and likes the colour of the bathroom now, and says he's sorry he didn't get round to painting it,' I suddenly add. Why I said that I don't know. God, I must be tired.

'He does?' Valerie says, her tone happy. 'I painted it yellow. He always hated it when it was lilac,' she chuckles. 'Said it looked too girly.'

Well, blow me away! Now I am really freaked out. Don't show that you are freaked out, Samantha. Don't show that you're freaked out, I tell myself.

'Really?' I say instead.

'Oh, thank you so much. Look, I had better let you go. I've taken up too much of your time already,' Valerie says. 'And thank you again. I'll try not to keep calling you. I feel I can move on with my life just a little bit more now.'

With my new-found confidence, I tell Valerie that she can call me any time. I smile and hang up. Another successful night and another £323 to add to my income!

CHAPTER EIGHT

The next few weeks pass by in a bit of a blur. I can't quite believe how good I am at this fortune-telling lark. In fact, Miracle has said on a number of occasions, that people have actually requested me for a reading, so I must be doing something right. I've spoken to that many people over the past fortnight that I tend to forget who's who. The only person who sticks in my mind is Valerie, who calls as regular as clockwork at three o'clock every morning. In fact it's so regular now that when I work the night shift, I don't log off until four, knowing that Valerie will be calling and will be disappointed if I don't speak to her.

I've discovered a lot about Valerie over the weeks. I know she now lives on her own, she has one son who lives in America and doesn't come to see her that often. I also discovered that Valerie was a seamstress before she retired and that she still sews when she gets the time. In fact, Valerie doesn't bother to ask me to read her cards for her or to tell her fortune anymore. Valerie just wants to talk and I do feel guilty that it is costing her money to talk to me, but the headaches I get when talking to her compensate for my guilt a little bit. I do wish she would phone earlier in the evening. By three o'clock my head starts banging and all I want to do is go to sleep.

In the space of a month, I've managed to pay off one of my credit cards and paid my rent with two weeks in advance to Ms Morris. Not that her ladyship was grateful for it mind you, telling me that I was lucky to have such an understanding landlady and that I would have been out on my ear if it wasn't for her. She also berated me for allowing Missy to use the banister as a scratch pole. I'm sure is wasn't Missy. Missy is too posh to do such a thing. Oh, and did I also realise that animals were actually prohibited in the building as a rule, and if Missy did it again she would also be out on her ear. At least she's stopped wearing that bloody anorak and I'm sure she's had something done to her hair.

As Ms Morris rabbits on and on about tenancy agreements, I don't seem to be able to shift the headache from the night before, and I'm tempted to shout, 'Oh shut up, you old bag!'

But at the end of the day my little Victorian flat, with its high ceilings and ornate fireplaces, is my home and I do need somewhere to live, so best not voice my opinions just yet. My mother did once suggest that I move back in with her now that she is on her own, but I think that this was more out of politeness than anything else. We both know that we would drive each other round the bend within a day.

So, Ms Morris, bless her, was not in as good a mood as I was that day, but I didn't care. My rent was paid up and in advance, meaning I didn't owe her anything and didn't have to deal with her for another two weeks either – yippee!

I don't know what Jack has that makes Ms Morris invite him in for coffee and not me... well I do, Jack has unashamed cheek and won't take no for an answer. With his boyish good looks and overflowing charm, Jack could sell coffee to Starbucks if he really wanted to, and it annoys the hell out of me that he can sweet-talk *my* landlady into giving him a cup of tea whenever he pops round, and yet she's a complete dragon to me.

'Oh, she's all right, as old people go,' Jack says.

'Ha! Yeah, right,' is my usual response.

'You've just got to play the cheek with her sometimes. She's quite a sweet old gal,' he says.

Sod Ms Morris and her lack of gratitude. I'm in a very good mood, and as it's my day off I intend to spoil myself rotten with my hefty pay-cheque.

Having showered and dressed I text Jack at work to see if he wants to meet me in town for lunch. With meeting places mulled over, I decide to head into town in search of some retail therapy.

With half of Miss Selfridges under my arms, I have no free hand to carry my new Cath Kidston lampshade – but balanced on the top of my head, as lampshades go it does make quite a good hat. In this state I tumble through the doors of Pizza Hut.

The waitress looks at me as if I'm clinically insane and should be committed immediately. I blush, apologise for the noise and scan the room for Jack who is sitting in the corner, hiding behind a huge menu, pretending he doesn't know me.

'Hi,' I breathe as I drop my bags to my feet.

'Do I know you, you weirdo?' Jack asks, for which he gets a thump in the arm.

'Right, I'm starved. What are we having?' I ask.

We tuck into a huge Margarita pizza with salad and wedges and catch up on the past week's events.

'So, Bree told Orson that she didn't want to marry him, and then Gabrielle went on a date with some new guy who turned out to be an alien! Oh and then, you're not going to believe this, Sam, Edie's implants exploded on the Matterhorn Bobsled ride in Disneyworld…' Jack says updating me on the latest goings on in Wisteria Lane that is *Desperate Housewives*. I had to work, and although I was trying to watch it, people just kept calling and interrupting me (the cheek of these people) and I have to admit, I did wonder why Edie was pulling such a funny face as she screamed down the tobogganing attraction. Now I know. Her boobs exploded – ouch, painful.

'Well, I think Edie deserves everything she gets,' I muse. 'She's a right tart anyway. So, do you want to do something at the weekend? Go to a club or something? I hear that new one in Bristol is opening on Saturday night. They're doing half-price cocktails all evening,' I say between mouthfuls of rocket and shredded carrot.

'Ummm…' Jack replies.

I look up with leaves hanging out of my mouth. Ummm? What does ummm mean? Jack never says ummm to me. Jack never turns down the chance to go out for a boogie on a Saturday night.

'What?' Jack says, fidgeting in his chair.

'You, that's what. Since when have you had to consider going out on a Saturday night?' I ask. 'Have you got a gig?'

'Ummm...'

Of course Jack hasn't got a gig. If Jack had a gig I would have known all about it. Whenever Jack has a gig he always, always, phones me in an excited manner to tell me when, where, and what is going to be on the Set List.

'Right, what's going on?' I ask, stabbing my fork menacingly into a cherry tomato.

'Nothing. Nothing's going on.' Jack fidgets again in his seat and studies the pizza menu.

'Ah, I get it. You don't like me anymore and have found a new best friend to spend your Saturday nights with.' I laugh a little too nervously in case it might be true.

'No, not at all. Well, not a new best friend... a... a girlfriend actually,' Jack says, looking down at his own salad and blushing like the cherry tomato I've just pierced and eaten.

'What? You? But you don't have *girlfriends*,' I say. It's true. As long as I've known Jack, he has never had a girlfriend as such. I mean he's not gay or anything like that and he has *had* girlfriends if you know what I mean, but they have always come second to the band and Jack's friends. Jack's previous girlfriends have always had to fit in around whatever plans the band or his mates were doing. Jack's previous girlfriends have *never* been a priority over a Saturday night out. *Never*. Not ever.

'I know, it's just Jasmine, that's her name, she's well... she's different and I promised that I would take her to see that new French film, Noir something or other,' Jack says. I know he's embarrassed.

'French film? Since when did you like French films? You can't even speak French, let alone understand it,' I say and I do have a point. Jack's idea of speaking French (or any other language come to that) is to talk *very* loudly and *very* slowly – in English.

'It has subtitles,' Jack says in defence of the French film industry.

'That's even worse,' I laugh. 'You're joking right?'

Jack shakes his head and I feel, well, I'm not sure quite what I feel really. Let down, abandoned like an unwanted puppy three days after Christmas. Angry that my best friend who I do *everything* with, has decided I'm surplus to requirement now that he's met some floozy woman who is named after a bloody flower.

'You'll like Jasmine. You're welcome to come to see the film,' Jack adds by way of compensation, but it only reminds me that I don't have someone of my own to take me to see a French film.

'No, you're all right,' I say, sullenly.

I know it's not like Jack and me are ever going to become an item, or anything. I mean, Jack and me! Ha! And I don't know why I feel like this, but I do. Maybe it's because we have done so much together that I'm over-protective of him? Like a worried parent, I wonder if he's going to be OK when he goes out with this... this jezebel, whoever she is. Regardless, I feel a bit put out that he's now got someone and I haven't and I will now probably have to spend Saturday night listening to Amy tell me all about her new gorgeous boyfriend, that's if she's not arranged to go to Scotland this weekend of course. Why does everyone else have a significant other and I don't?

'I've never reacted like this when you've had boyfriends. Most of them were dickheads but did I say anything?' Jack protests.

'Yes you did Jack, as it happens. Or have you forgotten about the time you texted James from my mobile and told him that he had BO and his breath smelt like a ten-day-old haddock? Or the time you called Andrew and told him that I had been rushed to hospital with some horrible tropical disease, and to not go to the hospital because it was touch and go, just because you wanted someone to watch the latest Steven Seigal film with. Which, by the way, in my opinion, was really crap. You made me believe he'd stood me up so I never called him again. For all I know he probably thinks I never made it and am ten foot under right now!'

'Oh yeah, that was really funny,' Jack laughs. 'And you're right...' Jack says.

'I am?'

'Yeah, I have to agree, it wasn't his best film to date.'

Instead of a punch on the arm, Jack is rewarded with a sharp poke of my fork to his left hand.

'Ouch! That really hurt!' he whines.

'Good,' I huff.

'Look, I tell you what, why don't we do something together Sunday night? Jas has to work then. She's a nurse. We could rent a movie if you like. One of your choice this time,' Jack says, trying to win me over into liking his new... whatever she is.

'Whatever,' I shrug, assuming the identity of a stroppy teenager who has just been told she's been grounded for a week.

CHAPTER NINE

My Saturday night is spent in McDonalds of all places with Amy and Kenzie. I think Amy felt a bit sorry for me and invited me out. Well, when I say invited me out, she actually asked me to come and watch her at work. When I say work, Amy doesn't actually work as such; she just walks around in a stroppy manner, bossing poor students around all evening.

'Anyway, I thought you said that hell would freeze over the day you and Jack became more than best friends?' Amy says as she passes by with a Happy Meal box and a Big Mac in her hands, and plonks it down if front of two teenagers. 'Sorry for the delay,' she hisses at them – Amy hates teenagers more than she hates students. She winks at Kenzie, who I have to say, lives up to all the gorgeousness that Amy has told me about him. He is sitting next to me, doing his best to look happy at the prospect of spending his Saturday night in a fast-food outlet.

'No! God – I'm not saying I fancy Jack. I mean, ewww Amy! That doesn't even come into the equation. The fact of the matter is, it's me. You've got Kenzie. Jack has this Jasmine whatever her name is, and me? Who do I have? Saturday was always *our* fun night. We have *always* done something on a Saturday night. It's like... well, it's the law. It's something we've always done and this floozy pops up and clicks her fingers and suddenly Jack is spending *our* Saturday nights watching bloody French films.' I say all this between mouthfuls of chicken nuggets. That's the best part of having a best friend who works at a fast-food restaurant – you can eat as many chicken nuggets with sweet and sour sauce as you like.

'Well, you can always come out with me and Kenzie later on if you like, can't she hun? – Darren! I'm not paying you to sit around and talk to your girlfriend all night you know!' Amy shouts at a youth in a burgundy cap who is obviously so in love that he's forgotten what he's there for.

Don't you just hate it when people in full coupledom mode make that kind of ahh-poor-single-no-one-wants-her type of gesture?

'No, you're all right. I've got some paperwork to do anyway,' I say, trying to sound as if I am very, very busy.

'Where are the two of you going anyway?' I know that this will instantly take the focus off me and my sad, lonely life. It's all Amy can talk about these days and I'm sure I know more about Kenzie than he knows about himself. Amy pulls one of those in-the-first-throes-of-love looks, not too unlike Darren the teenager actually.

'We're going to try that new club in Bristol, aren't we darling?' she gushes.

'You're welcome to tag along if you want, Sam?' Kenzie drawls in his Ewan McGregor-esque accent. He's very good looking and I would guess a couple of years older than Amy and me. He's also very kind and charming, but I still feel as though everyone in McDonalds feels sorry for me.

'Oh, show Sammy our holiday snaps of us on the boat, darling. Kenzie's dad is a professional photographer, isn't he, hun?' Amy says as she hands over a stack of prints of her and Kenzie all loved-up on the beach, of her and Kenzie all loved-up in the restaurant, of her and Kenzie... well you get the idea, her and Kenzie all loved-up basically.

Kenzie opens the pouch and produces a stack of photographs; she passes them over for me to look at while Amy goes into the kitchen to sort out a problem with the milkshake-mixing machine.

'And that's Amy at the surf-bar. She looks cute in that one, don't you think?' Kenzie drawls.

God, why oh why did I come here tonight? I feel like a right old Nancy-no-mates and looking at these photos is not making me feel any better right now.

'So, how's it all going in the world of psychic-fraud-hotlines then?' Amy asks when she returns to the table. She's still looking gorgeous despite having tackled the milkshake machine into submission.

'Will you keep your voice down?' I hiss. 'It's not a fraud. It's a genuine service.' After all, I am providing a service to people and so far I haven't had any complaints. In fact how does anyone actually know that I'm not psychic?

'You know I'm only joking, hun. I'm very proud of you. It's a good way of earning money whether you're psychic or not.' Amy laughs, and I guess she's right.

'Well Miracle says...'

'Miracle!' she screams.

'That's her name, well... I think it is... Anyway, Miracle says that everyone has psychic abilities, you just have to tap into them,' I say, trying to sound as though I have the faintest idea of what I'm talking about.

'Well, if that's what makes you happy and fulfilled.'

'Have you been reading those self-help books again?' I ask.

Amy nods, shamefaced.

Amy has grown into one of those women blessed with tanned flawless skin, a thin waist to match her thin thighs and a huge pair of boobs – basically, every man's dream. She is also a closet philosopher. Although she would never admit it, Amy has an entire bookcase full-to-bursting with self-help books with intriguing titles such as, *Improve Your Self-Esteem* and *Be Happy, Stay Happy*. Amy's latest attempt to lead the perfect life is with the help of a book (with a free CD) called *Happiness and Fulfilment Forever*.

You can't blame her. If I had a mother who had spent the majority of my childhood leaving me with neighbours and friends in favour of travelling on cruise ships, I think I would need a few self-help books myself. Thankfully my own mother didn't become an independent woman until she had dedicated 18 years of her life to us children.

'Right, I've got to get going,' I say. 'Paper work to do and all that.' Again, trying to sound like I'm a very important person. The fact that I'm going to stop at Blockbuster on the way home and get a huge box of popcorn, a DVD and a box of Roses, and slob out on the sofa with Missy is beside the point.

Amy gives me a big hug and kisses me on both cheeks – something she learned on a weekend trip to Paris and has since adopted as her way of saying, 'I love you and goodbye.'

'Have fun you two and I'll call you tomorrow,' I say, blowing them a kiss.

'Oh, we will and don't work too hard sweetie,' she calls back, before berating a couple of teenagers for sharing a cup of coke.

When I get back to my flat I discover three messages flashing on my answer phone. One is from my little brother Matt to tell me that he is coming to see me next weekend – well, what he actually says, between giggles (Mum obviously filled him in on my new job) is more like, 'You probably know what I'm going to say, you being a fortune-teller and all that, but can I crash at yours next weekend, Sam?' Oh yes, that's very funny Matt. Not.

Actually, I get on very well with my little brother. Despite being a complete nerd, he's really quite worldly wise for all his 23 years. Even when he was at school, he decided he was never going to work for anyone else and would make sure that he made a lot of money doing what he enjoyed doing. Matt was the one who held the family together when Dad died. Matt was the one who arranged the funeral, and it was Matt who was the one whose shoulder everyone cried on at the service. To this day, he hasn't spoken about losing Dad at such a young age and I don't think he ever will.

Paul on the other hand, despite being 28 and the eldest of the three of us, is the one who always gets himself into trouble, but somehow always manages to get someone to get him out of it again. You wouldn't trust Paul to look after your hamster let alone anything else – he would probably sell it on eBay given half a chance. I do admire Paul though because he is thick-skinned and doesn't give a toss what people think of him. So long as he has his sun, sea and surf, he's happy. He keeps telling me I should give up my flat and move to Australia with him, but his pace of life is way too chaotic for my liking. Paul's idea of life is to live one day at a time – literally. For example, he doesn't go to a supermarket to get his food, but manages to blag free meals from the local beach restaurants. He doesn't do any washing. Instead, he surfs in his clothes and then lays them out in the sun to dry. Paul doesn't do any kind of planning whatsoever, and he's happy with life like that.

I remember when we were kids, it was Matt who would always stick up for me whenever I needed sticking up for, which was quite often. I was a bit of weed actually, and if Amy wasn't there, it was Matt who I would go running to if someone in the year above me so much as looked at me. Paul was hardly ever at school to take much notice whether I was getting my dinner money nicked or not. He only ever did one full week at secondary school, and that was because he had a crush on some buxom blonde in the sixth form. He soon got tired of getting up early in the morning to catch the school bus, and no amount of ample bosom was going to make up for it.

The other two messages were from Miracle asking me to ring her back as soon as I got in. It's supposed to be my night off and I bet someone has rung in sick. To be honest, I don't feel up to talking to strangers tonight. Hmmm, ring Miracle for work, or stuff my face with chocolate and popcorn and recline flat out on the sofa watching Johnny Depp in *Chocolat*? No contest really. I unplug the phone and opt for slobbering over the delicious Johnny Depp.

By the time the film has finished, I have popcorn stuck to my dressing gown, chocolate smeared around my mouth and tear stains down my cheeks – always a stickler for a romantic movie, me.

It's not until I plug the phone back in the following morning, that I realise I now have six messages from Miracle. Having fallen asleep after the film and woken up as sticky as a six-year-old with a candyfloss, I decided to have a bath and leave the phone unplugged. I was half hoping Jack had left a message to say that he was sorry for abandoning me and our usual fun-filled Saturday nights, and that he had dumped Pansy, or whatever her name is, and would I please forgive him for being an inconsiderate pig. As I lay in the bath surrounded by white bubbles, I smugly thought that he had probably left several messages on my answer phone by now, and at least three on my voice mail.

He hasn't, of course. The only messages on the machine are from Miracle. The first one is asking me to call her back. The second is asking me where I was last night, and to please call her as soon as I get this message. The third is Miracle repeating what she had already said on message one and… well, you get the idea. At 8.30 in the morning I wonder if it's too early to return her call? If someone called in sick she probably had to work last night and wouldn't have got to bed before four this morning. Whilst I am pondering this thought the phone rings again, making me jump.

'Hello?'

'Samantha, where have you been?'

It's Miracle, sounding mightily pissed-off with me. I'm tempted to point out that she is the professional psychic here, so surely she should know that I was busy covering myself in popcorn and chocolate last night, but the desperation in her voice prevents me from doing so, and the fact that although I've never met her, I quite like Miracle.

'I was at home watching a movie, why?'

'Why didn't you answer your phone? I've been ringing all night,' Miracle asks.

'I thought you were calling for me to work,' I say, sheepishly.

'Work? No, well, not for last night anyway,' Miracle says.

'Look, I'll get straight to the point. How do you fancy being on the radio?'

'Me? Radio? Doing what?' I think she has gone a bit mad.

'Well, I've been asked by a radio station to do a live psychic phone-in and I can't do it – I'm going to see a flat in Brighton and I thought, since you are one of our best psychics and...'

'Me?' I almost choke on my Weetabix. I daren't tell Miracle that half the stuff that I tell the callers, I tend to make up as I go along.

'You're the only reader our callers phone specifically to speak to, Samantha, so you must be doing something right.'

'But where is this radio station and what do I have to do?' I'm actually panicking a bit now. I mean it's one thing to chat away to strangers in your living room, but quite another to have your conversation broadcasted on radio to the entire nation, isn't it?

'Oh, it's really easy, Sam. You'll be asked to go to your local studio where they will link you up with all their other stations and people call in, just like what you've been doing on the phone lines.'

'Only it will be live and on air to thousands of people,' I remind her.

'Well, yes, but...'

'And may I ask when this radio call might be?' I ask, knowing what Miracle is about to say next.

'Um, this lunchtime,' I can feel her wince as she says it.

'What? *This* lunchtime? As in *today*? As in just *four* hours away?' I say, my voice getting higher and higher.

'You'll be fine, sweetie. Just do what you've been doing all these weeks and you'll swing it, no problem. You need to go to *Town FM* in Weston-super-Mare, and be there by 11.45am. You'll be great,' she assures me.

'No problem? You're giving me just three hours notice to prepare for a live phone-in and you're saying it's no problem? Oh, I don't think I can do it, Miracle. I really don't.' And I don't. I mean I only started doing this so that I could get a bit of money to pay the bloody rent! These are *real* people, on *real* radio. I know the people I talk to on the phone lines are real, but well… they're not the same, are they?

'Look, Sam. I know you've only been in the job for a short time, but in that time people have come to respect you and they know you are for real. I've had so many people call and say they want to speak with you and refuse to take a reading unless you're available. I've come across a lot of readers in my time and believe me, I've never had such a high response to anyone else in this way. You are naturally gifted Samantha. I know you don't think you are, and you don't think you can do it, but trust me, you can. And besides, you have to because it's your fault that I've got to go to Brighton to view a house.'

'My fault? Why me?'

'Because it was you who said that I would be living by the sea, remember?' she laughs. I did, didn't I? I'd forgotten all about that.

'Well… I…'

'Please Sam?'

'Oh, God. OK, but just this once and if anything goes wrong, and I end up a laughing stock, it will be all your fault,' I say. Oh why, oh why do I give in so easily? I ask myself.

'Oh, Sam, you're a darling.'

CHAPTER TEN

Having been briefed by Miracle as to what to say, and more importantly, what not to say, for example that someone is about to suffer an untimely death, I sit nervously in the foyer of *Town FM* radio station, awaiting my meeter and greeter to come and meet and greet me. The walls are lined with photos of minor celebrities – some so minor that I haven't got a clue who they might be – all of whom have been guests of the radio station.

There's a woman I vaguely recognise from Blue Peter, I think. Oh, and there's Jordan aka Katie Price, with the chap who sang 'Mysterious Girl'. There's a bloke with a moustache and I *really* haven't a clue who he might be. There's also the obligatory shot of Pudsey Bear, with his poor bandaged eye – I wonder why he hasn't got that mended yet? Year after year he has that red and white bandage on his eye – with some radio DJ (or at least I think he's a radio DJ) sitting in a bath of baked beans, giving the photographer the thumbs up.

I'm not sure if I'm correctly dressed for the occasion, plumping for black jeans and a black t-shirt; seeing as it was radio I thought it wouldn't matter what I wore. The smart looking receptionist at the front desk obviously thinks differently because she looks me up and down and says, 'Oh, you don't look like a psychic. I thought you'd be older.' Maybe if I'd clamped a huge pair of curtain rings to my ears it would have given the right effect.

'Mystic Crystal?' A young woman in a beige suit and a bright smile approaches me with a clipboard in her hands.

'Sorry? Oh yes, that's me,' I say, feeling a little foolish for forgetting my 'stage' name.

'Hi, I'm Sarah-Jane. You're on in...' – Sarah-Jane checks her watch – '...exactly seven minutes. If you'd like to follow me,' she says and hurries towards the lift with me hurrying behind her.

'Sorry it's a bit of a rush,' Sarah-Jane says over her shoulder, 'our last guest, a Bollywood actress, ran over slightly and we're behind schedule, hence why we have to fit you in between the gardeners' slot and the news bulletin,' she asks breathlessly as we make our way to the fourth floor, 'Have you done live radio before?'

'Um, no, first time,' I say, nervously. I don't think you can count the live comedy sketch me, Jack and Amy did for the local hospital radio for Red Nose Day one year...

'You'll be fine. Well, I expect you already know that – you being a psychic and all that,' she laughs.

God, I wish people would stop saying that. It makes me so annoyed, not to mention guilty. Oh, I hope I don't screw this up. Still, at least they don't know my real name, and if I lower my voice a little, I'm hoping that no one will recognise it's me. When I was younger I could impersonate all sorts of celebrities. I should have auditioned for Britain's Got Talent just on the basis of my fantastic Cilla Black impression. Maybe I should do my readings in the style of Cilla for this phone-in. 'We've got a lorra, lorra dead people coming through...'

Town FM covers most of the south-west area and has a listening figure of around 300,000 – I know this because I quickly looked them up on my iPhone prior to making the 25-mile trip from Bath to the touristy seaside town of Weston-super-Mare – and I'm just praying that none of my friends or family listen to it.

'Right, go straight through there. Annette is waiting to take you in. Just be quiet when the red light is on. I think they're winding up Colin the Carrot Man now, and then you'll be on,' my meeter and greeter tells me. 'Have you got your crystal ball?' she giggles.

'Um, no... I don't use one of those,' I reply. Oh bugger! Maybe I should have invested in one for effect, although I have no idea where I might find a crystal ball and what did she mean by winding up Colin the Carrot Man, I wonder? Do they taunt him about the size of his carrots? I also wonder if Colin knows of anyone who has a fear of the orange root vegetable, which he might be able to refer me to.

'Hi, you must be Crystal,' a woman I presume to be Annette whispers, holding her hand out to shake. 'Won't keep you a minute, just finishing up with Colin here,' she smiles. Colin the Carrot Man, who, funnily enough has ginger hair, nods and I nod in return. Annette flicks a few switches and places a set of headphones on her head.

'Well, thank you for that amazing insight into the humble carrot, Colin. I will look at my carrot cake in a whole new light from now on,' she laughs. 'And Colin will be here next Sunday to tell us all how the carrot can cure the most amazing ailments. Now, coming up we have the one and only Mystic Crystal. She's here to answer all your spooky questions, so get calling. We now have Katy Perry with 'Firework.'' Annette flicks another switch on the multi-switch dashboard in front of her, takes her headphones off and smiles at me. My stomach flips as I hear the tinny sound of one of Jack's favourite singers coming through the headphones. I wish Jack were here to give me a bit of moral support. Mind you, he's probably too preoccupied with his new girlfriend to be thinking about what I'm doing today.

'OK, thanks Colin. See you same time next week.' Annette practically pushes Colin out of the studio. 'So, have you been on live radio before, hun?' she asks me. I shake my head.

'No matter. It's a piece of cake. I used to be in insurance – the most boring job in the world – and if I can do it, then anyone can.'

Annette is small in frame and a naturally pretty woman. At a guess I would say she's in her early 40s. As she talks she moves various switches up and down as though she knows what she's doing. Annette pushes her long fringe out of her green eyes and passes me a set of headphones.

'Pop these on and speak into this microphone,' she instructs. 'If you want to talk directly to me without the listener hearing, just push that button, but try not to do it when they are in mid-sentence as it mutes them on the live feed. Old ginger-nut does it to me all the time,' Annette laughs.

'OK,' is all I can manage to say.

'There's a glass of water there – unless you want something a little stronger?'

'No, water's fine, thank you,' I manage to say.

Come on Samantha, be brave! I tell myself. No one knows who you are, so just do what you do on the phone lines.

'Right, you ready?' Annette's words shake me out of my face-your-fear thoughts. I wish I'd read Amy's self-help collection now.

'OK,' I say nervously.

Annette puts her finger to her mouth and flicks another set of switches on her dashboard, which resembles something from the Starship Enterprise. I always thought that radio stations were massive, but this one is no bigger than a box bedroom, with smoky glass panelling. Behind the panelling sit two other people – one I learn is Jeff the news reader, a middle-aged man who looks a bit like Sean Connery. The other is a rather handsome looking sound technician called Liam. He gives me the thumbs up. I smile nervously and thumbs up him back, then put my headphones on.

'And that was the lovely Katy Perry with 'Fireworks,'' Annette says through her mic as she winks at me, 'and if you're one of the many Perry fans out there, you'll be glad to hear that she will be touring in the UK soon, so listen out for the chance to win some signed stuff. Now, before you shoot off in search of some carrots, we have a very special guest here with us today. Everybody give a big hand for our very own *Town FM* psychic, Mystic Crystal!' Annette shouts. I can see Liam and Jeff opposite rattling football rattles and cheering, as a wave of cheering and applause shoots through my headphones.

'Now, Crystal,' Annette looks at me, 'I understand you have

the ability to tap into the unknown and reveal our futures, is that right?'

Errr, I have no bloody idea actually, I think to myself.

'Yes, that's right,' I say instead in my lowest voice, hoping that I don't sound too much like a man.

'So, you can talk to the dead?' Annette enquires.

Oh crikey!

'Well, sometimes,' I say, remembering what Miracle told me when I first phoned up for the job. If I'm honest, I haven't got a bloody clue how this talking to the dead stuff works.

'Wow! That must be amazing. So do you tell your own fortune? Do you know when it's worth getting out of bed, or when you're going to win the lottery?' Annette laughs.

'Um, no. It's very difficult to predict your own destiny,' I say. I have this on good authority from watching hours and hours of *Charmed* on Channel Five. 'And although I can advise you what the outcome will be given a certain situation, nothing is set in stone. We all have our own free-will,' I add, feeling quite pleased with myself thanks to Aaron Spelling's supernatural series.

'Fascinating. Well, I can see we have a lot of callers who want to speak to you, so let's get started.' Annette flicks another switch which in turn sets the soundtrack from the film *The Sixth Sense* ringing into my ears.

'OK, our first caller is Hazel from Wales. Hazel, what would you like to ask Mystic Crystal, hun?'

'Oh, hello Annette, hello Mystic Crystal.'

'Hello,' we both say in unison. I shuffle my cards nervously, praying that Hazel from Wales isn't going to ask me when her boyfriend is going to propose to her or some other such I-haven't-got-a-clue question.

'I wonder if Mystic Crystal can tell me if and when my boyfriend and I will get married please?' Welsh Hazel asks.

Oh crap!

'OK. Well, Mystic Crystal, is Hazel going to marry her man

soon?' Annette asks.

I feel faint. Why, oh why did I agree to do this? Bloody Miracle! My hair is sticking to my face and my t-shirt is stuck to my back, due to my excessive sweating.

'Well...' I say, fumbling with my cards and trying to think of something to say next. In a split second I have a flash in my mind. I can see a hot beach, somewhere like the Bahamas, with beautiful palm trees in the background. I can also see a couple, but not their faces. Their backs are turned to me, but I'm sure this is the woman who has phoned in.

'Crystal?' Annette asks.

'Yes? Oh, sorry, yes... um... Hazel...' I say as I turn three cards over. 'Yes, you will marry your boyfriend soon, but I don't think it will be in this country. I have a feeling, and I could be wrong, but I think you will marry abroad and it will be somewhere very hot,' I venture. God, this sounds so bloody vague. I bet she thinks I'm a right con-artist.

'We will?' My first caller says excitedly.

I suddenly get a buzzing sound in my ears, which makes me jolt. I look across at Annette who doesn't flinch. The buzzing is like one of those white noise sounds that you get from an old TV set or a radio when you are trying to tune it in to a station. Out of nowhere a woman's voice whispers into my headphones.

'Tell her they have my blessing.'

I look at Annette again.

'What?' I say out loud. 'Who the hell are you?'

Annette looks quizzically at me and mouths 'are-you-ok?'

'I'm her grandmother, Winnie,' the voice says.

'Bloody hell!' I shout out loud. Oh my God! No, this can't be happening, I think, while all the time I can hear some woman's voice in my ears and it's not Annette or Hazel. Oh God, please don't let this be a dead person. Please don't let it be a dead person. Please let it all be in my head.

'She has had a hard time over this relationship and not everyone has

approved, but tell her not to worry. It will all be OK,' the woman's voice says to me. Holy crap!

'Um, we seem to have a little technical hitch, Hazel, could you remain on the line, hun?' Annette asks, panic rising in her voice. She flicks a load of switches and signals to Liam to play *The Sixth Sense* jingle again.

'Crystal! What are you doing? You can't swear on live radio!' Annette hisses at me. I suddenly realise where I am.

'Shit! Sorry Annette. Is the caller still on the line?'

Now I'm panicking and am not altogether sure of what I should be doing.

'Yes, we told her we have a technical hitch.' Annette nods to Liam to kill the jingle and link us back up.

'I'm sorry about that, folks. A slight technical hitch there. Hazel, are you still there, hun?'

'Yes I am. Is everything OK?' Hazel replies.

'Yes fine. Um, Hazel,' I venture, 'do you happen to know anyone by the name of Winnie?'

'Yes. My grandmother was called Winnie – well Winifred, but everyone called her Winnie. She died two years ago,' Hazel confirms.

My stomach does a flip. Oh I feel so sick. Right, hold it together, Sam. Oh great, now I feel faint. I don't want to talk to dead people. I try to think of how Miracle would handle this. I remember her telling me all about different psychic abilities and clairaudience, where you can hear dead people talking, was one of them. Oh great, I'm a freak who can talk to dead people! I'm a talking-to-dead-people freak!

'OK... um... well um, I have someone here called Winnie and she wanted me to pass on a message to you. She says that you have her blessing. She knows it has been difficult for you and many people have not been supportive, but you have her blessing and she says it will all be OK.' I say it as quickly as possible. I've already sworn live on radio, what does an old woman's voice in my head matter?

I hear Hazel gasp.

'Does that make sense to you, Hazel?' I ask. Annette is excitedly clapping her hands.

'Yes, yes it does,' Hazel replies. 'You're right, my grand-mother was called Winnie and she's right, people haven't been very supportive. My fiancé and I come from two very different cultures and it has been difficult for us to stay together. He was supposed to go into an arranged marriage, but... well, we fell in love with each other...' Hazel says quietly.

As I listen to Hazel, I turn the three cards over and sure enough there are hearts galore on all three.

'Well, I don't think you have to worry, Hazel. As your grand-mother said, it may not be easy but stick to your guns. I think you and your fiancé are a match made in heaven,' I say, smiling to myself. How nice to be the bearer of good news, even though I have no idea of where that lot came from and I'm more than a bit worried that I can now hear an elderly woman chuckling inside my head. Maybe I should make an appointment to see the doctor after all this?

'Thank you so much. We've been planning to get married for so long and it's nice to know that it will finally happen,' Hazel says. Annette swivels around in her chair and gives me a high-five. I look over at Liam, who gives me another thumbs up.

'That was brilliant!' Annette says after she's flicked a few switches and puts 'Ghost Town' by The Specials on to play.

'Thank you,' I say. 'And sorry about swearing. Hazel's grand-mother took me a bit by surprise.' Well, she did!

'Right, are you ready for your next one? We've got calls coming out of our ears here!' Annette says.

'OK,' I reply, wondering just what I've let myself in for.

CHAPTER ELEVEN

OK, so now this is getting even freakier. In the space of 20 minutes, I've done seven readings, live on radio. I've had the voice of an old man yelling into my ear, shouting obscenities at me for not passing on a message to his sister quick enough. I've had a little girl telling me to tell her mummy that she loves her, and a young man telling me that he didn't realise that the drugs would actually kill him and that he was sorry, he only took them for a laugh.

Annette is looking very pleased with the way this show is going and keeps pushing me to take more calls from people who want to know what their future holds or want to hear from someone they have lost. In all honesty, I don't know how much more I can take of this. Caller after caller comes through all wanting answers to their questions. Apparently, according to Miracle, what I have indeed just experienced is called clair-audience – in a nutshell, I can now hear dead people. Smashing.

'And next on the line we have Becky who wants to know if she will leave her job soon. Over to you, Crystal,' Annette smiles.

I give my cards a quick shuffle. No matter how many calls I take, I always dread the next one coming. Once again I pick out three cards for the caller.

'She's pregnant, you know.' A voice says in my ear. Despite having now heard numerous voices since coming into the studio, I still look at Annette to make sure it isn't her talking to me through the headphones. Annette is currently talking to Jeff in the opposite window. I'm not too sure if I like having other people's voices in my head, to be honest with you. It's… well it's just not right, is it?

The cards I draw are family cards. I have no idea how old this girl is, but she sounds quite young.

'Becky, I'm not sure how to say this, but I'm being told that you are expecting a baby,' I say, hesitatingly.

'Me? No way!' Becky answers.

Suddenly I'm at a bit of a loss for words. I look at Annette and wonder if it is her who's expecting.

'Umm... well...' I stutter. I haven't been wrong up to now, and Miracle did say to go with your first thoughts. Despite feeling as if I am going quietly mad, what with hearing voices and all, I still feel as though this girl is expecting a baby. 'Well, I'm being shown a baby, so if you're not pregnant, then there is someone around you who is, Becky.' I know it sounds as though I'm clutching at straws, but I don't know what else to say. Any moment now I'm half expecting her to say that she is actually not called Becky, but Brian and that she/he was testing me and that I am a complete fraud. Oh, give me back the good old days when all I had to worry about was curing someone who couldn't stand the sight of a cabbage!

'Well, *you* still haven't answered my question,' Becky snaps.

'OK, well...' I randomly pick out another three cards. One shows a pregnant woman – better not even go there. The next shows a sharp pair of scissors cutting a string and the third shows the Fool – fresh beginnings and a new start.

'Your cards do show that you will be cutting ties with someone or something and within a year your life will be very different from what it is now,' I say. 'So in answer to your question, yes I do feel that you will leave your job, Becky.'

Annette pokes her tongue out at the microphone and then smiles at me. I blow my fringe out of my eyes. Is it hot in here, or is it just me?

'Well, that's all we have time for, folks. Apologies to those who couldn't get through, but we hope Crystal will come back next week to answer all your mystical calls.'

I look puzzled at Annette who smiles again. Liam and Jeff are both doing thumbs up to me, which I take to mean that the show went well. I feel like wee Jimmy Krankee with all this thumbs up business. Any moment now I feel as though I should shout out 'Fandabbydozey!' at the top of my voice.

Annette introduces the news bulletin and signals Jeff in the opposite room that it's his turn to take over.

'Well!' Annette turns to face me, 'That was bloody brilliant, Darling!' she says.

'Oh, thank you. Sorry about swearing on air. Something took me by surprise.'

'So, will you come back next week? I asked the producers if we can have a regular Sixth Sense slot and they agreed... please?' Annette begs, 'The producer said he has never had so many calls for a phone-in and they do pay well, talking of which, here you go,' she hands me a sealed envelope embossed with *Town FM* on it. Inside is £300 in cash.

'They're willing to pay you that every week if you agree to come in every Sunday,' Annette says with a pleading look in her eye.

'Well... I'm not sure, Annette. I wasn't supposed to be here at all. I was only covering for my boss,' I say. 'I'll have to check with her that it will be all right.'

In all honesty I don't think my nerves are really up to this live radio lark every week. But then again the idea of getting paid £300 for an hour's work is very appealing.

A woman's voice comes into my head: *'Tell her to get the brakes checked on her car.'* Oh, not again. I do wish this would stop happening. There's a name for people who hear voices you know! I am *not* a psychic. I am just a good judge of character and a good guesser. I am *not* hearing voices in my head! *'Tell her!'* The voice demands. Oh bollocks!

'Well, have a chat with your boss and call me tomorrow, but I really do want you to come back. I bet the producers will pay you more if you want me to ask them?'

'Oh, no, it's not about the money.'

'Well, ask your boss and see what she says.'

'OK, I will and I'll call you tomorrow. Thank you so much for making it a nice experience, Annette. Oh, and by the way…' I venture, 'I'm being told to tell you to get the brakes on your car looked at,' I smile nervously just waiting for Annette to tell me that she doesn't actually own a car and she is in fact an environmentalist who cycles to work every day. Instead she looks a bit shocked and then nods.

As I sip my latte in the *Town FM* canteen, while texting Miracle about my concerns at hearing voices in my head, Liam the sound technician plonks himself down in front of me. As previously mentioned, Liam is one of those men who could easily come under the category of naturally good looking – he has natural blonde hair that is spiked at the front and dazzling green eyes. He has an air of quiet confidence about him and like me, Liam is a jeans and t-shirt kind of person. Also like me he has a penchant for coffee.

'I thought I would find you here,' Liam says, smiling. 'How did you find it, your first live performance?'

'Good. A bit nervous,' I say, licking the coffee froth from my top lip. Oh no! I hope he doesn't think I was licking my lips in one of those, you know, those suggestive-licking-your-lips kind of ways. Suddenly my face feels almost as hot as my latte.

'You did really well, considering it was your first time.' Suddenly I feel very self-conscious. 'So how long have you been a psychic?'

The dreaded question. Do I admit the truth and tell him six weeks and I'm not actually a psychic, that I'm just good at guessing and I hear departed people in my head? I blush again.

'Not that long. Still learning the ropes,' I offer, which I suppose isn't too far from the truth. I *am* still trying to fathom out how and why I have started to hear voices in my head. Maybe it's because I spend so much time in my own company. You see it all the time in the papers. The nutter who claims to hear voices – they all turn out to be loners, you know. Note to self; must get out more.

'So, what do you think?' Liam asks, shaking me from my thoughts.

'Huh?'

'About coming to this new wine bar tonight. We get VIP tickets in return for mentioning it on air and I thought...' Now it's his turn to blush. Oh, he is lovely.

'Umm... yes I'd love to. Thank you.' Blimey, it looks like I, Miss Lonely-Hearts-Club, just got myself a date!

CHAPTER TWELVE

'So, what you been up to then? I've been trying to get hold of you all morning,' Jack says.

'I know,' I reply. Having checked my answer machine, I found no less than 16 messages, 15 of which were from Jack wanting to know where I am and what I'm doing at such an ungodly hour on a Sunday morning. The other message is from my mother to tell me some obscure fact about the humble radish and to also enquire as to my whereabouts. Huh! I don't lounge around the flat till lunchtime *every* Sunday you know!

'Just fancied a run,' I lie to Jack.

Jack does that girly giggle that really doesn't become him.

'You? Running? Bollocks!' Jack manages to splutter between laughing.

'Yes!' I snap a little too defensively. I sometimes forget that Jack has known me for the past God knows how many years and also knows when I am lying.

'So, what have you *really* been doing from eight this morning until two-thirty, Miss Ball?'

'I can't say,' I say. If I try to lie again I will just make a complete hash of it. If I tell Jack the truth he will probably go and tell Amy, my mum and the whole of Bath come to that and then mysterious Mystic Crystal will not be very mysterious at all, will she?

'What do you mean you can't?' Jack says, sounding like a wounded kitten.

'I just can't, all right? Anyway, how did it go with what's-her-name and the French film?' I ask, changing the subject completely. I know darn well what her name is, but I'm still smarting from being dropped like a hot potato last night.

'Oh no you don't. I'm not telling you anything until you tell me what you've been up to,' Jack says. I sigh. He's not going to give up on this, is he?

'If I tell you then you have to promise you are not going to blab to anyone – and that means in particular my mother and Amy,' I warn, 'and you have to promise not to laugh,' I add, knowing what Jack is like as soon as I mention anything remotely connected to psychic things.

'Cross my heart and swear to whatsit,' Jack promises.

You see, unfortunately I'm born with that mysterious gene that prevents you from being able to make up convincing stories and well, lie. I've never been any good at it. I mean I start well, you know, with the little white lie, but then I can't just leave it at that, I have to embellish it a bit more, in the hope that it sounds convincing. Then just to make sure it's realistic, I throw in that one of my relatives has just died. People must think I'm very careless given the amount of times I've 'lost' them.

'I was on the radio this morning. *Town FM*,' I venture sheepishly – another grandmother-death-in-the-family is not going to cut it with Jack, given the fact that he knew my grandmother and actually attended her funeral.

'Oh yeah, doing what?' Jack doesn't sound convinced.

'A live psychic phone-in, if you must know,' I say huffily.

'What you? On the radio? Live?'

'Err, yeah,' I confirm – God, Jack can be so… grrrr sometimes!

'What live? On the radio?'

Do we have Little-Sir-Echo on the phone here?

'Yes Jack. Me, live, radio. As in "Welcome to *Town FM*",' I say in my best radio presenter's voice.

'What THE – *Town FM*?'

I'm not sure what part of I-was-live-on-the-radio Jack is not getting here.

'Yes Jack.'

'Bloody Hell!' Ah-ha, the penny finally drops. 'How come?'

'Because my…' – I was about to say psychic advisor, because I guess that's what Miracle is really – 'boss, Miracle, couldn't do it and asked me to cover for her.'

'Cool! So what was it like?' Jack asks.

I don't want to freak him out by telling him that I have since discovered that I am the grown-up version of the 'I-speak-to-dead-people' kid from *The Sixth Sense*.

'It was good, I just did some live readings, that kind of thing.' I play it down a wee bit.

'Cool. You reckon you can get a demo of the band played for us then?' Jack says.

'I don't know. They've asked me back next week, well every week actually,' I say, feeling quite proud of myself.

'Double cool! So you're gonna be like a psychic DJ?' Jack laughs.

I do wish Jack would take me seriously sometimes.

'So are you coming to The Lion tonight or what, Mystic Sam? The band's playing,' Jack says.

I'm about to say 'yes' when I suddenly remember that I'm already booked.

'Can't, sorry. *I* have a date.' I smile as I say it. In fact it has been so long since I've dated anyone that I have to admit it does sound good. I-have-a-date!

'What you? A date? Who with?' Jack says as I get a sense of deja vu coming on.

'Well, don't sound so bloody surprised! I'll have you know I am in fact quite a catch!' I say a little too defensively.

'I know that. I just meant... When did this happen? Who is he? Where did you meet him and can I come too?'

'None of your business and no, you can't come too. You've got a gig remember and even if you didn't have, I wouldn't let you come anyway,' I reply.

'Oh right. OK then. I'll call you tomorrow.' Jack sounds all forlorn, which serves him right for trading in our Saturday nights in favour of some... some floozy Florence Nightingale.

'Bye then. Loves ya,' Jack says.

'Love me too. Bye Jack.'

I feel a bit of a cow-pat for being off with Jack, but it serves him right. Now, what does one wear to a posh wine bar?

I feel somewhat overdressed. Actually overdressed is an understatement. The wine bar in Trenchard Street is heaving with bodies – and they are all dressed in t-shirts and jeans. Having spent the best part of three hours squeezing myself into my little black dress – the one and only designer item I have in my wardrobe, thanks to a shopping trip in New York that Amy won as area manager of the year – and a pair of killer heels, I now remember that the dress code for a trendy wine bar is casual wear. Still, I do look good, even if I say so myself, and even if I do stand out like a sausage at a vegan conference.

The Glass Half Full wine bar is decorated in a beautiful trendy style, what is currently referred to as minimalist, or in other words, as if they don't have two kidneys to rub together. It reminds me of the student bars Amy and I used to frequent. The floors are bare, save for a coat of clear varnish; the walls are un-plastered, favouring instead the trendy-loft-apartment-breeze-block look, with a few canvas prints that look nothing like their subject, hung at interesting angles so that you have no option but to strain your neck in a bid to make out what the subject is meant to be, and even then you still have no idea.

I spot Liam almost immediately. Did I mention that Liam is six foot four, so it's not that hard to spot him in a crowd, or a dimly-lit room for that matter – bit of a problem for him though, I imagine, should he be playing a game of hide and seek.

'Ah, here she is now,' Liam says as I push my way through the jean-clad crowd. Isn't it funny how any other evening I wouldn't think twice about walking into a wine bar on my own? Tonight however, I feel nervous and I'm sure everyone is looking at me – which, considering I look as though I've just taken the wrong turning to an Oscar party, they probably are.

'Excuse me, excuse me, excuse me,' I mutter to the backs of

people as I make my way to the main bar.

'You made it then?' Liam smiles as I finally reach him. I feel as though I'm on the verge of overheating. I'm sure it's illegal to have so many people gathered in one room so lacking in ventilation, you know. I blow a stray curl out of my eyes.

'Hi,' I say, somewhat out of breath – did I memo myself a reminder to get fit?

'Anya, this is Crystal.' Liam introduces me to the woman standing next to him, as he hands me a glass of white wine. I momentarily wonder what they give you in a wine bar if you don't drink wine. I suddenly realise that Liam just referred to me as Crystal and doesn't actually know my real name. He actually thinks my name is Crystal. Do I correct him now or just keep quiet? And anyway, do I really look like a Crystal?

Before I have time to say anything, Liam's companion, Anya, has already launched into a conversation aimed at me.

'Lovely to meet you, Darling. Loving the dress! I've heard so much about you, Crystal. In fact I heard you on *Town* today; you were very good and so accurate. I particularly liked the bit with the woman who wanted to know if her fella was going to marry her – amazing! How did you know that?' Anya says.

Anya, also dressed in a t-shirt and very tight skinny jeans, with lots of trendy rips in them, exudes confidence and as well she might – she empowers gorgeousness – tall, willowy and graceful are just three adjectives that would sum Anya up. At a guess I would say she was in her early thirties. Her long ebony hair flows like a river down her back and she has the most perfect complexion a girl could ask for. Life's really not fair, is it?

I blush as Anya enthuses about *Town FM's* new Sixth Sense programme. Liam, unable to get a word in edgeways, nods in all the right places and keeps us topped up with wine. I'm surprised he's not bored out of his mind by now.

'So are you going to become a regular for us then?' Liam asks, as soon as Anya pauses for a moment to take a sip of her drink.

'It looks like it.'

Having phoned Miracle to update her with recent events and voice my concerns that I suddenly keep hearing voices in my head, she was only too eager for me to do the regular slot for *Town FM.* 'I see big things coming your way, Samantha, so grab as many opportunities that are thrown at you, sweetheart,' she encouraged. Miracle then proceeded to tell me that if I was going to make it as a professional psychic I would have to put up with the voices, and something about opening and closing my chakras properly, whatever they are. She also assured me that the voices I have heard are real dead people and I'm not imagining things, nor am I going mad.

According to Miracle we all have the ability to tap into our sixth sense and it's only when we open ourselves up to that possibility, that the non-living feel comfortable in contacting us. This is all way outside of the box for me at the moment, but it *is* earning me lots of money. As if this sort of thing happens to everyone every day? She then went on to tell me all about the fabulous flat she has found with an equally fabulous sea-view and that the estate agent wasn't all bad either!

'Great, I can't wait,' Liam says with a gleaming smile. Ooh, I think he likes me!

'So now you're a pro at this game have you ever thought of getting into TV, Crystal?' Anya asks.

'TV? Oh God no. I've only done one session on the radio.' I laugh at the very idea.

'So? You've obviously made a good impression with the show's producers. They wouldn't have asked you back if you hadn't would they, Liam? So what do you think?' Anya Asks. I look puzzled.

'Anya is a producer for the BBC. Shows like *What Your House Says About You,* that kind of crap,' Liam laughs.

'It is not crap. It is real life media, I'll have you know. I'm telling you, Crystal, if we got someone like you on board our viewing figures would go sky high. What do you think?'

'Oh I... ummm... I don't know,' I stutter.

Miracle's words echo in my brain telling me to grab opportunities and I know if it was Amy she would have bitten Anya's
arm off within nanoseconds, but I'm not Amy and I don't know
what to do. Maybe I should ring Amy. It's all very well doing a
radio phone-in, but on telly you're there in full view of everyone
who wants to prove you're wrong. There will be letters of
complaint, questions, and people wanting me to prove myself all
the time. Oh I don't know!

'Have I got some news for you!'

A voice I recognise calls over to me and I'm thankful for the
diversion that is Annette. She sashays her way over to me and I
say a silent thank you to whoever might be listening – and as
things stand that could be just about anyone up there at the
moment.

'Annette, lovely to see you,' I say, and do the mwoah, mwoah
thing that is so fitting nowadays. In my student days I used to
laugh at the likes of Paris Hilton and Lindsey Lohan and their
air-kisses, but I've since noticed that it is an essential part of
social greeting etiquette between women who wish to great each
other and it's also a very effective way to keep your lip-gloss in
tact.

'You are not going to believe this!' Annette says excitedly. 'Hi
Liam, hi Anya,' she adds as an afterthought. 'You know that girl
that phoned in today? The snotty little madam... what was her
name? Becky, that was it. The one you said was expecting a
baby?'

I nod, remembering what a challenge she was.

'Well, it turns out she is indeed pregnant! You were right,
Darling! She phoned the studio to speak to you, but you'd
already left. She said that after she spoke to you, she and her
friend went out and bought a pregnancy test and it turned out to
be positive! You were right all along. She's only 18. Silly girl,'

Annette muses.

'Blimey!' Anya and Liam say in unison. I blush and take another gulp of the very pleasant wine.

'See, I told you she was good. My little star!' Annette says smugly to Anya.

'I know, and I'm trying to persuade your little star to come on to one of the day-time shows,' Anya smiles back. Forgive me, but it looks to me as though these two have a bit of rivalry going on here.

'Well, it's up to Crystal, of course, but you know how fickle TV work can be and just remember, I saw her first,' Annette warns.

I look at Liam to help me and thankfully he gets the message. He holds out his arm.

'Shall we?'

'Yes please,' I reply.

CHAPTER THIRTEEN

You would think having just come back from a date after being 'on the shelf' for the past 18 months I would be on cloud nine, wouldn't you? Wrong. Liam was lovely, don't get me wrong. He did all the right things, said all the right things, and yet... After all this time of being a singleton, you would have thought that I would have been only too happy to have a date with a gorgeous, tall, sound tech, and I was happy. We had a very nice time at a small Italian restaurant in the town, but there just wasn't that spark that I thought there would be, or should be. Maybe I've become a cynic over the years of failed relationships, but from what I remember, aren't you supposed to have butterflies in your stomach or thunderbolts of lighting? The only feeling in my stomach is that of hunger, and the only thing that is going to cure it is a bacon sandwich.

Liam is most definitely not married. He is most definitely gorgeous looking and yet... well, why don't I feel anything for him? I think I really must be going mad – that or I have spent way too much time on my own of late.

As I search miserably in the fridge for something that resembles a packet of bacon, I wonder if I'm destined to be a spinster for the rest of my life. All my friends are either engaged or happily settled down with just the one boyfriend by now. Maybe I'm being overly fussy and I should accept any offer that is put in front of me – after all, I don't think prince charming is out there anymore. Men don't seem to aspire to being prince charming, the kind of man who sweeps women off their feet. More like charming for all of two weeks and then they get bored with all that opening doors and paying for dinner malarkey. Two weeks in, and you get the door shut in your face and you have to 'go Dutch'. Gosh, do I sound cynical? If I don't sort myself out, I just know I am going to end up like Ms Morris upstairs – oh God, what a thought!

I must give Liam the benefit of the doubt and make more of an effort if I am not to end up like my landlady, I memo myself. I promised I would call him before Sunday when I am due back in the radio studio. Now where's that bloody bacon I bought?

I'm back at work and am finding that the more phone calls I take the easier it gets. I still get someone other than the caller rabbiting to me in my ear, but strangely enough I've got used to them and I actually find it quite odd when I don't hear voices in my head. My phone rings for 20th time. Although I'm prepared for my next call, I'm not prepared to hear that it is in fact my mother on the other end of the line – you'd think I would, being a psychic and all that, wouldn't you?

'Samantha. It's your mother here.' Uh, oh, sounds like I'm in trouble.

'Mum, I'm working. I can't take personal calls when I'm working, I told you that,' I say as nicely as I possibly can, praying that Miracle isn't trying to get through with a caller.

'Well this is important.'

'Go on,' I sigh, 'but make it quick, I've got calls to take.'

'What's this about you being on national radio?' My mother asks. OK, so who told her?

'Mum, I can't really discuss it right now. I'm working.'

'Well, is it true? Oh, please don't tell me you're going under your own name?' My mother sounds as though she is going to faint.

'No, Mum. I'm not disgracing the family by going under my own name.'

'Well, Marjorie said that she recognised your voice immediately. She had to go to the garden centre to get some compost and one of those things you put in fish-tanks – now what did she say it was called? Oh, it will come to me in a minute. Anyway, she said she couldn't believe it when she heard your voice coming out of her radio. Of course, I told her it was nonsense and it must have been someone that sounded like you, but she was adamant that it was you. Oh Samantha, what are you doing with your life?' My mother sounds very disappointed in me – again.

'Look Mum, I don't think it's any of Marjorie's business what I do on my weekends.'

'So it is true then?'

My mother would make a very good interrogator for MI5.

'Yes, Mum. I was filling in for my boss who had to go somewhere, and if you must know, I did a very good job. And it's not national radio, it's local radio. I was way better than Colin the Carrot Man.' Well I was.

'Colin the what?' my mother says, sounding intrigued. Mention anything relating to vegetables and you've got her attention.

'The Carrot Man. He does a gardening slot just before my Sixth Sense programme.' Ooh, hark at me, *My* Programme!

'Ooh,' my mother says. Nice one, Sam. I think I've taken the focus off me for the time being. 'Oh, and I met someone – a man – called Liam. He's the sound tech at the station,' I add for effect. 'Look, Mum, I'll call you later and tell you all about it. I have to get back to work now.'

'OK, but you make sure you do. I want to know more about this carrot man and this young man you've met. Oh, yes, that was it, a filter. For the fish-tank. That's what Marjorie had to go back for,' my mother says before she hangs up and lets me get on with my work.

It's Friday before I remember to phone Liam, and I do wonder why he hasn't called me first. Surely if he was that interested then he would have picked up the phone first? Or maybe he's secretly read *The Rules* and has decided that *he* will make *me* wait. Maybe he just doesn't want to see me again? It wouldn't surprise me. I did give out some negative vibes on our evening out together that said I wasn't interested in him. Either way, if I don't phone him it's going to be pretty difficult on Sunday when

I go back into the studio. I give myself a mental slap and punch out his mobile number.

'Hello?'

'Hi Liam, it's me... Crystal,' I say, suddenly remembering that he still doesn't know my real name yet and would probably say 'Samantha who?' if I said it.

'Hello stranger!' Liam's tone brightens – that's a good sign – yes?

'I'm sorry I didn't ring earlier,' I say. 'I had loads of work to do.'

'No probs. Are you in on Sunday again?' he asks.

'As far as I'm aware.'

'Cool. You won't be with Annette though; you'll be on with Jeff this weekend.'

'Oh, why?'

'Didn't you hear? Annette was involved in a car crash on Wednesday,' Liam explains.

What? I feel sick to my stomach.

'Is she hurt? What happened? Is she OK?'

'She's out of hospital now, but has a broken arm and her neck is in a brace. Apparently she was on her way to the garage to get her car serviced and she hit an oil patch on the road. The brakes gave out and she went crashing into the reservation barrier.'

'Oh, no! I told her...'

'Told her what?'

'Oh, nothing, at least it's not worse,' I mutter. The spookiest thing is I *did* warn her, didn't I? Why, oh why don't people listen when you give them a warning? I mean it's not like I give out warnings all the time to all and sundry. This is all new to me too, but you would think that if someone who had proven they could talk to dead people as well as the living had told you to get the brakes on your car checked, then you would get your bloody brakes checked.

'Yeah, she was really lucky. She's going to be away for a few weeks, but should be back in full working order soon. You'll just have to put up with Jeff and me. We'll take good care of you, don't worry,' Liam laughs.

I should laugh too but for some reason I don't. I feel a wee bit freaked out by all of this right now.

'So...' Liam says to break the silence between us. 'Do you fancy going to the cinema tonight? That new Nicole Kidman movie is on at the Showcase.'

I know, I know, I should give the guy a chance. I mean he's nice enough, he's good looking, charming *and* single, but I just can't bring myself to get excited at the prospect of going to the cinema tonight. I really don't know what's the matter with me.

'Yes, that would be great!' I say instead. 'I've got my brother coming to stay this weekend, but if we catch the early showing that should be fine,' I hope that I sound as though I am grateful for the offer.

'OK, great. I'll meet you there about five then. Oh yeah, I forgot to say, you know Anya you met in the wine bar the other night? The TV producer?'

Oh yes, who could forget Anya.

'She wanted me to pass on a message to you. She said the other producers are interested in meeting with you to see about joining a new lifestyle programme they are doing for the Beeb. Can you give her a ring asap? Hang on, I'll give you her direct line,' Liam says. He fumbles about with some papers on his desk and reels off Anya's number.

My stomach does another flip once I put the phone down to Liam. Anya wants *me* on her TV programme – yikes! Now don't get too excited, Sam. It doesn't necessarily mean that she actually wants you to appear on a TV show. All he said was that some producers wanted to meet you – that's all. Nothing more.

CHAPTER FOURTEEN

It's Friday night and the queue for the cinema is about a mile long. I feel as though we've been waiting here for ever, as we shuffle slowly forwards in the queue in a bid to see Nicole Kidman's latest blockbuster.

As we queue up again for popcorn, sweets and crisps, I suddenly notice Jack in front of us. A girl with long, blonde hair, who I assume must be Jasmine, has her hand tucked into his back pocket. What's Jack doing here? I thought his new girlfriend was into French films?

'Jack?'

Jack turns round with a shocked look on his face and looks at Liam for a moment.

'Hey you! How you doing? Jas, this is my... my best mate...'

'Crystal!' I shout, as I hold out my hand to Jack's girlfriend. Jack looks puzzled and then amused. His girlfriend ignores my greeting.

'Jas, *Crystal, Crystal*, Jas,' Jack says by way of introduction.

'Hi,' I say, as I suspiciously look her up and down. She's very thin. Actually bony would be a better description *and* she has a crooked nose which bends at a slightly funny angle. I don't quite know what I was expecting her to look like, but this wasn't it. I thought she would look more, well... I don't know... more nurse-like, I suppose. She looks more like a bony, long-nosed, thing. Nothing like a nurse.

'Hi,' Jasmine says, as she flicks her hair from her shoulders – she looks at me in a suspicious way, as if I have some inside information on Jack.

'Um, Liam, this is Jack, my best friend. Jack, this is Liam,'

'Nice to meet you, mate,' Liam shakes Jack's hand. Jack smiles and shakes Liam's hand.

'Are you going to see the film?' I ask, in an attempt to break the silence between the four of us.

'That's what cinemas are for, aren't they?' Jasmine trills with a slight laugh.

'Of course,' I add, thinking how nice it would be to shove popcorn up her great hooter right now.

'You can sit with us if you want?' Liam offers. Jasmine raises her eyes to the ceiling.

'What did you do that for?' I ask, a little too defensively.

'Oh, no offence,' Jasmine says, 'it's just Jack and I would like to be on our own date if you don't mind. We don't do double-dates, do we Jacky?' Jasmine says. It's more of a statement than a question.

I look at Jack who is looking down at his feet. Bastard! Why doesn't he stick up for me and tell the big-nosed bugger to be nice?

'No problem. Enjoy the movie then,' I say haughtily as I grab Liam's arm and march into Screen 2 with him.

As we watch Nicole Kidman battling to save the planet from another alien invasion, I feel really peed off that Jack didn't say something to Jasmine and my mind is not on the film at all.

My mind isn't on Liam either when he drops me off at home and suggests he could come in for a coffee.

'Sorry?'

'Coffee? You want me to come in?' Liam asks again with a twinkle in his eye.

'Oh sorry, Liam. My brother will be here. Another time?'

'Sure thing,' Liam smiles. 'I'll see you on Sunday then?'

'Sure. Bye and thanks, Liam.'

I am so annoyed with myself for allowing Jack to make me feel irritated and ruin my evening with Liam. I bet he thinks I'm a right joy to go out with! Oh, why can't love be easy? Now I'm going to have to ring him and apologise for a crap night out. Normally the first person I would phone for relationship advice would be Amy, but she is spending the whole weekend in the Highlands with the lovely Kenzie, and I don't want to ruin her weekend by moaning and groaning about my disastrous attempts at getting a man.

Amy's love life has in the past been more spectacularly disastrous than my own. Unlike me, Amy didn't have a habit for attracting married men. She did once get engaged to a transvestite – although she swears she didn't know he had a fondness for cross-dressing until she found him trying to squeeze his size tens into a pair of her size five, open-toed sandals.

So I'm pleased that she has finally met someone who a) seems normal and b) makes her happy and c) doesn't try her shoes on.

Added to this, I have to have a serious think about this TV opportunity. It's probably not the best time to talk to my mum about it. Given that she already thinks that I've brought shame on the family with my vocal chords, I think she would be absolutely mortified if I asked her whether it would be a good idea to go on national television as a performing psychic. She still hasn't got over the shock that I went on local radio.

Fortunately Matt has arrived and just in the nick of time – well my little brother actually arrived while I was out, but has been asleep on my bed claiming that he was suffering from jet-lag, despite not actually flying in from anywhere, rather driving his BMW from London to Bath – poor soul.

When Matt finally decides to grace Missy and I with his presence, I'm just finishing off a call for Mystic Answers. Matt smirks as he listens to me waffling on about new beginnings and new possibilities being just around the corner for my caller.

My brother looks very similar to me – in fact if I were a boy we could be mistaken for twins. Thankfully Matt doesn't have the same sort of wild and wayward mane of hair that I do and I don't wake up with stubble on my chin like he does – yet. Matt's hair is smartly cut into some sort of trendy spiky style called something like an Emo Funk, whatever that might be. Whatever it's called it requires copious amounts of hair products with macho names such as Rock Gel and Granite Foam.

'And your final card is the ten of cups, which signals that things really are going to get better for you, Shelley. I really feel as though there is light at the end of the tunnel here and that despite having had a hard time, you are nearly there. I'm getting a yes to this from my guides too.'

'Thank you so much, Mystic Crystal. You've really made my day and I hope you're right. I could do with a bit of good luck after all I've been through,' Shelley, my caller, says.

'Well, you know where I am if you need me. If you need any more advice, just call Mystic Answers and ask for Mystic Crystal.'

Matt snorts and puts his hand over his mouth. I give him one of the looks that our mother is so fond of giving. Matt removes himself to the kitchen so that he can laugh out loud.

'You're up then?' God I sound like our mother. Matt smiles and opens his arms to me.

'So, Mystic Crystal, how's it all going and can your crystal ball tell me where you keep the Marmite?' Matt asks, opening cupboard doors.

'It's going fine and I don't like Marmite,' I say closing the cupboard doors behind him. 'There's plenty to eat in the fridge if you want it.' I raided Tesco late last night and stocked up on all Matt's favourite foods – well, except for Marmite.

'You do realise that your name is now Mystic Crystal Ball,' Matt laughs as he dives into the fridge in search of food.

'Yes, I have been told. Very funny, I though of all people you would be more intelligent than that,' I retort.

'I'm only kidding. I think you're doing great,' Matt says, blowing his long fringe out of his eyes. Why have a long fringe when you a) can't see where you are going and b) when you spend most of your day blowing it out of your eyes?

'You do?' I'm slightly aghast that someone in my family is

finally on my side. I know Jack is kind of on my side, but he's still out of favour for not standing up for me in front of Miss-Naughty-Nurse and Amy would be on my side if she could drag herself up for air from Kenzie for five minutes.

'Yeah, I think it's great. I mean just think of the potential of this,' Matt says, scratching his chin. You know when Matt has an idea when he starts scratching his chin as if in deep thought. 'You could be huge, Sis,' Matt adds. 'If you're good enough to be on the local radio, you must be good at all this psychic stuff.'

'Well…' I hesitate, 'don't say anything to Mum, or Paul for that matter, but I went on a date the other night with the sound tech from the radio station…'

'What you? A date?' Matt looks shocked.

Why does everyone think it's amazing that anyone would want to ask me out?

'Yes me, actually. Anyway, I was invited to a VIP wine bar thingy they were holding for *Town FM* and this producer came up to me and asked me if I might like to appear on a new programme for the BBC.'

'Really? Bloody hell! You must be better than I thought!' Matt stops eating his Dairylea and pickle sandwich that he's haphazardly knocked together, and scratches his baby-faced chin again. 'You know, we need to act on this right away, Sammy,' he says. 'Seize the moment. Come on.' He darts back into the lounge, sandwich in one hand, the other hitching up his low-slung jeans – why is it that men his age insist on wearing jeans that are too big for them, consequently showing off their Calvin Klein's or even worse, their hairy bottoms? It's like when girls of a certain age insist on showing off their g-strings, or when builders show off their builder's bum – it's just not attractive. Oh great, I am turning into our mother.

I hustle out to follow Matt into the lounge to find he's already logged on to my computer – bought I might add with my third week's salary – yay me! Being a computer wiz Matt is quickly pressing keys and talking to someone called 'Spudulike' on some instant messaging thingy, as pages upon pages of cryptogram whizz up through my computer. They go so fast I can barely read what's on the pages. I do hope he isn't downloading anything sinister on to my computer.

'What are you doing?' I venture, trying not to sound like a total technophobe in front of my little brother.

'Hang on,' Matt says through a mouth of bread and cheese. I watch patiently, occasionally nodding and saying 'hum' as though I have the slightest idea what the hell he's doing – which I don't. I'm quite capable of finding a website or creating a spreadsheet, but anything outside of that and I'm at a complete loss. Matt clicks the mouse a few times, presses a few classified keys, apparently known only to computer nerds, and a new screen, sorry a new 'window', pops up. He clicks on a little box in the right-hand corner and a website comes up.

'What do you think? It's only in beta at the moment, but give me a few hours and we will have the psychic world at our feet.'

What do I think? Bloody amazing! That's what I think. In the matter of fifteen cyber minutes, Matt has managed to create a website. *International Psychic Mystic Crystal Ball – as seen on TV. Here to answer all your questions and to guide you to inner peace and happiness.* It must be the time of the month or something because my eyes start to well up with tears. Against a cobalt blue background, with silver stars flashing intermittingly around it, the white text looks amazing. Matt has managed to place a beautiful crystal ball slap bang in the centre of the screen, upon which reads *'enter'*. I can't believe what he has done in a matter of minutes.

'Matt, that's brilliant… but…' I hesitate as he looks expectedly at me. 'I'm not an international psychic.'

'Not yet, you're not, but you just wait and see,' Matt says with a huge grin on his face. 'You see this box down here?' Matt points with his cursor. I nod. He clicks the mouse again and up pops another box with a list of hundreds of names and questions in it.

'Who are all these people?' I stare in amazement as the list goes on and on and... well, you get the idea.

'Contacts of mine, from all over the world. You're not working tonight are you?' Matt asks.

'No, I took the night off to be with you,' I mutter as I try to read all the names that are going way too fast for my poor little eyes to take in.

'Good, because you're going to be busy answering one question from every one of these contacts. In return they are all going to give you credibility for your website, which in turn will give you more credibility as a renowned psychic,' Matt says. 'Did you know psychic sites are the second most popular sites searched worldwide? *And* did you also know that there are four times as many psychics in France as there are Catholic priests?'

'Blimey. What are the most popular searched sites then? And how the hell am I going to answer a question from all these people? There must be thousands of them! And how do you know all these people anyway?' My eyes are going funny as I try to read the questions that keep on flying off the page.

'Porn,' Matt says.

'What?'

'Porn. It's the most popular searched for subject on the Internet. So if you want to get rich quick, you need to have a porn site. Otherwise become a psychic,' Matt laughs.

Might have known.

'And, if you want to gain a reputation and prove to the world that you're not just some charlatan trying to make a fast buck, you are going to have to put a bit of time into this, Sis,' Matt adds. Time? Time? What is this thing he talks about? I don't have much free time on my hands as it is. If I'm not answering people's questions at some ungodly hour in the morning, I'm answering them on live radio. I don't get enough sleep as it is!

'Once you're on the TV people will automatically Google you

to see what other people think of you,' Matt adds as he types.

'Ah, well, I haven't decided whether I want to be on TV or not,' I say, and I haven't. I mean this was never in my grand life plan. Not in a million years did I think my career would involve talking to dead people. My original dreams were along the lines of listening to folk who actually had a pulse, lying on a couch telling me why they would run a mile if they saw a broccoli floret, not listening to dead people and passing on messages, which quite frankly, the living don't bloody well adhere to anyway!

'What? Are you barking mad?' Matt looks at me as if I surely must be. 'Don't you see what an opportunity this is for you, Sam? They are asking you to appear on national TV and you haven't decided whether you want to be on there or not?' Matt shakes his head – evidently I must be mad.

'Yes, but...' I stutter. It's OK for Matt; he's taken risks ever since he could type with two fingers. The problem with Matt is, he sees an opening for an opportunity and there's no stopping him. I say it's a problem; it's not a problem for Matt. It's a problem for me. I'm more of a 'hmmm, let me sleep on it' kind of a girl and find people who take the bull by the wotsits without thinking things through very worrying. I mean, what if it all goes wrong? What if this Anya doesn't think I'm suitable for TV? What if I'm too ugly to be on the telly and am better suited to being the unseen voice of radio?

'But what?' Matt says challengingly. 'What's the worse that can happen, Sam? You've been given this great opportunity by basically blagging your way through it and you're thinking about turning it down?'

Put like that I do sound a bit pathetic, don't I?

'You have to do this, Sam. I mean think of the big picture here!' Matt adds. That look of excitement on his face reminds me of when he was just 14 and realised the potential of creating affordable websites for small businesses. I remember clearly the day he suddenly decided he was going to take the small business world by storm. He was sitting with his head bent over his Amstrad computer when he suddenly looked up and shouted, 'I've got it!' Me and Paul looked up from *Top of The Pops*, looked at each other and shrugged. Little did we know that what he had 'got' was going to turn into his first business, which now employs fifteen staff to keep up with the new clients which contact him daily.

'I know, but…' I can't think of another valid reason as to why I shouldn't pick up the phone right now and ring Anya and yet this is way outside of my comfort zone. I mean, I was quite happy taking calls from people like Valerie at three o'clock in the morning. I've already registered myself as self-employed with the Inland Revenue and I was quite happy to listen to people to my heart's content. Of course if a time came when a high-profile celebrity confessed that they were terrified of veg… at this point the subject of lachanophobia would be thrown into the spotlight and I would become the world's leading authority at curing lachanophobics.

'No more buts. Now get me another sandwich while I get on with this website of yours,' Matt instructs. Blimey, anyone would think he was the older one here!

'How's Jack by the way?' Matt asks as he types and clicks at the same time. Why does everyone in my family always want to know how Jack is?

'Fine, I think,' I say, trying to sound as if I don't care less.

'I thought you and him usually got together on a weekend?'

Yeah, me too.

'He's got a girlfriend – a nurse,' I say, as if somehow her chosen career has any relevance on the matter.

'A nurse, eh?' Matt smirks.

Great. What is it with men and nurses?

'So, you're peeved because he's made other arrangements for his weekends now,' Matt says.

'No!' I say a little too defensively. 'What Jack gets up to is his business. In fact I have a new boyfriend myself,' I add for effect.

'What, an actual boyfriend?' Matt looks at me in surprise.

'Why does everyone do that?'

'Do what?'

'That! Look so surprised when I announce that I have a boyfriend. I'm not an ugly, wrinkled old prune you know!'

'No, I didn't mean that. I'm just surprised, that's all,' Matt says a little sheepishly.

'Well, maybe, just maybe, for once I want to keep my business my business,' I add all huffily.

'Right. What's his name then?' Matt asks.

'Whose?'

'The new boyfriend,' Matt gives me that look – you know the one when someone doesn't believe a word that is coming out of your mouth.

'Oh… um… it's Liam.'

'Liam, hey? And you met this Liam where?'

'I told you, he's the sound tech at the radio station. It was Liam who put me in touch with the TV producer, remember? And if you must know, we just had a fabulous time at the cinema,' I add, just a little bit smugly.

'Cool,' Matt says. 'He's not married then?'

'Oh hardy ha, ha! No, he's not married.' Well I don't think he is.

By the following morning Matt has a) managed to convince me that appearing on national TV is a jolly good idea and b) has created the most amazing website known to man – or woman, seeing as we have to be so politically correct these days.

On my all-singing-and-all-dancing website is a forum where members can get together and chat about the meaning of life; a free three-card computer-generated reading; lots of twinkling stars and even an exclusive members only bit, where for the subscription fee of £25 a year, a member can have a free in-depth reading and access to the forum, where they can chat with other like-minded members about, well about whatever they want to, really. Where Matt thinks I will get the time to keep this thing going I do not know.

I phone Anya and leave a message on her mobile. Within minutes she has called me back and arranged a meeting for me in London for Monday morning. Matt is going to cat-sit for me while I take the coach up there on Sunday, after my afternoon slot on the radio.

The Sixth Sense show goes relatively well, despite Jeff having a fit of the giggles when an elderly woman phones in and asks me to contact her dead pussy – her words not mine, I hasten to add – to the point where he has to put another track on before he can compose himself again to introduce the next caller. Unfortunately the next track just happens to be the Pussycat Dolls with 'Don't Cha', which sets him off again. Oh dear.

CHAPTER FIFTEEN

Thankfully I didn't hear any meowing in my head – otherwise I would be worried. Instead, I reassure the lovely old dear that her cat is fine and playing happily with all the other cats in feline heaven. The show is more popular than I first thought and I didn't realise that it is broadcast to all the other local radio stations within the south-west, so the phones are ringing like mad with people trying to get through.

My next call is one that, if I'm honest, I would rather not have taken, but as Liam only has a vague idea of who the next caller is going to be and what they are going to ask, there is nothing to stop a caller changing his or her mind once they have been put through to me.

'Our next caller is Tanya. Are you there, Tanya?' Jeff asks into the microphone.

'Yeah, I am,' the female voice answers. No sooner do I hear her voice, I get a stabbing feeling in the top of my back, followed by a numb sensation in my left arm.

'OK, Tanya, and you want to know if Mystic Crystal can contact a dear friend of yours, is that right?' Jeff says with all the professionalism of a radio presenter.

'Yeah, that's right,' Tanya says.

'OK, over to you Crystal.'

The pain in my left shoulder is more intense as I listen to the caller, to the point where I'm in agony and wince with pain.

Liam looks concerned and mouths 'are you all right?' I nod and try to concentrate on what Tanya is saying.

'Baz was me best mate,' Tanya says, 'we always did every-thing together. I just wanna know he's OK,' she adds.

'Yeah, no thanks to her, stupid bitch!'

A man's voice comes into my head, along with another sharp pain in my shoulder. Who are you? Are you Baz? I mentally ask.

'Yeah, and that bitch killed me.'

The man's voice says. My mouth drops open. Oh my God! Ouch!

'Crystal?' Jeff asks.

'What? Oh yes, sorry... um... right. Um... Tanya, do you happen to know how your friend Baz died?' I ask.

'No. Why would I know that? I mean I wasn't with him or nothing like that,' the young woman answers.

'No, I wasn't suggesting anything like that. I just wondered if you knew how he died because I keep getting a stabbing pain in my back. Was your friend Baz stabbed, do you know?' I ask. I'm not enjoying this call one bit, not to mention I could well do without the empathic pain right now, thanks very much, Baz.

'Yeah, well I don't know... I think so. I hadn't seen him for a while and someone at the centre said they thought he got stabbed,' the woman mutters. 'I just wanna know he's, you know, OK.'

'Oh, she knows all right. It was her who stabbed me in the back – literally. She's a druggy, you see. I couldn't get her any gear, we got into a fight and she stabbed me.'

Holy cow! I do not like this at all. What do I do now? I've just been told that the woman who is on the phone is a murderer. This is all very *Most Haunted*, isn't it?

'Um... Tanya, I do have Baz here and he's very worried about you,' I venture.

'Like fuck am I. She's gonna end up dead like me anyway if she carries on like she is doing.'

'He wants you to get help. He says you will know what he means,' I say.

'Tell her you know she's a murderer. Tell her you know she knifed me up.'

I can't say that. Oh help. I really don't want to be taking this call.

'Well, I'm fine, I am getting help, but tell him... tell him... I did love him,' Tanya says quietly.

'*Ha, now she tells me!*' Baz laughs. '*Why couldn't she have told me that before? I would have married the silly cow and we could have got off the drugs together. Silly cow. I know she didn't mean it,*' he says light-heartedly.

'Baz is saying he wished you had told him before. He says he would have married you and you could have both got... better together,' I add. This is all very rock and roll. I've got a woman on the phone who stabbed her boyfriend over some drugs and the boyfriend in my ear is forgiving her. I wonder how Miracle would handle this if she had such a call. I mean do I call the police and say they should arrest this woman? But then who am I to sit in judgement? I'm just the messenger, surely?

Slowly the pain in my back eases as I feel as though Baz is smiling.

'Well... um... you know... thanks... for, you know, getting hold of him for me,' Tanya mutters quietly.

Oh no problem. Any time. That's what I'm here for – to contact people you've murdered, I want to say. It doesn't matter how uncomfortable I feel about all this, at the end of the day I guess I'm just the one who passes these bizarre messages on to folk. Oh why, oh why did I take this job on in the first place?

Once I've managed to get Tanya off the line and Baz out of my head, I tell Jeff to wind the calls up. Tanya's call has taken the sails out of me and I don't think I want to take any more today.

'Can you just take one more?' Jeff asks. 'Liam says the next caller, Annie, is distraught and desperate to talk to you.'

Liam looks pleadingly through the smoked glass window.

'Oh go on then. Just this one and that is it for today.'

Liam smiles and winks at me.

'Hello, I'm Mystic Crystal, how may I help you, Annie?' I ask as soon as Liam connects the call through.

'Oh hello... I... um...' a woman says quietly.

'*That's my mummy.*' A little girl's voice comes into my head.

'*She's really sad. It was my birthday today,*' the little girl says.

What's your name? I ask to myself.

'*I'm Emma. I was eight when I went to heaven,*' my little spirit girl says confidently.

'Um… Annie, I think I have your daughter, Emma, with me,' I add, praying that she does indeed have a daughter called Emma.

'Oh my God!' is all Annie stutters.

'She's telling me she was eight years old when she passed over, is this right?'

'Yes, yes she was,' Annie says quickly. 'Is she OK?'

A little chuckle of laughter rings through my head.

'*Tell Mummy I'm fine here. It's a bit strange not being able to be there with her anymore, but Granma Dee looks after me here, and I have made lots of friends my own age here. They're all dead too,*' Emma says with another giggle.

I pass on the message to Annie from her daughter. Tears sting my eyes as I listen to the most angelic voice in my head.

'*Oh, and can you tell my mummy that there is nothing wrong with baby Freddie. He's just looking at me, that's all,*' Emma says matter-of-factly.

As I relay Emma's words, her mother Annie gasps.

'We thought he might have some problems hearing us. I miss my little girl so much,' Annie sniffs.

'*I miss you too, Mummy, but don't worry, I am always around you and will wait for you until we are together again. It wasn't the man's fault. I shouldn't have run out into the road after the ball. I do know my Road Safety, I just forgot,*' Emma says. For an eight-year-old she sure is a bright kid.

Trying to stop myself from bursting into tears, I look ahead of me to see both Liam and Jeff welling up.

'*Oh, and can you tell my mummy to let Freddie have all my toys, and tell her to give my Polly Pockets to Victoria – she was my best friend and she's been sad too because she doesn't have as many Polly Pockets as me,*' Emma adds.

I pass on the final message to Annie who chuckles.

'I can't thank you enough, Crystal,' Emma's mum says between tears.

'Any time,' I say before I switch my mic off and burst into tears.

When I finish my stint I'm pleased to find Colin the Carrot Man in the canteen having a glass of tomato juice and a slice of organic flap-jack. I sit opposite him with my latte and smile. Colin doesn't return the smile and just looks down at his cake.

'Are you OK?' I ask.

Colin, who ironically looks a bit like the comedian Jasper Carrott, replies with a shrug. Colin is small in frame and is of that generation when men always wear a shirt and tie regardless of whether they are pottering about in the garden or telling people how to grow mammoth carrots. Like my dad, Colin probably doesn't own a t-shirt, let alone one with a humorous slogan on it.

'Anything I can help you with?'– I know, but I just can't help myself sometimes.

'I doubt it,' he mumbles.

'Try me,' I say in my best therapist voice.

'Do you think I'm attractive?' Colin suddenly blurts out.

Uh-oh!

'Well…' I begin wondering whether to say some cliché about inner beauty or beauty being in the eye of the beholder, but I don't think this is the right time somehow. Everyone knows what you're actually saying is, no, you're a right ugly bastard.

'Oh, don't worry, I'm not trying to chat you up. I just wondered, you know, if you were a woman…well, I know you *are* a woman, but I mean, you know, a woman of a certain age – a lot older… whether you would think I was attractive?' Colin explains.

I actually quite like Colin – not in that way I might add. I purposely went in early today so that I could pick up some tips from him about talking to people live on air and despite looking a cross between Jasper Carrott and Percy Thrower, he's really very good and soon puts people at ease when they phone up worrying about problems such as white-fly on their vegetables. I do wonder how he would have handled some of the calls I took today, mind you. In particular the woman with the dead cat and the drug-addict murderer – all in a day's work, hey?

'Umm... Well I guess if I were a *lot* older, I would ...' Oh heck, I don't know what to say to him. 'Yes, I mean yes. I would say you were attractive to the old... um, more mature lady,' I venture. My cheeks feel as red as Colin's hair.

'Really?' Colin looks relieved.

'Really,' I smile, happy that I've just made his day. I just hope he doesn't follow me home.

'It's just that I never feel as though I've connected with anyone before. You know on every level, I don't just mean sexual...'

Ewww! I don't think I want to hear any more, thank you very much.

'But on an intellectual level. I've never met a woman as passionate as me about vegetables,' Colin muses.

'Ha, well you've never met my mother then!'

'What, your mum is a gardener?' Colin asks. I'm sure there is a sparkle in his eyes.

'Well, yes and no,' I add. 'She's writing a book at the moment about how many miles our food travels to get to our plates, but yes, she is a qualified horticulturist too.' Yep, there's definitely a spark there.

'It must run in the blood,' I add. 'I chose to specialise in lachanophobia when I left uni, but I didn't realise that there aren't actually that many people who suffer from it,' I say.

'The fear of vegetables,' Colin smiles.

'Yay! You are the first person I have met besides my college tutor who actually knows what it is! You know, there were only three people in my class at uni – me, the tutor, and some vegetarian girl who decided it was un-cool to be pale and became a carnivore and dropped out of class.' I feel so relieved that for once I don't have to explain what the word means.

'It was rather embarrassing towards the end of my final year – there was only me and the tutor in the class,' I add, and it was. Just me, Professor John Summers and the galling fact that he was gay.

'I have a cousin who suffers from it,' Colin tells me. 'His GP thinks it's all nonsense though; basically told him to snap out of it.'

I feel quite excited that I have finally found a person who really does suffer from vegetable phobia!

'Well, I can tell you it is a real problem,' I say, sounding most authoritative on the subject as well I might – I did study the subject for three bloody years! 'You'll have to put me in touch with your cousin,' I add. It's got to be better than talking to dead people.

'And you will have to introduce me to your mum,' Colin says in return.

Humm, now there's an idea...

CHAPTER SIXTEEN

The last time I visited London was over five years ago with Jack. We had heard on the grapevine that the over-60s were planning a coach trip for the day. Jack had it in his head that we could borrow some clothes from his uncle, and dress up as pensioners in order to blag a free trip. I, on the other hand, had a better idea and volunteered the two of us to help out – just in case anyone decided to have a turn outside Buckingham Palace and required CPR.

A lot has changed since then. I'm sure there wasn't this much traffic five years ago, you know. Jack and I got ourselves into a bit of bother the last time we were here, well I say Jack and I; it was actually *Jack* who got *me* into trouble. He dared me to go up to one of the sentries outside the Palace and kiss the Queen's guard on the cheek. Always one to take up the challenge in those days, I applied a fresh coat of lip-gloss, practised my pucker and sidled up to the very handsome guard in his black fluffy busby. No sooner had I got within a metre of him than he raised his weapon to me – no, not *that* weapon – and shouted, 'Step back!'

Jack practically wet himself laughing as I almost jumped out of my skin, tripped over my own feet and landed flat on my face. When I finally got up, Jack wet himself again when he noticed that the gravel from the parade forecourt had managed to stick itself to my Cheeky Cherry glossed lips. I looked as though I had been tarred and feathered. I was lucky to escape with just the humiliation and a pair of puffy lips, rather than being thrown into the Tower of London and fed to the ravens. I still shudder when I think about it.

Obviously one dare deserved another, so in return for my public shaming, I dared Jack to stand in the middle of Piccadilly and sing 'The Devil Went Down to Georgia' in the style of Elvis Presley. Not one to face a double-dare, Jack, who brought along his guitar to amuse the old folks on the coach, practised his pelvic thrust, much to the old dears' approval, pushed up the collar of his polo shirt, made a funny shape with his lip and started belting out the great hillbilly folk song at the top of his voice. Being a musician, Jack is a naturally good singer, unlike me, who can't carry a tune in a bucket. What I didn't realise is that he is also a very good Elvis impersonator. Within seconds he had a Chinese tour group surrounding him, taking pictures on their digital cameras and encouraging him to do more – which, because Jack actually needs no encouragement to perform, he did. Jack made £253.28 that day, so I made him treat each of the 52 old-aged pensioners to a punnet of strawberries with clotted cream on the way home. Well, it was his own fault for being a show-off and giving me puffy lips.

I walk hastily past Buckingham Palace, shielding my face with my hand, just in case the guard in the box recognises me and decides to shoot first and ask questions later. I look at my *I Love London* pocket guide and wonder where on earth the Park Plaza Riverbank hotel is. I'm sure somewhere along the line from leaving Victoria Coach Station and here I've managed to take a wrong turning – it was probably when I was practising my Lambeth Walk.

Just as I am looking like a right bloody tourist and turning my map round in circles, my mobile rings into life. It's my mother. Again.

'Hi, Mum,' I say, trying to sound ever so confident and not at all like a tourist lost in the middle of London.

'Are you there yet, Sammy?' she says with motherly worry in her tone.

'Yes, Mum. I'm just at... well, I've just gone past Buck Palace.' God, I wish I knew which way I was meant to go.

'Ooo, have you seen the Queen yet?'

I squint up to the huge building I have just left behind.

'No, I don't think she's in today. I'm just on my way to the hotel.'

'I wish you'd have let me come with you, Sammy. I don't like to think of you in the big city on your own. You know what you're like with directions.' I'm sure she thinks I'm still 10 years old sometimes. And it was only the once that I took the wrong turning to the school disco and ended up at the local Greek restaurant, and got in a panic, thinking that they were going to use me in a kebab. By the time my mum and dad had figured out where I was, I was propped up on the bar tucking in to a plate of lachano carota salata and a glass of Coke.

'Remember what I said, don't go getting into any taxis with foreigners in them, you don't know how legal they are.' Always politically correct, eh, Mum?

'Yes, OK. Look, I'll call you when I get to the hotel,' I say. I wish I hadn't told her that I was going to London now, but then I had little choice because Mum wanted to know if Matt and I were going over to hers for Sunday tea, so I had to say something, and as we've already established, I am hopeless at lying.

'Yes, you do that. Oh, Amy says to say hi and good luck.'

'Amy? What, she's there?'

'Oh, she had a bit of a ding-dong with Kenzie over him going to France to do some photo shoot. I think she was a bit lonely. She didn't realise that you were going to London and thought you were home today. I told her all about you going to see this producer,' my mum whispers into the phone.

Aww, poor Amy. I must call her when I get back. I was going to tell her about this trip, but I don't want people to think I'm getting big-headed and the fewer people who know about it the better because sure as eggs is eggs, it will all go horribly wrong. Oh, I really hope that Kenzie isn't going off Amy. Still, my mum will look after her. They have always got on well together and Mum has kind of become Amy's surrogate mother since her own is never anywhere to be seen.

It's always been the same; every school play, every karate

grade, every parent/teacher evening, Amy's mum would always have something else on that she just had to go to. It was always my mum, never Amy's mum, Lorraine, who would be there in the background clapping for her, cheering her on, or speaking to her teacher.

'Oh, OK. Must go, Mum. Tell Amy I'll call her later,' I say as I dodge a black cab driving past at a hundred miles an hour.

By the time I actually find the Plaza, it's six o'clock and I am starving. I thought I would treat myself and book into somewhere a bit posh and the Plaza doesn't disappoint. I'm sure I read somewhere that the Beckhams frequent it, so it must be OK.

First impressions are very good. A smartly dressed porter escorts me to the huge oak reception desk and despite my being dressed as though I'm about to go on an SAS operation – black combat trousers, black t-shirt and rucksack on my back – he doesn't bat an eyelid. I must just look as though I can afford to stay here, I guess.

After checking in at reception I head off to room 181. My room, I hasten to add, not someone else's. And my room is so much more than I expect – it's huge! I bet you could fit my entire flat into this room alone. The bed is the biggest I have ever had the pleasure to jump on. I throw myself down on the soft mattress. The view over the Thames is stunning, as the sun slowly sets and casts a red glow over the shimmering reflections from all the tall buildings surrounding it.

Having taken advantage of room service and ordered myself a dinner of smoked salmon in a dill sauce, followed by a chocolate orange mousse in cream (mmmmm), I take a very long and luxurious bath with the complimentary bath bombs and scented rose petals and settle on the bed wrapped up in one of the hotel's fluffy bathrobes. I wonder whether I should phone Jack or just leave it. He texted me while I was on the coach to see how I was getting on. Apparently he had called round and Matt had told him where I had gone and told me to call him once I got to London.

I press the speed dial button on my phone.

'Hi, smelly! How's London?' Jack answers.

'It's as busy, if not busier than the last time we came here.' It's nice to hear a familiar voice in this place where I know not a soul.

'You should have let me come with you,' he says.

'Not bloody likely! I have an important meeting tomorrow and I don't need any distractions.'

'Moi? Distraction?' Jack says in his best French accent.

'Err, yes, you. So how are things there? What have you been up to?'

'Well, I caught you on the radio at lunchtime – you were like a real pro. I especially liked the old woman and her pussy, was that for real?'

'Oh yes, it was for real all right. Jeff couldn't get her off the line quick enough. I hope my mum wasn't listening.'

'And who the hell was that weirdo woman – the one who called about her friend? She was well off the wall!'

'Occupational hazard, I'm afraid. For every genuine caller there are fifty nutters,' I say quickly. I daren't tell Jack that the woman in question just so happened to have murdered her boyfriend. 'So what else have you been up to?'

'Well, Matt refused to make me lunch so I went and pestered your landlady instead,' Jack says proudly. I don't know how he does it, I really don't.

'I went to band practice and I'm now in the middle of watching *Midsomer Murders* and eating a pepperoni pizza,' Jack informs me. 'I'm sure it's that Barnaby who does all these murders, you know.'

'He's the bloody detective, you fool!'

'Ah, that's what they want you to think!' Jack says. 'How come he's always the first at the scene of the crime then, eh?'

'Because he's the bloody detective!'

'Well, I still think he's the one that does it.' Jack is not budging on this theory. 'For starters, he's always first there at the scene of the crime and secondly, he always looks shifty…'

'Shifty?'

'Yeah, as though he knows something we don't know,' Jack muses.

'That's because he's a detective, Jack. He's supposed to know something we don't. He's supposed to look shifty.'

'Well, I don't trust him,' Jack says. I've figured that Jack has far too much time on his hands today.

'So where's what's-her-name tonight then?' I ask casually, if nothing else to shut Jack up about *Midsomer Murders*.

'Jas? Oh, she's working tonight,' Jack says matter-of-factly, giving me no clues as to whether this is going to be a long-term thing or not. Mind you, when people start shortening other people's names it's a sure sign that they're getting on well. Damn I'm good; I should be partnered with Detective Chief Inspector Barnaby.

'Oh, right,' I say, hoping that I sound as though I don't care a jot. I don't care, you know, it's just I'm still smarting at the way people drop their nearest and dearest at the first sign of a big-nosed woman in a nurse's uniform and besides, I have Liam now, don't I?

'You should see the hotel I'm staying in, Jack, it's amazing,' I say, quickly changing the subject. 'It has its own pool, gym, sauna, and you should see the size of the bed I'm lying on – it's massive!' I spread myself out to see if I can touch the ends of the bed – I can't.

'I wish I was there…' Jack says quietly and almost in a serious tone.

'What?'

'We could have a massive pillow fight and get pissed on the mini-bar,' he adds quickly.

'Yeah, me too.' I'm a bit unsure what Jack meant there. 'Look,

I'd better go, got an early start tomorrow and I want to go through my notes before I go to bed. I'll text you tomorrow and let you know how it goes.'

'Cool. Catch you tomorrow!' Jack says.

'OK,' I say and hang up. I just realised that for the first time since I met Jack he didn't say 'Loves ya!'

I suddenly feel very lonely and very far away from home. I do wish Jack were here, or even Amy; we would have such a laugh together. It's all very well staying in a fancy hotel, but if you haven't got someone to raid the mini-bar with, it doesn't quite feel the same raiding it on your own somehow. I should have invited Liam to come with me, and I don't know why I didn't now I come to think of it. Oh well.

CHAPTER SEVENTEEN

I slept like a baby – well, a good baby who sleeps for seven hours at a time, that is – and having had a hearty breakfast of French toast, something that resembled scrambled eggs but had a fancy name attached to it, and a cup of coffee, I feel ready to take on the world of visual broadcasting.

I have to admit I feel very nervous at the prospect of meeting and greeting producers and other TV people and in some respects I wonder if I'm doing the right thing here. I mean, this is all happening so fast. One minute I'm so desperate for money that I will do anything – yes, including phoning up for a job as a psychic phone reader. The next, I'm appearing live on radio taking calls from all sorts of strange people and have even had the offer of being on the telly. I guess I must be doing something right otherwise people wouldn't keep phoning up and asking for readings from me, but all the same, this telly business is a little too far outside of my comfort zone.

Despite never having met Miracle in the flesh, I instantly knew it was her waiting for me outside the studio. As soon as I saw the larger-than-life lady with long red hair flowing down her back, dressed in a black and purple dress with a matching shawl, I just knew it was her.

Miracle wanted to wish me luck before I headed off to London, just to assure me that it will all run smoothly, but I had the feeling that her mind was on other things, such as a certain estate agent by the name of Max, who keeps phoning her up to show her other properties.

'Oh, he is lovely, Sam,' she gushed, as if she were in the first throes of love.

'But?'

'I just don't want to get hurt again. When Roy left I felt as though my heart had been ripped out.'

'I don't think Max is going to do that to you,' I assured her. That's the problem; being a psychic you would think that you would know what's going to happen in your life, wouldn't you? Unfortunately it doesn't appear to work like that. I tried to read my own cards once, but didn't get anything from them that meant anything to me, and besides, sometimes I wonder if it's best to not know what the future holds.

'Well,' Miracle said as she hugged me to her, 'you just have a good time and enjoy yourself. This is your opportunity to shine, young lady, so take it. Now, I must get going, Max is taking me to Bath Spa for lunch and to look at some wonderful Georgian houses.'

'But, you want to move by the sea. Bath is nowhere near the sea.'

'Oh, I know that. I just wanted to be taken out somewhere nice for lunch and where better than Bath?' Miracle laughed.

Having asked one of the hotel porters to call me a cab, I take the short ride to the BBC Television studio in Shepherds Bush and wait while a portly security guard checks my papers. I can't help it, but ever since I've heard voices in my head, I have a bad habit of looking at people to see if I can get any messages for them – a habit I really must stop because if I don't remember to keep my mouth shut, one of these days I'm going to say something and someone is going to either have me committed or punch my lights out.

As the security guard checks I am who I say I am, I chuckle as I see an image in my head of him struggling to get into his uniform trousers. A woman, who I presume is his wife, is laughing at him and teasing him about losing weight.

'It's not a laughing matter, Samantha,' another woman's voice comes into my head – oh will I ever get used to this? I must have one of those bemused looks on my face because the security guard looks at me and asks if I'm all right.

'Um… yes, fine, thank you,' I mutter.

'*Tell him if he doesn't lose weight soon, he will have a massive heart attack,*' the voice continues. Oh blimey! I can't tell him that!

'Nice day today isn't it?' I venture.

The guard, whose name badge reads Gerry, looks up from my paperwork and nods. Oh dear, this is going to be more difficult than I thought.

'Think I might go for a run later,' I say, looking up to the sun in the sky and dramatically stretching out my arms. 'Do you run?' Now I bet he thinks I'm taking the piss out of him.

'Eh?' The guard says, looking at me as if I'm stark raving bonkers.

'Run. Do you go running?' I ask, praying that he isn't going to clobber me over the head with his truncheon or spray me in the face with pepper-spray.

'Do I look like a runner, Miss?' Gerry asks.

'Well… you could always start. Did you know it only takes 30 minutes a day of gentle jogging to burn up 300 calories? I mean, you don't need to run if you don't want to, you could always walk… quickly, if you prefer…' I say, desperately trying to sound cheery and not condescending.

'Oh, right,' the guard seems unimpressed.

'There are lots of parks round here, you could use one of those.'

'Yeah, right. There you go. Make sure you wear this pass at all times because they will check you inside,' says Gerry.

I don't think I'm making a big impression on Gerry the security guard, but I did try. I mean short of saying, 'Oi, fatty, lose some weight or you're gonna die!' I don't know what else to say. I thank him and walk inside to the TV studios.

I have to say I am looking suitably cosmic-happy-ass in my attire of a long black and purple panelling dress, with my pointy black boots just poking out at the bottom of my skirt and a nifty little black shawl. Actually the dress and shawl came from last year's Halloween costume where I morphed myself into the evil witch from *The Wizard of Oz*, courtesy of Jack's uncle, but obviously having disappointed the staff at *Town FM* by turning up in jeans and a t-shirt, I thought I had better make the right impression this time – it is TV after all. I just hope people don't take one look at me and start shouting 'Burn the witch!'

Having located Anya and her posse on the sixteenth floor – another memo to myself to get fit – I do my best impression of someone gliding sophisticatedly into a room. It is a typical meeting room. The walls are white and beset with framed black and white photographs of brick walls – odd.

It's only 8.30am and the building is already buzzing with activity. Tours around the studios start from eight o'clock and it looks as though the first coach party consisting of many Americans, a few media exchange students and the odd pensioner have arrived and are assembled in the car park below us.

Anya is already in the meeting room ready to greet me and does so with a great show of enthusiasm, throwing her arms around me as if I am a long-lost friend.

'You look gorgeous, Darling!' she says, holding my arms out and looking me up and down. Anya is equally gorgeous in a black trouser suit – in fact Anya could look gorgeous in a Tesco carrier bag. This woman just oozes gorgeousness. She's one of those people who doesn't need to try to look gorgeous – unlike me who needs a good three hours of plucking, moisturising, exfoliating and scrubbing to look as though I'm alive and not an extra on Dawn of the Dead.

'Oh, thanks,' I say, a little embarrassed.

'Now before the production team comes in, I wanted to brief you on a few ideas,' Anya says as she shows me to one of the fourteen chairs that surround a huge oak table placed in the middle of the room. She passes me a bottle of mineral water and sits down next to me. Her place at the table is littered with folders, paperwork and an official looking BBC clipboard from which she flicks sheets of paper up and down. 'Since Trisha defected to Channel Four, we've been filling our morning slot with programmes like, *How Much for Your Junk* and *Pet Disaster* and all that sort of crap. Anyway, the people at the top have decided to have something similar to *This Morning* on ITV. They know it's going to be tough competition, because Phil and Holly have such a huge following...' I'm tempted to tell her how much I love Phil and Holly from *This Morning* and that they have been my life-line to sanity for the past year or so, but seeing as they are the opposition I think better of it.

'We need to have the best lifestyle magazine programme going and being new we are going to have to make a big visual impact,' Anya says. All this media speak is going way over my head, so I just nod in agreement. 'Now, in two weeks' time we are going to be launching a new morning programme called *Morning Latte* – I know, not my choice of name, but there you go – anyway, if we are going to be bigger and better than *This Morning* we are going to have to recruit bigger and better guests and have some regular lifestyle slots. The current trend is leaning towards healthier lifestyles, mind, body and spirit and all that malarkey, so what the creative team are looking for is someone who can do live readings, initially one morning a week, probably on a Wednesday... ah, here's the team now,' she says, as a number of media types enter the room.

There are eight of them and they all look as though they have just stepped out of a student disco – maybe I should have just worn a t-shirt and jeans after all. I'm introduced to one after the other by Anya and they all seem friendly enough.

'So guys, this is our little mystic star, Crystal. I've quickly briefed her as to what we are going for here, so shall we start with a questions and answers session?' Anya says, clapping her hands in an authoritative manner. The team sit down and help themselves to water and shuffle various bits of paper around in front of them. A small oriental woman stands up first.

'Hi Crystal, I'm Honey, the features development editor for *Morning Latte,*' she says with a smile, 'Anya has filled us in on your recent radio experience, but what I want to know is how you think TV work is going to differ from that?'

'Well... obviously I'll be on screen rather than just being a voice,' I hope I don't sound like I'm stating the bloody obvious, but I didn't realise I was auditioning for Question Time. 'So presentation is very important,' I add.

'Good. And how do you feel about millions of people tuning in to see you?' Honey asks.

'Oh fine,' I say. Actually I'm not sure how I feel right now at the prospect of millions of people watching me, though pooping myself comes to mind at this very moment. I mean, how many millions are they talking here? And what if all my skeletons come tumbling out of the closet? Have I got lots of skeletons? I should look in my closet. Well, Amy and I did try smoking a joint at the back of the youth club once. Oh and then there was that time when we went into the corner shop and nicked a Milky Bar and a bag of jelly babies...

'Good, because we have a feeling that once we feature this slot, you are going to be inundated with requests for readings.' Honey smiles as she writes down some notes on her official BBC issued clipboard.

The meeting goes very well, as one by one the various members of the team fire questions at me. Anya spends most of the meeting writing down my answers and nodding in agreement with the rest of the team. I have to say, there is a huge amount of positive energy in this room and I don't know why I was the least bit worried about meeting these people. In fact, by the end of the meeting I feel positively happy here and excited at the prospect of appearing on their new programme.

Once the team have been dispatched to their various offices, Anya goes through the official-looking contract with me, including what I can be expected to be paid for what turns out to be 25 minutes of work on a Wednesday morning – £750 plus expenses such as travelling up to London. I do a quick mental calculation. Bloody hell! That works out at £30 per minute! Because the BBC don't have advertisements, Anya warns me it might be hard going to talk continuously for 25 minutes, but she is going to try to get a break thrown in and feature other highlights of the day's show then. I nod in agreement and go through the rest of the contract with her.

CHAPTER EIGHTEEN

So now I am really, really nervous. No, really, I am. I have just signed a contract with the BBC to present the Mystic Crystal slot on *Morning Latte* live, every Wednesday morning starting in two weeks' time and I am so anxious, nervous and any other negative adjectives you can think of ending in 'ous'. In a moment of panic, I call Miracle as soon as I get out of my meeting with Anya.

'That's wonderful news!' Miracle screams down the phone. 'I am so proud of you!'

'Is it? Are you?'

'I told you, Sam this is your vocation in life. Didn't I tell you that you were looking for things in the wrong place when you first phoned Mystic Answers? Didn't I tell you that you were a natural at this?' she reminds me.

'You did... but TV, Miracle! I mean, what if I mess it up? It's going out live to millions of people every morning,' I say, feeling as though I'm going to be sick.

'Why do you think you're going to mess up? Have you ever messed up on the phone lines? Have you ever messed up on your regular radio slot?'

'Well no, not really,' I say. What I don't add is that on the majority of the readings I have done, I have been very lucky and managed to blag my way through them all. OK, so I hear voices in my head now, but do I really? I mean no one else can hear them, can they? It would be a different kettle of fish if other people could hear them too, but I appear to be the only one here that can hear them. Now, being a qualified therapist I think I have enough training to know that one of the classic signs of being one strawberry short of a full punnet is that you can hear voices in your head! So with this in mind, I frequently ask myself, am I going mad?

'Well, there you go then.' Miracle interrupts my thoughts just in the nick of time, before I slam the phone down and ring for the men in white coats to cart me off. 'You are going to be fine, and if you feel nervous just ask your dad to help you,' she says. My initial reaction is to remind her that he is in fact dead. She knows this of course.

'OK, but if I mess this up I'm going to blame you for telling me to go for it.'

Miracle laughs her hearty laugh.

'You do that then. Now let me tell you all about my day in Bath...'

The rest of the week passes in a bit of a blur and soon my nearest and dearest all know about my impending debut on TV thanks to Matt, who has a complete inability to keep anything a secret.

'Well, they're going to see you on the telly next week, you muppet, or were you contemplating putting a bag over your head so they wouldn't know who you were?' he says when I tell him off for telling Mum, who in turn told Amy, who then told Jack, who then told all the band members, who told everyone in our local... At this rate the whole of the south-west will know that I'm gong to be on TV and in fact it's not long before they do.

Come Sunday, just before I'm about to do the Sixth Sense show on *Town FM*, Annette, who is back after her accident with the dodgy brake pads, announces live on air that everyone must tune in to see me on Wednesday at eleven o'clock on BBC1 – Aghhhhh!

'Annette, I didn't want the whole world to know, you know,' I protest.

'Oh it's not the whole world, just the whole of the south-west, that's all,' she says matter-of-factly. 'And, besides, I'm so proud of you and still feel very foolish for not taking your advice about the car,' she adds, pointing to the neck brace decorating her neck. 'I was going to get it serviced – I even had a post-it note stuck to my fridge – but I kept putting it off. That will teach me, won't it?'

'Yes it will and thank you, but in future, if I tell you something make sure you listen!' I say, waggling my finger like my mother does when she is making a point.

And speaking of mothers, at this very moment mine is sitting in the staff canteen with none other than Colin the Carrot Man! Having spoken to my mum at length about his carrots and his desire to meet her, my mum took no persuading in clambering in my car this morning, notebook in hand and hitched a ride to the studio with me in order to meet the elusive Colin.

My mother listened intently in the reception room to Colin's explanation of the theory that if you ate nothing but carrots your skin would turn orange. I do hope Mum doesn't try this at home. Apparently it's true. A student at the local college tried it. She wanted to test the theory and spent the following two months eating nothing but the orange-coloured root vegetable. And she did indeed turn a nice shade of orange thanks to her diet of carrot cake, carrot soup, carrot juice... well, you get the idea. Whether or not she turned back to normal after her unusual experiment, that is after she made herself look like she'd been Tangoed, I'm not sure, but I bet she saved a fortune on food – a diet of carrots surely can't cost that much.

Colin went on to explain the composition of pesticides and what they actually do to carrots and my mum scribbled away in her notepad, listening attentively to his wise words of the vegetable world.

Meanwhile, I am busy chatting away to callers who all want to know, a) when they will meet Mr or Miss Right, b) when they will win the lottery, c) when they are going to become famous, or all/any of the above. What happened to finding your spiritual path in life? Or inner peace? I chat easily to most of them and find that I'm finally getting the hang of reading the cards.

'So do you think I'm doing the right thing?' a caller named Emily asks, in relation to whether she should continue chasing after a man who has obviously no interest in her whatsoever.

'I'm being told that you are fighting a losing battle here, Emily,' I say, and surprisingly enough I am being told! A little voice in my ear keeps saying, *'Tell her to stop pissing around with this guy and go out with Richard.'* The voice in my ear is a woman and I try mentally asking her what her name is. Finally she tells me she is called Maria.

'Do you, or did you know someone called Maria?' I ask the caller and wait with batted breath.

The line goes quiet for a moment.

'Emily?'

'Sorry, yes, I do. She's... she was my best friend. She died in an accident last year.'

'Well Maria has just told me... oh, I'm not sure if I can say this on air...' I look at Annette who mouths 'No swearing' to me. 'Well, I won't say the exact words, but Maria just told me to tell you to stop messing around with this guy and to go out with Richard instead.'

'Richard?' Emily shrieks. 'But he's just a friend.'

It amazes me that Emily doesn't sound the slightest bit surprised by the fact that I've just had her dead friend rabbiting in my ear telling me to pass on a message to her, nor the fact that I just mentioned her male friend's name! I'm still not used to this talking in my head. I'm sure it's not right, but obviously other people assume it's something that happens to people like me every day of the week.

'Well, Maria says you should give him a try.'

'Oh well, if Maria thinks I should...' Emily muses down the line.

'Yes, she does. And she also says that she doesn't mean to be rude, but she doesn't like your new hair-cut. You should have left it long, but not to worry, it'll grow back again.'

'OMG!' Emily shrieks. I can imagine she is holding on to her hacked locks as she does so. 'Is it really that bad?'

'I haven't a clue, I'm not that good a psychic, you know,' I laugh. 'But your friend obviously thinks it's sh... no, I can't say that... thinks it looks better longer,' I say, hoping that I haven't spoilt the poor girl's day.

'Oh, I thought it looked quite nice. But Helen... the hairdresser I usually have... was on holiday and I had to have some girl who had just started. I knew she wasn't very experienced...' Emily says. As conversations go, this will go into the, one-of-the-most-unusual-conversations-I-have-had-to-date pile – having said that the one with the girl who murdered her boyfriend is probably still at number one right now.

The rest of the show runs smoothly as one caller after the other is put through on the line. I look over to Liam who is in the sound box and he winks at me. I smile shyly. What is the matter with me? This guy is young, good looking, single and kind and yet I don't get that excited feeling you're supposed to get at the start of a relationship. Grrr, me!

Right, that is it. I am damn well going to give this guy a chance. He's got everything I'm looking for. I have to make the effort to be nicer, I tell myself. After the show I will ask Liam if he wants to go out this evening.

'We are just breaking for a moment to give Crystal a breather and then we will be right back to take more of your calls. The lines are very busy at the moment, so if you can't get through immediately, just keep trying,' Annette says in her best radio presenter voice. 'Here's Queen with 'Radio Ga-Ga'.' She flicks a few switches and slumps down on her chair.

'Another successful show,' she says and smiles happily at me.

I too slump down in my chair. I'm exhausted. All this talking has made my throat hurt.

'How's your neck now?' I ask concerned as she winces and massages her neck brace with her un-broken arm.

'Oh you know, painful,' she laughs. 'I will heed your warnings next time. I promise.'

'She's doing too much and needs to take a break.'

The same voice I heard before whispers in my ear. Oh bum!

'Maybe you should take a holiday?' I offer.

'Yeah right, like that's going to happen,' Annette laughs. 'With Sharon on maternity leave and Simon with his bad back, I'm the only one left to run this ship at the moment,' she says and then looks at me. 'Oh, is that another piece of advice I must listen to?' I nod and smile.

'You've been doing too much lately and you need a break. Jeff can always cover for you. He was very good the other week.'

'Wel,l maybe I might just do that then. Thanks, hun,' Annette smiles. 'Right, back to business.' She flicks a few more switches and pops her headphones on.

'OK, so now we are refreshed, let's have our next caller. Hello, what's your name and how can Crystal help you?'

'Err, hello... my name is... Stu... Stewart,' a man's voice says nervously and then he coughs. 'I would like a reading from Mystic Crystal, please.'

Oh my God! I know this voice. It's Jack! I feel as though I'm going to faint and suddenly go all cold. I cannot believe he is phoning up pretending to be someone else! I mean this is my job, it wouldn't occur to me to try to screw things up for him at his place of work.

'Well Stewart, is there anything in particular you would like Crystal to focus on?' Annette asks, completely oblivious to the fact that this is my so-called best friend playing a prank.

'Errr, no, not really,' 'Stewart' says.

'OK Crystal, it's over to you.'

'OK, *Stewart*,' I say, not sure where I'm going to go with this. 'I'll draw some cards for you and I'll see what comes up,' I add. I'm not sure whether I should be doing this. I mean, what if something comes up that I'm not expecting? Am I too close to Jack to be able to do a proper reading for him? I take a deep breath and draw three cards.

'Well... we have quite a turbulent time going on here for you,

Stewart,' I begin. 'You're not where you are supposed to be in love or in life and have recently let down a few people who love you.' I keep picturing Jack with his naughty nurse and can't seem to shake the image from my head. If he wants to mess around then he's going to get what's coming to him. 'You will move on soon, both in your career and love life. What you thought you wanted is not what you want now. But just remember who helped you along the way.' I pause for a moment to collect my thoughts.

'You're on the right track. You're doing just fine,' a voice comes into my head. *'Don't worry, he won't be with her for long, she's a right bimbo. Tell him he's going to be a star!'* the voice urges. *'And then he will realise just where his love lies.'*

'OK, I'm getting a message for you here Ja... Stewart,' I correct myself. I wonder if I should refer to his girlfriend as a bimbo – maybe not. 'I'm being told that things are going to change and soon and that you will soon be a star.'

'Cool! Anything else?' Jack aka Stewart asks.

'Yes, I'm being told that you should remember your old friends on the way up, because you might just meet them on the way down again.' Well, you can't blame me for getting just one dig in, can you?

'Uh, OK,' Jack mutters. He knows that I know it's him and not someone called Stewart – and where he got that name from God only knows!

After Jack, I have one more caller to deal with, called Beryl, who wants to know when she is going to win the lottery and is pissed off that despite buying a Daily Play every day, plus tickets for the Lotto, the Thunderball and the other one I can't remember the name of, she still hasn't won a penny. I try to advise her that I can't predict a lottery win and that she might be better off using her money in more productive ways, but she just rants at me about not winning anything.

'Tell her to be careful what she wishes for because she will get the

money she wants, but not in the way she expects,' a man's voice tells me.

'You will get the money you want,' I say, 'But...'

'Oh brilliant! When?' the woman demands.

'I don't know, but please try to focus on other things besides money, because this money might just come to you in a way you don't want,' I try to advise.

'The important thing is that I'm gong to be rich! That's all I wanted to know, thanks!' the woman says and hangs up on me. Oh well, I did try. I've come to the conclusion that I can only try to forewarn people. It's up to them whether they take my advice or not, and more often than not they seem to take no notice of me anyway.

'Great show, once again, hun!' Annette says. 'And I will take your advice about having a holiday. Promise.'

'Good. Make sure you do,' I say as I tip out the contents of my bag on the desk in order to retrieve my Strawberry Crush lip-gloss. 'Right, I'm just going to speak to Liam and then reclaim my mother from carrot-loving Colin and then I'm off. I'll see you same time next week.'

CHAPTER NINETEEN

Having searched the entire *Town FM* building, I finally track my mother down in the local supermarket of all places, where she is busy analysing just how fresh the carrots really are, with Colin in tow. The pair of them have their heads buried in the vegetable section, sniffing bunches of carrots. Sniffing for what exactly I'm not sure, but they have already gained the attention of a member of staff and a security guard who are looking at them as if they have just been released into the community.

'Um, Mum?' I say, tapping her on the back, 'I'm ready to go, and what on earth are you doing sniffing the veg?'

'Oh, hello darling!' my mother enthuses as she fondles another root vegetable. 'Be with you in a mo, just doing a bit of research with Colin for our book.'

'Yes, well, that's all very well, Mum, but people are beginning to think you're a pair of nutters and that I'm your carer, so come on.' I guide the pair of them away from the fruit and veg section of the shop. 'And what book? I thought you were halfway through one?' See, I do listen to my mother sometimes.

My mother dramatically waves her arm in the air – it's no wonder people think she's out of her tree half the time.

'Oh yes, darling, but the food mile one is almost finished. Colin and I are going to be working on a book all about... guess what?

'I have no idea.'

'Carrots!' My mother is obviously excited at this prospect – but hang on one cotton-picking minute, what's all this about Colin writing a book with my mum? They've only just met.

'What? You're writing a book *with* Colin?' I ask the obvious.

'Oh yes, Colin's a mine of information on carrots. You didn't tell me just how clever he was, Sammy,' my mother announces, a little too loud for my liking. OK then, let's just make our way quietly to the exit, I think to myself as I escort the pair of them out of the store.

My mother is on cloud ninety-nine that she has at last met someone who is as passionate about vegetables as she is, and has arranged to meet up with Colin next week to discuss the dynamics of other coloured vegetables, including the beetroot and of course the 40 odd varieties of cabbage. Oh dear, I don't like the sound of all this, but then again she is a grown woman and who am I to question who she spends her time with?

'Samantha, I told my cousin Clive about you and he said he would give you a call. You never know, you might be just the one to cure him,' Colin says.

'Thanks Colin, that's great,' I say as I try to usher my mother into the car. However, before I can get round to the other side of the car, she has spotted a dried fruit stall on the other side of the road.

'Colin, look!' she says as she scurries across to it, dragging Colin with her.

'We could do a follow up on how beneficial dried fruit really is,' I hear her enthuse as the pair of them proceed to sample half a dozen varieties of dried fruits.

'What do you think of the cranberries?' my mother asks as she pops one into Colin's open mouth. I think his mouth probably dropped open because he couldn't quite believe his luck in meeting my mum – who, it has to be said, is still a darn good looking woman – and what's more she is passionate not only about fruit and veg, but equally about life too.

I know she can come across as, well... how can I put it... a very British Eccentric, but beneath that ditzy exterior lies a survivor. My mother hides it well, but throw anything at her and she will handle it in her own way, bless her. I decide it's better all round if I just quietly drive off and leave them to their food testing.

For once I have the evening off. I am very tempted to unplug the phone, but before I can, it rings. It's Amy in a bit of a state.

'I don't know what else I can do!' she wails down the phone.

'Look, hun, it's not the end of the world. You've got loads more options. I mean, it isn't the only place that needs area managers, you know.'

'I know, but I haven't any real qualifications. At least if I'd stayed on at college and qualified, like you, I'd have something on paper.'

'Ah, but as I have proved there are no jobs out there for qualified therapists – which is why I'm talking to dead people for a living,' I joke. 'Look, in all seriousness, why don't you come round and we'll open a bottle of wine and embellish the truth on your CV. And you don't even know if you are going to be one of the area managers who has to go yet,' I add. Amy has heard on the Big Mac grapevine that her bosses are having a reshuffle and they might have to lose some of their area managers.

Amy sighs, 'No, you're all right. I know it's your only night off. I'll be fine. I'm going to call Kenzie and get an early night.'

'All right then, but you know I'm here if you need me.'

'You too, hun,' says Amy.

My next caller is Miracle who asks if I might consider swapping my evening off in favour of filling in for her so that she can have dinner with Max – er, let me think… no. I haven't had a night off in ages and, as much as I love Miracle, I am not trading in my precious night off in favour of love's middle-aged dream – especially when I am still young and kind of single!

Liam calls to tell me that he's got VIP tickets to see Band of Gold next week. This man is so sweet, it's untrue. When we were out earlier, I'd mentioned that my favourite band was Band of Gold and hours later he's managed to get tickets to see them! I have promised myself that I will make more of an effort with Liam and make a point of telling him how grateful I am.

The one person I expected to hear from and haven't yet is Jack. Well, I say I expected him to call, deep down I didn't really since

I sent him a bit of a snotty text, telling him that I knew that he and Stewart were as one and that he could sod off and I never wanted to see him again. I am so mad at him! It was a really crappy joke to play on me, especially live on air. Besides, I expect he's too busy entertaining Miss Naughty Knickers to phone up and apologise.

Just as I'm about to settle down to watch *Mrs Doubtfire*, the phone rings again. I hesitate as to whether I should answer it. I wish I had Caller Display on my phone, then I could screen all my calls beforehand and only speak to the people I want to speak to, instead of trying to guess who they might be. Funny how psychic powers don't come into play when you really need them, isn't it?

'Hello?' I answer with trepidation.

'Hello, is that Samantha?' a man's voice enquires.

'Yes it is.'

'Hello, Samantha, you don't know me but I'm Colin's cousin, Clive. He said you wouldn't mind me calling you,' the man says.

'Oh right, no not at all Clive.' I'm not sure whether I really want to hear any more about vegetables today to be honest. 'How can I help?' I say instead.

'Well, I expect Colin has already told you that I suffer from lachanophobia?'

'Yes, he did Clive, and please don't be embarrassed about it. It happens to a lot of people,' I lie. 'How serious is your condition?' I ask. I lift Missy off my lap and grab a pen and notebook. Missy gives me one of her looks and huffs out of the lounge.

'Well it's – pretty serious. The mere thought of... veg... vegetables makes my stomach churn. I can't even look at a picture of them in a magazine without feeling sick.'

'Humm... OK. Look Clive, I think I might be able to help you. If you'd like to come round to my place on Friday I'll see what I can do. It won't be something that will happen overnight, but with a few sessions I think we might just be able to cure you of this,' I say brightly.

'Really? That's brilliant!'

'I'm sorry I can't make it any sooner, but I've got a really busy week ahead.'

'Yes, Colin told me that you're going to be on TV,' Clive says. 'I hope it all goes well for you.'

'Yes, thank you, me too.'

I make arrangements for Clive to visit and tell him my rates and put the phone down.

Wow! My first real client! You never know, once one comes out of the cupboard more might follow suit!

CHAPTER TWENTY

I'm nervously standing outside the BBC TV studios waiting to go into the building, doing a double check that I have everything I need. I've had to stick artificial nails over my own nibbled stumps, because I spent most of yesterday chewing them down to nothing. I can't believe I can get so nervous over appearing on a TV programme – but I am.

A car picked me up at six o'clock this morning to take me to the studio. To be honest I would have preferred to take the train, but they insisted on sending a chauffer-driven limousine to pick me up and drive me to London. The driver drops me right outside the main entrance and I sit there for a few minutes, gathering my thoughts.

As I leave the luxury limo I notice someone jogging towards me. It's Gerry the security guard. Despite looking as though he's about to have a heart attack on the spot, Gerry has a smile on his face – or maybe it's more of a grimace.

I stand watching as he puffs his way towards me. He stops and bends down, placing his hands on his ample thighs.

'Hello there!' I say.

Gerry holds a hand up in the air as he catches his breath.

'Hi... again,' he says finally, 'I... took... your... advice.'

'So I see! Well done you!' I say encouragingly. Gerry must be 19 stone in weight and the short jog to work has obviously taken it out of him, but he looks so pleased with himself.

'Two miles,' Gerry wheezes. 'That's how far it is from my house... to here.'

'Well done! You'll feel better a few days into it,' says she who only has to look at a treadmill to feel faint.

'Well, I'd better go and get changed. Martin will sign you in. Oh, and good luck with your TV thing,' he says.

'Thanks, and well done,' I smile. I'm so pleased he took my

advice.

I get signed in by Martin, another portly security guard, and momentarily wonder whether I should offer him the same advice as I gave Gerry. If this TV stuff doesn't work out, I could always become a fitness trainer to portly security guards. How come all security guards are generously proportioned? I wonder. Well, I guess not all security guards are like this, but the ones that I've come into contact with – two, to be precise – are.

I decide not to offer Martin any advice and make my way into the Green Room to wait to be called for make-up. I was told not to wear any whatsoever because the make-up girl will only scrape it off and put fresh on anyway, so I did as I was told, despite resembling something out of the *Thriller* video.

A make-up artist called Becky works her magic on me as she natters on about natural cheekbones – what are unnatural cheekbones then? is there such a thing? – and flawless complexions. I haven't a clue if she's referring to me or not, she just keeps randomly throwing words like 'exfoliation' into the conversation. Apparently my choice of attire is not suitable, according to the wardrobe department. The silver thread in my black and silver top will reflect on the camera and cause the viewers' eyes to shrivel up into dried walnuts – or something like that. Whatever the explanation for my dire wardrobe malfunction, I'm escorted to the wardrobe department for a complete new outfit which consists of a full-length black gypsy skirt, a ruffly kind of top, also in black and a black and diamond choker. Not my idea of a day-time outfit, but they obviously want me to look the part and with my black kohl and silver eyes and silver lipstick I look suitably mystical – I could just as easily be mistaken for a wench out of a Charles Dickens novel, but not to worry, if nothing else it will cheer Amy up and give her a laugh.

Now that I look the part, I sit and wait in the Green Room to be called into the studio. The 'Green Room' is a misleading expression as it turns out it isn't green at all. In fact it's a nice shade of lilac with a huge wide-screen TV set into one wall so that guests can watch the show they are about to appear on. The not-green-room, as I will refer to it on the grounds that there is not a hint of green in it, contains three plump two-seater sofas, and a glass coffee table with a huge vase of flowers placed strategically in the middle of it. It's comfy yet rather clinical and I daren't look at one of the glossy magazines that have been so carefully laid out for fear of disturbing the feng shui going on in here.

My nerves are getting the better of me as I look up to the TV screen to see the hosts, Billy and Suze, two C-list presenters, telling viewers to get busy phoning if they want to have their fortune told, because coming up soon is Mystic Crystal who will reveal all. I'm slotted in between Dr John – a doctor, in case you hadn't guessed – who is currently talking about how an in-growing toenail grows inwards – humm, nice. After my slot is the Style Guru with what to wear if you have a fat arse – OK it's not called that, but that's the gist of it.

I watch as Billy, a cross between Elton John and Ricky Martin – no, seriously – looks as though he's really interested in foot fungus. He has one of those orange perma-tans favoured by the likes of David Dickinson. He nods enthusiastically as Dr John demonstrates how a toenail grows right into the foot. Eww! I wish I hadn't had breakfast this morning.

Suze, an ex-rocker from the 80s, a kind of a mixture of Suzie Quatro and Chrissie Hynde – is beautiful in a kind of mature rock-chick way, and despite being almost fifty she refuses to leave her black leather trousers at home for fancy-dress parties only. She epitomizes rock and roll, and I'm sure she could easily drink any man under the table.

I feel as though every pore in my body is oozing sweat right now as I wait and wait for Dr John to wind up talking about gross nail fungi.

A young woman with a clipboard and a headset comes in to

the not-green-room and smiles at me.

'Don't worry, it's not as bad as it looks. I'm Tina by the way, production assistant.'

Tina holds out her slender hand. I wipe my own sweaty paw down my skirt and return the handshake.

'Easier said than done,' I say with a nervous smile.

'You'll be fine. Now, you're on in ten so if you come with me, I'll show you to the set,' Tina instructs in a very production assistant kind of way.

She escorts me to a set that holds a small comfy chair, a matching double sofa, a table with a black silk cloth thrown over it and a huge crystal ball placed slap bang in the centre. The backdrop behind me is another black silk throw, only this time, tiny twinkling stars are dotted all over it – very pretty, despite giving it the feel of a Gypsy Rose Lee's caravan. Oh God, I think I need the loo again!

'You'll be just fine,' a man's voice echoes in my head. It sounds very much like my dad's.

'Dad? Is that you?' I ask out loud.

'Sorry?' Tina says, looking at me as if I've gone mad.

'Huh? Oh no, sorry. I was just…'

'We're on in five,' Tina says as someone attaches a small microphone to my top, while another fluffs my face with a huge blusher brush.

'Shut your mouth,' the same voice in my head tells me and I realise that my jaw has dropped open.

'Are you OK?' Tina asks. I shut my mouth.

'Err me? Yes fine.' Please, Dad if that was you, please let this go well for me. I think of all the things that can go horribly wrong; I might freeze up, say something I shouldn't, faint, or even worse, fart – oh no, what if I fart? Now that *would* be embarrassing. Why, oh why, have I agreed to do this? What if I say the wrong thing? What if I say shit on air again? It will ruin my TV career before it's even started!

'On in four, three, two and go!' I hear in my ear. All my preparation has gone out the window, and I look like a rabbit caught in the headlights.

'And if we walk over here to our specially designed mystical set, we will find Mystic Crystal and her mystic crystal ball,' Suze says as she walks from her set and sits next down to me.

'Crystal, hi,' she says with easy professionalism.

'Hello,' I croak – I wish I had a glass of vodka to hand. Instead I have a glass of genuine BBC tap water and I take a shaky sip of it in a bid to drown the frog in my throat.

'So,' Suze says as she places her notes on her lap, 'tell us how this works then. I mean, do you really hear spirits?'

'Yes I do – sometimes,' I add, 'not always. I have no control over whether anyone will come through to me or not.' Nice disclaimer, Sam.

'And these are tarot cards?'

'Yes, I use these as a tool to help me to connect to spirit,' I say, trying to sound authoritative on the subject, when in fact I got all my information about why psychics use tarot cards off the web.

'I see.' Suze smiles a comforting smile. 'Viewers may or may not be aware, but Crystal is a highly reputable psychic, who not only dedicates her nights to answering calls for the psychic hotline that is Mystic Answers, she also has her own radio show on *Town FM* and her own website which will be coming up at the bottom of your screens shortly. Now, we have lots of callers on the line already, so we won't waste any more time. Let's see Crystal do her stuff,' Suze says excitedly.

'Tell Suzanne to make it up with her sister before it's too late,' a woman's voice comes through in my head. Oh, not again! I mentally tell whoever it is that this is not really a good time for me right now and could she possibly come back later?

Mystical music is played over a scene of tarot cards fluttering around the words 'Ask the All Knowing Mystic Crystal'. I know this not because I am psychic but because to the left of me is a TV monitor showing exactly what the viewers can see. Suddenly I see myself come into shot and yep, I still look like Bugs Bunny with a truck heading straight for him. You know, I'm sure they're right; TV sure piles the pounds on you.

CHAPTER TWENTY-ONE

'OK, so let's not waste any time and go to our first caller. Caller number one, are you there?' Suze asks.

'Yes, hello Suze, hello Crystal. Great first show by the way Suze!' A man's voice echoes round the studio.

'Thanks love and you are?' Suze asks.

'Oh sorry, yes, I'm Steve,' the man answers.

'OK then Steve, how can Crystal help you today?'

'Hi Crystal.'

'Hi Steve,' I say, thankful that this time it isn't a voice I recognise.

'Right, well, I wanted to ask you something really, if that's OK?' Steve asks.

'Sure, fire away,' I say.

'OK, well if, like you say, you can prove that there is life after death then why don't you tell the spirits or whatever you like to call them that they should only take old people and let young people live their lives to the full?' Steve asks.

Oh blimey! I just knew I would get one of those impossible-to-answer questions and I have to admit it has thrown me a bit. Why *do* the young die? I don't bloody know, do I? I mean a few months ago it never even entered my head. It was only the fact that I didn't have any money that meant I even wondered about there being an afterlife.

'Oh, for fuck's sake!' a male voice comes into my head and I visibly jump. *'Just tell the idiot that it was my time to go. I'd done everything that was planned for me and nothing would have changed it. It was my time to go,'* the voice says.

Err, who are you? I ask in my head.

'I'm his best friend, Darren. We had a crash. He survived, I didn't, end of story, and he's been beating himself up about it ever since,' the voice continues.

'OK, Steve,' I begin, 'I know how upset you are feeling about things right now...'

'Did your crystal ball tell you that then?' Steve says with a huge dollop of sarcasm. Don't you just hate it when people don't allow you to finish a sentence?

'No, Steve. Darren has just told me,' I say somewhat smugly – ha, that told you didn't it smug-ass!

'What?' Steve says, almost aghast.

'I'm afraid I can't say on air what Darren's exact words were, but he told me that there was a car crash and that you survived and he didn't and that you have felt guilty about it ever since.' The line goes quiet and Suze looks at me.

'Steve, are you still there?' Suze asks.

'Um, yes, yes, I'm still here,' Steve says quietly. 'Um, wow! Um, did he say anything else?'

'Yes, he did. He told me to tell you that nothing you could have done would have prevented it happening and that it was his time to go and nothing could change that,' I offer.

'Tell him to stop being a plonker and to get on with his life. All he does is sit in that flat of his and stare at the fucking walls. He's got to snap out of it,' Darren says in my ear.

'He liked to swear a lot, didn't he?' I laugh.

'Oh yeah,' Steve says.

'Well, I'll take out the swearing, but he is telling me to tell you to stop being a bleep bleep, and to get on with your life. You have to stop sitting in your flat staring at the bleeping walls,' I add.

'Oh, right,' Steve says.

'Does all this make sense to you, Steve?' Suze asks to camera one.

'Yeah. God yeah.'

'Would you like to share with us?' Suze encourages Steve like a professional counsellor coaxing a client to open up, 'Would you like to talk about Darren, Steve?'

'Daz and me have been best friends since primary school,' he says. 'We went everywhere together. We were both involved in a car crash six months ago... I was driving,' Steve says quietly. 'I wasn't drink driving or anything like that,' he adds. 'I took a bend too quickly and flipped the car. When I got out Darren wasn't moving,' he says.

Suze nods sympathetically to the camera. I feel as though I'm about to burst into tears.

'Don't you start fucking crying too!' Darren says in my head. *'Tell him I'm always around him, oh, and to clear that shit-hole of a flat up!'* he laughs.

'Steve?'

'Yeah?'

'Darren says he is always around you and, again bleeping out the unsuitable words, he says to clean your bleeping flat up. It's a right mess,' I laugh.

'Yeah, it is a bit,' Steve agrees.

'A bit? It looks like a fucking hand-grenade went off in there!' Darren says.

'Well, Darren says it's a bit more than a mess,' I laugh.

'Yeah,' Steve says.

'So, does that answer your question, Steve?' Suze asks with a warm smile.

'Yeah man! You're one cool dude, Crystal,' Steve says.

I don't think I've ever been called a dude before and a cool one at that!

'Well, thank you for sharing with us Steve and do as Crystal... and Darren says and get that flat tidied up and get out there and live your life,' Suze says.

'Well done, Crystal. So obviously you can prove to us that there is life beyond the one that we currently know, but do you often find that you have to prove this before people will take you seriously?' Suze asks me.

'It seems so, doesn't it?' I say with a chuckle. I don't say that I have no idea how all this psychic stuff works or that I only ever got into this because I was so desperate for cash or the fact that I am still getting used to hearing voices in my head.

'Well, you certainly proved it for Steve!' Suze laughs. 'Now shall we go straight to our next caller? Caller number two are you there?'

'Hello, yes I'm here,' a female voice says.

'And you are?' Suze asks.

'Michelle,' the caller says.

'Right then, Michelle, what can Crystal do for you today?'

'I'd quite like a reading please,' Michelle asks.

Michelle sounds as though she is in her thirties and clearly very shy.

'OK Michelle, I'll pass you on to Crystal,' Suze says.

'Hi Michelle. Is there anything specific you would like me to concentrate on?'

'Well, um yes. I'm not sure whether I should do something or not.'

'OK, well don't tell me anything else and let's see what I can get,' I say – Ooh, I'm getting good at this!

I deal out seven cards from my well-worn pack of cards and one by one I turn them over. The gypsy-style top they've put me in is made of some sort of itchy material and keeps scratching my skin. I bet I'll end up with a bloody great big rash the size of Poland by the end of the show. I look puzzled by the cards for a moment. They are all female cards.

'*She's one of those lesbians,*' a voice says to me. Thankfully I've managed to prevent myself from shouting out shit, fuck, or other suitable shock-inducing profanities when I hear voices in my head and merely sit there with my gob open.

'*She is you know,*' the woman's voice in my head insists. '*That's why you've got all those frilly cards. She hasn't come out of the wardrobe yet.*' Closet. It's closet not wardrobe, I say in my head.

'Crystal?' Suze says, 'Are you OK?'

Suze has every reason to question me as I have this inane grin on my face.

'Sorry, yes, I'm fine. Um, right Michelle,' I add, trying to think of where I left off. 'OK, this decision you're not sure about deciding on...' God, how do I say this? 'Well, I have an idea of what it is, but I don't think you want me to state it on air, do you?' I venture.

'Um... well, if it's what it is, then no, I'd rather you didn't.'

'OK, well if I just said it's to do with a woman and a special woman at that, would that be correct?'

'Yes, that's correct,' Michelle says somewhat hesitantly.

'Right, well the cards are telling me that you should take the chance and go for it...'

'*Tell her she's a long time dead,*' the woman's voice giggles and I find it hard not to laugh. '*Her aunt Lilly was one of those you know. Never told anyone, mind you. Wasn't done in our day, but everyone knew about it.*'

'I'm also being told you're a long time dead and that your auntie Lilly had the same... um... situation as you have now. Don't take any notice of anyone else and follow your dreams, Michelle,' I add.

Michelle gasps.

'You're right. My auntie Lilly was a... Did have the same problem. I know that because I remember my mum and dad talking about it.'

I actually feel very sorry for Michelle. Despite us living in a modern society and for all our claims of freedom of sexuality, it is still a very difficult thing to do to 'come out the wardrobe', as my dead friend so eloquently put it.

'Thank you so much, you've made my day,' Michelle says, her voice sounding so much happier than when she first phoned in.

'You're very welcome.' I smile most sincerely into the camera – I can't believe I just did that!

After taking twelve more calls and being asked everything from careers advice to 'is there life on Mars?' my debut is over. I slump lifeless into the comfy chair while Suze waltzes over to another set to introduce a woman who is an expert in big butts. She's describing what style skirt a woman with a big butt can, and can't, get away with without looking as though she has a big butt.

I'm still slumped in the chair when Billy introduces a band I've never heard of. They play as the credits for *Morning Latte* roll up the screen – poor buggers, I bet everyone has switched over for the news now.

'How do you feel?' Suze asks and I open one eye to respond.

'Bloody knackered,' I say honestly and I do feel bloody knackered as it happens. I never knew TV work could be so exhausting! Suze hands me a cup of coffee and sits down opposite me, kicking off her biker boots to reveal a pair of purple and black stripey socks underneath.

'I've heard that it can be hard work… you know, connecting to spirits.'

'It is,' I agree. 'Oh, before I forget. You know when you were introducing me?'

Suze nods.

'I had a message for you, but we were about to go on air.' I'm still a little hesitant about telling complete strangers that dead people have given me a message for them.

'For me?' Suze says excitedly. Good, a positive response.

'It wasn't much. A woman told me to tell you to make it up with your sister before it's too late,' I say and hold my breath. I may have opened up a can of worms here.

'Oh,' is all Suze says.

'I take it you do have a sister?'

She nods.

'We fell out when my mum died. It was over something really stupid like what sort of flowers she liked best, or something. We haven't spoken to each other for four years now.' She looks sad and melancholic.

'Well, why don't you call her, or write her a letter? Someone's got to make the first move.'

Suze looks down at the cup in her hands.

'Maybe I will. Thanks.' She smiles at me. My work here is done!

CHAPTER TWENTY-TWO

I'm well and truly knackered and my very first client, Clive, is due to come round in twenty minutes. After my first successful show, the producers have said that they want me back next Wednesday and also want to talk about the possibility of having me on five days a week. One day of travelling up to London and back I can handle, but five! I think if I agree to this then me and Missy are going to have to think about relocating, and soon.

Having done my end of month accounts, I am happy to say that I owe nothing to anyone and, believe it or not, for the first time in my life I have no credit card debts. My bank manager has probably had to cancel his holiday now he can't rely on the huge amount of interest he's been raking in from all the overdrafts and credit card charges that I've been paying.

I am in credit with my rent to Ms Morris. Now she just avoids me rather than threatening me with eviction, and thanks to my TV contract, which is paid in advance, I am well on my way to actually being able to save some money, rather than spending it all. Matt informs me that my website has had a 100,000 hits in two days since I appeared on *Morning Latte* and he has had to transfer it to its own server to cope with all the new members signing up to join the Mystic Crystal Psychic Club. He's had to recruit a member of staff solely to maintain the website and keep up with all the traffic it's generating – and they have people wanting to advertise on it coming out of their ears.

No sooner have I returned home from London than I receive several messages of congratulations from family and friends all saying how professional I came across – Jack wasn't one of them, I hasten to add. He must have seen the programme, but besides me neither my mum nor Amy has heard from him for two days.

Added to this a reporter from *The Daily Mirror* has phoned to ask if I will do a piece on psychic attack, whatever that might be

– memo to self, must ask Miracle that one – and three celebrity agents all want to represent me, one being Larry something or other who represents some of the biggest stars in show business. An agent indeed! What do I need an agent for? I wonder, as I tidy the flat by fluffing cushions and chucking everything that's on the floor into the cupboard.

My mum no longer thinks I'm working for Satan and despite some pointed remarks about too much eyeliner, I think she is actually rather proud of me being on the telly, although she still can't understand, or doesn't want to understand, how I have gone from being a psychology graduate to someone who talks to the dead. She didn't say as much, but the fact that she held a 'Samantha's TV Debut' Coffee Morning for some of her friends, including the influential Marjorie, who also just happens to be the Chair of the WI, speaks volumes.

'And Marjorie said she was so impressed with your presentation skills that she wondered whether you might like to come and do a talk to the ladies next week?' Mum says excitedly.

'Well, I'll see what I can do, Mum, but things are pretty busy at the moment,' I say as I push the cat litter tray under the couch.

The buzzer buzzes, making me jump – as it always does – and there stands the most unusual man I have ever seen.

Clive is well over six foot tall and has absolutely no weight on him whatsoever – a lanky streak of whatsit comes to mind. Actually Clive bears an uncanny resemblance to Willy Wonka from *Charlie and the Chocolate Factory*. Clive's face, which is almost skeletal, is framed by a pair of huge glasses, similar to those favoured by Timmy Mallett.

'Hi, you must be Samantha.' He extends a long arm towards me. Appearance is obviously not of great importance to Clive, who at a guess would be in his late 30s. The sleeves on his tweed jacket, complete with obligatory suede patches, end just after his elbows and he looks as though he's been shoe-horned into his brown slacks, which are very tight and short enough to show not only his yellow Simpsons socks but also his hairy shins.

'And you must be Colin's cousin, Clive,' I say, returning the handshake. 'Please, come in.'

Missy hisses at the extraordinarily tall stranger and runs into the kitchen to escape as I escort Clive into the lounge.

Clive sits himself down on edge of the sofa and immediately wrings his hands. He looks most uncomfortable. His eyes flicker around the room, rather than look me straight in the eye.

'Would you like a cup of tea or something?' I ask.

'No. No thank you.' Clive fidgets in his seat and pushes his large glasses back up his nose.

I've already prepared my first session which involves working out when Clive first discovered that he had a fear of vegetables, which I soon discover we have to call 'things' because even the word 'vegetable' gives Clive a nervous twitch.

'So do you think the reason you fear those 'things' could be because your mother walloped you around the head with a bunch of carrots when you were seven years old?' I say as I take notes and try not to picture this traumatic scene between mother and son.

'Yes I do. The damage she has caused...' Clive hisses, hatred in his eyes.

'But do you not see that it wasn't the carrots' fault and that maybe it was your mother's?' I add.

'Yes but...'

'I mean, the carrots didn't just jump up and hit you on the noggin, did they? The carrots didn't all gang up on you and say "Come on, let's all beat Clive up."'

This must be at the top of the list of the most bizarre conversations I have had to date – although the caller who asked me to contact his dead mother to find out whether she thought he should get circumcised or not comes pretty close to the most bizarre conversation I've ever had in my life.

'She was a very ill woman,' Clive says in order to justify his mother's desire to hit him around the head with an orange root vegetable.

'I'm sure she was, Clive, but can you not see, it was your mother who instigated this and not the carrots... um, I mean things?'

'You just don't understand!' he shouts and suddenly jumps up and holds his head in his hands.

'I think I do understand, Clive. You feel that it's the fault of the 'things', when in reality the 'things' just happened to be there at the time. Now, if your mother had hit you with, say, a newspaper, would you blame the newspaper and have a fear of them for the rest of your life?'

Clive continues to hold his head in his hands and just shrugs his shoulders like a child who has been asked how to spell Mississippi. I'm beginning to realise that there is more to his disturbance than just the simple fear of vegetables.

After fifty minutes of getting to the root – excuse the pun – of the problem, I decide that it's going to take more than one session to get Clive to realise that vegetables are not out to get him, so I book him in for another session for the next four weeks. I think I'm going to have to get another professional involved on this one and make a note to contact Professor Summers in the morning.

I'm sure Clive would stay all night if I let him. It takes some persuading to get him out of the door. Having calmed him down into sitting back down by bribing him with a chocolate digestive, Clive began to settle down and once we got off the subject of vegetables, he opened up a little about his life.

Clive lives alone and confesses that he has never had a proper girlfriend, but does have girls as friends, he assures me, and the only reason he's not married is because he is so shy. He works as a library assistant and spends a lot of his time reading.

By the time I finally ease him out of the door, Missy meows at me as if to say 'bloody loony' and I have to agree with her. Clive is a little odd, but then people who need therapy for their vegetable phobia have to be a little unusual, I guess.

With Matt back in London I'm actually terrified of logging on to the website he's created for me, but I know I have to. He is busy monitoring it for me and constantly sends me messages.

Mystic-Crystal-Ball.com is not just alive and kicking, it's positively doing the River Dance! The forum is buzzing with people discussing all sorts of mystical issues, we have already had 2000 members signed up, each paying £25 – that's… quick calculation in my head… Oh my goodness… that's fifty grand! Bloody Hell! I hope they don't all want a reading at the same time! I'm going to have to phone Miracle and get her to get some of the girls in to answer this lot.

A few phone calls later and I've managed to recruit fifteen girls to take on the majority of the calls, so I only have 200 readings to do myself. I've also managed to persuade Miracle to cover for me tonight so that I can catch up on doing these readings, as well as the more mundane things such as my laundry and cleaning the flat. That's the problem with having a job, you know, you don't have time to do anything else!

By the time Sunday rolls round again and I'm due back in the radio studio, my flat is gleaming like a new pin, all my laundry is done and Missy has had some much needed 'me time' with her mum. Despite my working last night and waiting up until four o'clock for Valerie to call in, she didn't, which I find odd. I hope she's OK. She's phoned every day at three o'clock in the morning since I've been working for Mystic Answers and last night was the first night that she didn't call. I wonder if Miracle can trace the calls and give her a ring to check that she's OK.

CHAPTER TWENTY-THREE

After another successful radio show with Annette, I have a meeting with the producers at the BBC to discuss doing my five mornings a week. I manage to persuade them to cut it down to four – I don't think I can manage to do any more, and I don't want to let Miracle down because she was the one who got me into this in the first place.

Just as I'm about to go and meet the reporter from *The Daily Mirror* there's a knock at the door. I was hoping it would be Jack, but it isn't. I really don't want to call him first because it is his fault that we are no longer on speaking terms, but I really thought he would have called by now, if only to congratulate me on my TV appearance.

It's Amy – and she's in a bit of a state.

'Can you spare five minutes?' she says looking somewhat dishevelled and the worse for wear. A comfy, bright pink tracksuit with *Barbie* written in silver across her bum, has replaced the smart black trouser suits Amy usually favours. It doesn't do justice to her lovely figure.

'Have you been drinking?' I don't know why I'm asking this because it's obvious she has.

'Can I come in?' Amy slurs.

I check my watch.

'I'm just about to go out, hun. I've got a meeting with a newspaper in twenty minutes but you're more than welcome to stay with Missy until I get back.'

Amy looks disappointed.

'I shouldn't be long. Look, come in and make yourself at home. Get a bath and some coffee down you and I'll be back as soon as I possibly can,' I say feeling, and sounding, really guilty for letting my friend down when she so obviously needs me right now.

Amy slumps onto the sofa and promptly falls asleep.

As I close the door and hurry down the stairs. I see Ms Morris coming the other way.

'Hi, Ms Morris. Lovely day,' I smile.

Ms Morris, who has replaced her anorak and is now wearing a new lambswool coat, doesn't even look at me and hurries on up to her flat with her head down. Rude cow-bag.

Just as I'm about to start the engine there's a tap on the window.

'Aghh!' I shout as I suddenly come face to face with Clive who has his long nose pressed against my window. He smiles, pushes his glasses higher on his nose and starts waving enthusiastically. I wind the window down.

'Clive. What are you doing here?'

'I was in the neighbourhood and thought I'd just pop in to see you,' he says with a grin on his face.

'Oh, I see, well, actually I'm just on my way out.' And if I don't get going I'm going to be late, I want to add, but don't.

'What time will you be back? I thought we could go for a drink later or something.'

'I don't know when I'll be back and I'm going out tonight. Sorry,' I lie.

'Some other time then?' Clive says looking disappointed in me. Oh dear, that's two people I've disappointed in a matter of minutes.

'Yep, I'll see you next week for your appointment,' I add, 'Bye!'

'Bye then,' Clive says and stands and watches me as I drive off. Missy was right – bloody loony!

After a successful interview about psychic attack with a very nice reporter called Candy – no, I don't think that's her real name either – I discover what is meant by psychic attack from Miracle, who actually experienced this herself when a malevolent spirit decided to turn her house upside down one night, causing untold damage. I had to ask if she was sure it was a spiteful spirit and not the result of a fight with her ex, and she assured me it was most certainly a spirit. Equipped with my new-found knowledge and a bit of Internet research, I managed to explain with authority to Candy how to protect yourself if you suspect you have a little gremlin in your house – all very Harry Potterish.

I get back to my flat within three hours and find Amy wrapped up in my fleecy dressing gown, slurping down a huge mug of coffee and watching an advert for *Morning Latte*.

'Hey,' she says as I flop down on the sofa next to her.

'I have to say you look better than when I last saw you. Are you OK?'

'Yeah, I've lost my job, but other than that I'm fine,' she says with a hint of sarcasm in her voice.

'Oh Amy, I'm so sorry. What are you going to do?'

'What any other self-respecting fast-food area manager would do of course – I'm going to defect to their competitors.'

'Really? Well, why not?' I say. It's good to see her again. It seems ages since we got together for a girly chat.

'I'm joking, Sam,' Amy says in all seriousness. 'I wouldn't work for them if you paid me.' I want to point out that they would actually be paying her to work for them.

'So what are you going to do then?'

Amy shrugs.

'God knows. You need any help with your psychic thingy?'

'Me?'

'Well, you seem to be doing very well for yourself. They just showed you on the advert for that new morning programme. Nice make-up, by the way. Surely you must be doing all right? TV deals, newspapers wanting to interview you, this website of yours…' Amy says.

'I don't think I'll be recruiting staff at any time soon,' I laugh. 'Besides, I don't think you're really cut out for all this psychic stuff.'

'What psychic stuff? All you do is make it up as you go along. You said as much yourself.'

'Well, not always...' I smile.

Despite her being one of my oldest friends, I daren't tell Amy that for the past four months I have not only heard voices in my head, I've also managed to be almost entirely accurate in all my readings, and to be honest, when Amy is in one of her sceptical moods, no amount of explanation from me is going to change her mind.

'So where's the lovely Kenzie today then?' I ask, praying that he hasn't dumped her as well.

'He's still in France. Doing some photo stuff with his father, on a magazine or something,' Amy sighs. 'I hardly get to see him these days.'

'Well, now you've got some time on your hands, why don't you go and stay with him for a bit?'

'Humm, maybe,' she sighs again. 'Have you heard anything from Jack?'

'Nope,' I say matter of factly, on the grounds that I will look as if I care that he's dropped me, and all his friends, for some big-nosed bimbo.

'Nor me. I wonder if he's OK. He's not answering his mobile.'

'He's probably too busy with his new girlfriend to care about us. Have you met her? She's a right cow,' I add.

'No I haven't. You know what Jack's like. He'll come to his senses soon and want to go back out with his mates,' Amy says. 'Come on, let's go out and get pissed.'

'Aww Amy, I can't. I've got to work tonight and be up early in the morning to go back to London. Any other night and I'd be happy to.'

'Oh great!' she huffs. 'And what am I supposed to do with myself while you're living it up in bloody London – baby-sit your stupid cat?'

'I'm hardly living it up, Amy. I'm working. And no, Missy is going to stay with my mum, but thanks for the offer.'

'Yeah, whatever,' she says in her stroppy teenager voice. 'Oh well, I know when I'm not wanted,' she adds and promptly huffs out of the door.

I don't like to tell her that she has just marched off looking like a bag lady in *my* dressing gown and *my* slippers.

CHAPTER TWENTY-FOUR

'Fancy another one in a minute?' Miracle asks.

'Oh go on then,' I laugh. This is the fifteenth call I've taken this evening. Since my introduction to the world of TV and radio, Miracle has kindly put my rates up on the grounds that it has increased her business tenfold since she started throwing in things like 'as seen on *Morning Latte*' and 'International Renowned Psychic' into her advertising.

And what's more, I am actually enjoying this job now. I know I initially said that it was just a stop-gap, until I could get to use my degree, but if I'm honest, I am much more confident about this job than I was when I first started, and many of my callers have become regulars and phone me on a fortnightly if not weekly basis. It's like I have a little club now and callers know which nights I work and will only call on those nights – I've even got a couple of people who actually pre-book their readings with me. I've done a fair amount of unusual jobs in the past, but this one tops them all and I'm surprised to say, I actually like it.

'Let me just grab a glass of water,' I say as I make my way into the kitchen. With more experience under my belt, I decided to invest in one of those cordless phones so that I can now walk around and talk – I can even take a pee while I'm on the phone if I so wish, although I don't just in case someone calls and wonders, is she having a pee?

'So, how's it all going with Max?' I ask as I reach for a cold bottle of water from the fridge.

'Oh, he is lovely, Sam...' Miracle coos. Anyone would think she was a teenager with a huge crush, not a 57-year-old divorced psychic. I'm really pleased it's all working out for her and, although I don't let on, I have a good feeling about this relationship.

I laugh as Miracle tells me about her recent date with Max to the London Eye and how he wined and dined her afterwards at The Ivy of all places – I thought you had to be a celebrity to get in there? Or maybe Max is a celebrity, disguised as an estate agent.

Dusk has claimed the light outside, I notice as I pull at the cord on the kitchen blind... Oh, shit! Is that who I think it is?

'Are you still there, Sam?' I hear Miracle say.

'Yes... um, can you hang on a minute, hun?' I mutter, as I press my head against the window pane. There sitting on the low wall that surrounds the house is Colin's cousin, Clive. He has a small set of binoculars with him, similar to the ones you take to the opera, and is... oh, shit! I duck down besides the sink unit and shuffle on my bum over to the door where the light switch is and flick the light off.

'Sam?' Miracle asks, concerned.

'Yes, sorry, still here,' I puff.

'Are you OK? You sound a bit distracted,' Miracle asks with concern.

'Yes, fine. You know that chap Clive I told you about? The one I'm treating for the vegetable phobia? Odd chap with the short trousers and strange socks?'

'Uh-huh.'

'He's only sitting outside my flat as we speak,' I say as I peep over the sink unit, 'and with a pair of binoculars in his hands,' I add.

'What's he doing that for?' Miracle asks.

'Well how should I know? You're the psychic here. Although actually I think he's got a tiny bit of a crush on me. He was outside the house earlier today, asking me if I wanted to go for a drink with him this evening. I had to make up the excuse that I was already going out.'

'Well, you're always moaning that you can't find Mr Right,' Miracle laughs. 'Maybe he's The One!'

'Oh, stop it! He's just strange. I only agreed to see him in the first place because my mother is…' – actually I'm not altogether sure what she's doing with Colin the Carrot Man – 'co-writing a book with his cousin, Colin,' I add. 'Oh crikes, he's looking right up here.' I drop down to the floor again and crawl, sniper-style along the cold kitchen floor.

'Maybe he's a closet astrologer?' Miracle suggests.

'Or maybe he's just a pervert?' I add. Miracle laughs.

'You are so funny, Sam.'

'This is no laughing matter, Miracle!' God, you hear of women being stalked all the time. Maybe I have my very own stalker!

'Do you want me to phone the police?'

I look out of the window again, but Clive is nowhere to be seen. Maybe he got bored of waiting for me and has buggered off.

'No, it looks like he's gone now. Right, where were we?' I hurry back into the safety of my lounge and throw myself on the sofa.

'Well, my sweetheart, I've got three callers lined up here asking for you, now stop bringing strange men home and get on with some work,' Miracle laughs.

'Hello and welcome to Mystic Answers. You're through to Mystic Crystal and I will be your reader for tonight. How may I help you tonight?' I say trying not to giggle.

'Hi Crystal! It's Amanda here,' a familiar voice says quickly. Amanda is one of my regular callers and despite being a highly intelligent, 45-year-old woman and a top London lawyer, she will not commit herself to anything or anyone unless she has a reading with me first.

'Hi Amanda, how are you?' I ask, pleased to hear from her again. Amanda is a nice person, if somewhat a bit too reliant on tarot readings. I'm sure it isn't good for you to constantly rely on other people's advice, but you can't tell Amanda. She says she spends the majority of her time having to make decisions for clients, but when it comes to making decisions for herself, this is where she falls down spectacularly – as in the case of when she had to decide what to wear to a charity ball and decided on a stunning Donna Karan number with more frills than a tutu, only to stand on said frills, lose her footing and end up head first in the punch bowl. Now she refuses to make any kind of personal decision without contacting me first.

'Well, you know me, as indecisive as ever, hun,' she says.

I shuffle the cards as we speak. I have thankfully got the shuffling business down to a fine art now.

'OK, so what is it this time?' I laugh.

'Right, well, you know I'm thinking about going into partnership with Barratt?'

'Uh-huh.'

'Only I don't trust him, Crystal. You always tell me to go with my instincts, and as you know, I'm useless at listening to my inner voice – that's if I could find it even,' Amanda laughs. 'Anyway, I don't know what to do. I need a partner to help me get the bigger clients and Barratt is a hot-shot lawyer, but...'

'But it doesn't feel right?' I say.

'Exactly, but I'm not sure why. Hence why I'm calling you – again,' Amanda says.

'Well, you know what I always say Amanda – trust that inner voice.'

'Ah, but I can't because every time I do, as we all know, I end up making the wrong decision.'

'OK, let's see what the cards make of Mr Barratt then shall we?' I say as I lay three cards out.

The first card tells me all I really need to know about this man's proposal of a partnership. The moon card is the first to be drawn and reminds me that it is a sign of deception. The following cards, all swords, confirm Amanda's initial instincts.

'Don't do it,' I say suddenly.

'Oh. OK then,' Amanda says.

I hope I haven't just lost her the opportunity of a lifetime here, but I get the strongest feeling that Amanda should have nothing to do with this man Barratt.

'At the end of the day, the decision has to be yours, Amanda, but the cards are confirming that you should be very wary of this man and his partnership offer. I sense nothing but trouble with him and he could bring you down with him.'

'Right, well that's fine by me,' Amanda replies. I do wish people wouldn't rely on my word so much. I just pray she doesn't phone back next week and tell me that another lawyer went into partnership with this guy and is currently sailing around the world on a yacht bought with their profits.

I go on to take another twelve calls consisting of a few more regulars; a few from women wanting men and men wanting women – sometimes I wonder whether I should start my own dating service instead; a few from people wanting to know if they are likely to win the lottery; and one from a woman obsessed with death who wanted to know whether it was possible for me to have her ashes made into an egg-timer – yes, I know, utterly barking mad that one. I advised her to contact her local funeral director. I tell Miracle that I'm taking a break for five minutes.

No sooner do I sneak back into the kitchen to put the kettle on than the phone rings again.

'I thought I told you I was taking a break?' I laugh into the receiver.

'And I thought you told me you were out all night?' a male voice snarls into the phone. Shit and bollocks, it's Clive!

'Ah, hello, Clive,' I stutter. 'How are you?'

'I'm extremely pissed off as it happens. That's how I am,' Clive replies. Oh boy!

'Look Clive, I'm working at the moment – from home,' I add.

'You're a liar!' Clive shouts.

I double-check the kitchen window to make sure he's not outside on the wall again.

'You told me you were going out tonight, remember?' Clive adds.

'Yes, well work called and asked me to work the night shift...' I say, feeling extremely pissed off by now. How dare he spy on me! 'And in all honesty I don't see that it has anything to do with you what I do with my evenings,' I add.

'It has everything to do with me!' Clive snaps. 'You are my therapist. I divulged a lot of secret and confidential information to you the other day and this is how you repay me!'

'Excuse me? You are my client, Clive, not my keeper, and I really think that if you are going to keep up this behaviour I will have no choice but to terminate our sessions.'

I have to say that despite having studied all the theory for dealing with difficult / barking mad clients, I am more than a little bit unnerved by Clive's tantrum, not to mention the fact that he was spying on me.

'You can't do that!' Clive shouts.

'Please don't shout at me, Clive,' I say, as calmly as I can manage.

'I'm sorry. I just... you can't just not see me,' Clive's voice falters.

'Look, Clive, I really don't think I will be able to help you. Perhaps I should refer you to another professional,' I say. The fact of the matter is that Clive has made me feel quite vulnerable and I don't need a stalker at this moment in my life, thank you very much.

'But...' Clive stutters.

'And please don't call me again. I will pass your number on to one of my colleagues.' I put the phone down and heave a sigh of relief.

Grrr to Clive and all the other stalkers out there!

It's times like this that I miss Jack – you know, those times when you need someone to chase the tarantula out of the bath, or as in my case, the weird, stalking lachanophobic. But I am not going to phone him. No, I am not! Despite desperately missing him and desperately wanting to hear what he's getting up to, I am still bloody furious with him and no amount of stalkers is going to make me phone him up first. Grrr, to Jack and the entire male species in general!

CHAPTER TWENTY-FIVE

OK, so I am now getting the hand of this media business and have since become Miss-Media-Savvy-Pants thanks to my new agent, Larry Jones – yes, I know, me with an agent! I still have to pinch myself.

Larry is a larger-than-life Yorkshireman and one of the most knowledgeable people I have ever had the pleasure of meeting. He instinctively knows what's a good deal and what's not. OK, so he takes twelve percent of my income, which is currently going up and up, but he has the media management down to a fine art and has already managed to secure me a regular column on two major glossy magazines. Larry is now in talks with four publishers about rights to a book entitled something along the lines of *I Speak to Dead People*.

I don't know how I managed to land myself an agent, or quite why Larry is so interested in me, but I'm thankful now that I returned his call because with all this work, I'm finding it incredibly hard to remember where I am supposed to be at any given time. Larry phones me, texts me and generally makes sure I am where I should be and with whom. He's more like a personal assistant than an agent – I swear, every girl should have one.

My week goes something like this at the moment: Monday to Thursday is spent working in London for *Morning Latte* and doing interviews, then I'm driven back to Bath on Thursday afternoon and spend Thursday, Friday and Saturday catching up with the website and working for Miracle. I'm going to seriously have to think about cutting down my hours with Miracle, but if it weren't for her, I wouldn't be where I am today.

And for the first time in my life I have proper cash in my bank account. I don't owe a penny to anyone and I can finally start to look at buying my own place instead of spending half my time cultivating the mushrooms that are currently growing behind the loo. And nowadays I get fan mail. I know! Me! Fan mail – now how cool is that? I, Samantha Ball, have fans!

'So what are you planning to wear then?' my mother quizzes me down the phone. Normally my mother has never bothered to question what I choose to swathe my body in, knowing full well that since the age of about 14 I would never listen anyway, but on this occasion and seeing as I'm going to be on TV, she sees it as her mission to make sure that I don't go out of the house looking like an unmade bed – or wearing too much eyeliner. The occasion in question being the Day Time Television Awards! I know, I can't quite believe it myself either.

Larry phoned half an hour ago to say that *Morning Latte* had been nominated for Best New Magazine Programme and the whole team has been invited to attend the awards – including me. This means that I, along with all the rest of the crew, will be sitting looking important in the middle of the TV awards, while listening to someone like a Paris Hilton look-a-like announce who the winner is.

Of course, as a professional psychic you would think that I would have been given some inside information about this from someone up there, but no such luck, so I guess I will be looking equally as shocked and surprised as everyone else there.

'Well, Suze is going for a posh-goth look,' I say to my mother, who naturally tut-tuts at the prospect of ex-rocker, Suze, dressing most inappropriately for the Day Time TV Awards, 'and most of the other people there will probably be dressed in long ball gown type dresses, I would imagine,' I muse.

Larry has suggested that I do a mystical thing at the after-show party, and before you can say abracadabra, has spoken to the organisers and arranged for me to give readings to the stars at £50 a head! He certainly has balls, if not the crystal kind.

'Well, you don't want to get anything off the peg, Sammy. I mean what a disaster, bumping into someone from Sevenoaks wearing the same frock!' my mother is outraged.

'*Hollyoaks*, Mum.'

'What?'

'It's *Hollyoaks*.'

'What is, love?'

'Oh never mind. So what do you suggest then?' I sigh.

'Well, it just so happens one of Colin's relatives is a wedding dress maker...' my mother says.

'Mum, I'm not getting married, I'm going to a TV award dinner and besides the last time I was introduced to one of Colin's relatives I managed to land myself a stalker, remember?' I say, shuddering as the thought of Clive enters my head.

'Yes, that was quite unfortunate, but Colin assures me he won't bother you again, dear. And anyway, you really shouldn't put yourself in that position, Sammy,' my mum warns.

'Me? Aghhhh! Mum, I did no such thing!'

'Yes, well, you just think hard in future who you invite back to that flat of yours. Now, anyway, Colin's step-sister's sister makes wedding gowns, but I'm sure if we ask her she will make something exclusively for your night out.' We? Since when did my mother and Colin become a 'We'? Oh well, I listen to her rabbit on for another forty minutes and realise that I have not only given her all my measurements, I've also committed myself to allowing someone I don't even know to design and make a frock for me for Saturday night! Oh no, what have I done?

'You've been speaking to my mother,' I say to Amy who is currently on the phone to me for the fifth time today.

'Well, I don't think it's fair. You're going to this bloody TV awards thing and I'm left at home baby-sitting the bloody puppy!' she whines again.

'Look, it's not up to me. Anyway, I thought you loved the new puppy Kenzie bought for you?'

'Well I did, that's before he shat in my shoes and handbag!'

'Who, Kenzie?'

'No, Brian!' Amy screams. I did tell her Brian was not really a suitable name for a dog and that he would only get teased in the park by dogs with more suitable names such as Fido and Tyson, but would she listen? No. Amy insisted that her adorable Andrex-ad-look-a-like puppy was going to be christened Brian, after Brian May from Queen – I know, you figure it out.

'Well, I can't help it, hun,' I say, trying to sympathise with Amy.

In an in-depth conversation with my mother, Amy discovered that I had been invited to the TV awards and ever since she has been badgering me to take her with me. I can't take her because… well, actually I daren't take her – Amy, alcohol and star-spotting could make for a very messy combination indeed.

'Anyway how's the job-hunting going?' I say, trying to get her to change the subject, and get off the phone so that I can have a bath.

'Huh, like you bloody care! Brian, get off that! Crap, if you must know, but I've just applied for a manager's job with Ann Summers, so fingers crossed,' she says, sounding a little brighter.

'Well, at least if you get that job you'll get lots of sexy freebies,' I laugh. 'Something will turn up and I do care, Amy. I just can't take you to this 'do'. It will probably be crap anyway,' I say, trying to ease the guilt I feel.

'Humm, is that what your crystal ball tells you, is it?' Amy laughs.

'Maybe. Look, have you heard anything from Jack yet?' I can't help but worry and wonder why he hasn't been in touch.

'Nope. Nothing,' Amy says. 'Well, I'd better let you get on with mingling with the rich and famous, I suppose.'

As Amy rings off, I'm not sure quite how to take that last comment. I know Amy is down right now, but there isn't a great deal I can do about it. I feel relieved that I can finally take a bath, but at the same time just a shade guilty. She's having a bad time, while for me, professionally speaking, things couldn't be better.

Once the ceremony is behind me, I'll devote myself to cheering her up, I decide. Maybe enlist Jack too – when he finally deigns to call me.

I have to say that Cilla, Colin's step-sister's sister, has surpassed my initial trepidation about my dress for the TV awards – I wonder why all Colin's family are named with the initial C? I'm sure there is some good reason. Anyway, the dress is made of a deep burgundy silk – strapless with a tight bodice to ensure nothing pops out at an inappropriate moment, and the full-length skirt makes my legs look as though they go on for miles. This woman certainly knows her stuff and I have to say I do look truly amazing in it. My hair has been curled into cute ringlets. The make-up artist has gone a bit overboard on the dark eye shadow, in order to make me appear even more mysterious than usual, but I have to say the whole look has exceeded my expectations.

I've had messages of good luck from everyone at the radio station, including Liam, which surprised me considering I haven't had time to see him all week. The two people I haven't heard from are Amy and Jack – surprise, surprise – and I have to say, I'm a little hurt that the two people who I considered to be my best friends have not bothered to wish me luck. Oh well.

The Grand Hotel that we – me, Suze, Billy and the rest of the *Morning Latte* crew – are ushered into, is absolutely massive. There are cameras everywhere you look and it reminds me a bit of *Big Brother*. There is no getting away with a quick nose-pick here. The entire nation could be watching you as you try a sneaky bat-in-the-cave moment.

I sit with my hands in my lap as though I were back at school. It's an uncomfortable feeling to think that the whole of the UK could be watching me right now, so I just sit there and laugh when everyone else laughs at the warm-up comedy act, even though I don't get the half the jokes. I feel like I shouldn't really be here. It should be Miracle, not me. It was Miracle who should have taken the radio job at *Town FM* and if she had she would have been asked to work for *Morning Latte* and in turn be sitting here to hear the announcements.

I'm desperately trying not to look star-struck and in awe of all the other people in the room. There are stars from my childhood sitting in the same room as me. All the old ones from Blue Peter are sitting at one huge table and I keep watching to see if they will whip out a shoe box and some double-sided sticky tape and produce a miniature hotel for Barbie and Ken. They don't.

There is a table dedicated to breakfast time newsreaders; a table for a bunch of children's TV presenters. I can tell that they're children's TV presenters by the way they are all dressed – they are *all* wearing very brightly coloured clothes and one of them who I vaguely recognise is actually wearing a pair of orange dungarees. You'd have thought, it being after 9pm and a grown-up event, that they would leave the brightly coloured costumes at home, wouldn't you?

Suze and radioactive Billy know everyone and I mean everyone! They wave at one table of presenters and then another, turn to each other and bitch about them – oh, the world of celebrities.

'She's had them done again,' Billy whispers as Suze waves to a surgically implanted woman who looks as though she is about to fall out of the two strips of material she calls a dress.

'Humm and she's had her cheeks chiselled by the looks of it,' Suze whispers back. Cheeks chiselled? How on earth do you have your cheeks chiselled? At any rate, it sounds very painful. I wouldn't want my cheeks chiselled or anything else for that matter, thank you very much.

'Oh look, there's Tony!' Suze points and waves to a man in the far corner of the room who looks like a conductor in his black dinner suit. He sends a regal wave back and then turns to the woman on his right and whispers something to her, as Billy does likewise to Suze. It's no wonder these people are paranoid if all they do is spend their evenings whispering about each other.

'And the winner of Best Breakfast News Programme goes to...' The Paris Hilton look-a-like pauses for effect. 'Wake Up!' she shouts into the microphone.

The table with the newsreaders cheers loudly and they all run up to the stage at the front of the room.

'Yeah!' one rather smartly dressed newsreader shouts, as the rest of them gather around the microphone, trying to get a word in edgeways so that they can thank their agents, producers, mothers... etc.

Once the newsreaders are ushered out of the room, the Paris-Hilton look-a-like looks at her notes.

'We're next,' Suze whispers to me. 'It's the Best Day Time Magazine Programme next, we'll nail it,' she says confidently.

'And the nominees for the Best Day Time Magazine Programme are...' the hostess pauses for effect, '...*Good Morning*...' – a huge cheer erupts and I sit on my hands so that I don't clap my all-time favourite programme – '...*Morning Latte*...' – another loud cheer goes up and this time I do clap my hands – '...and *Your Home is Your Castle*.' Unfortunately for the *Your Home is Your Castle* team on the table opposite us, the only cheers come from their own table. I think it's one of those programmes, I mean it's a bit like one of the soaps you have never heard of being up against *Coronation Street* and *Eastenders* – the only people who know what is going on in them, are the cast.

'And the award for the Best Day Time Magazine Programme goes to...' Ms Hilton lookie-likey rips open the pink envelope in her hands – '...*Morning Latte!*'

A big cheer echoes around the room and Billy punches the air, Suze screams 'Yeah man!' in a very rock-chic style and gives Billy a high-five. They both grab my hand and run up the stairs to the glittery stage with me in tow. Uh oh! Where are they taking me? Once again I am a rabbit-in-headlights as I stand looking out to the vast crowd with my gob open wide.

'Congratulations!' Paris, or whoever she is, hugs Suze as Suze waves a golden award in the shape of a star in the air.

'Thank you, thank you all!' Suze screams into the mic. Blimey, you'd think she was thanking Wembley. 'You know this wouldn't have been possible if it wasn't for the whole *Morning Latte* team and that includes our very special psychic, Mystic Crystal here!' Suze holds my arm high in the air – yikes, did I Immac my armpits? I feel that this could be that inappropriate moment when something that shouldn't pop out of my dress will do so. I blush the colour of said dress and look down at my very pretty shoes.

'And a very big thank you to our production team and Arnie, Penny, Lester…' Billy reels off a load of names I've never heard of but I assume they have something to do with the programme. Suze grabs the microphone from Billy who looks furious at her.

'And a huge thank you to our viewers. Without you none of this would be happening! Thank you all!' she screams again – once a rock star always a rock star.

After milking the applause for as long as they can, we are asked to leave the stage via the side curtains and the paparazzi photographers pounce on us and start snapping away.

'Crystal! Over here!' I hear a photographer shout as I turn. I smile as he shoots over and over again until I get flash eye.

I'm then bustled along to make room for the next award winners. I haven't a clue what anyone is saying, but I'm following exactly what Suze is doing. I'm pushed into a tunnel that leads back to the massive hall where all the celebrities are gathered waiting with bated breath to hear who has won the Best Actress award.

CHAPTER TWENTY-SIX

Before the after-show party is in full swing, I am ushered by Larry's PA into a private room which is to be my fortune-telling booth. Again no expense is spared and although I'm sure the organisers are taking the piss by making the room look like a fortune-teller's caravan on Blackpool seafront with a huge sign declaring 'Madam Crystal is in Residence', it actually proves very popular indeed and in no time at all the celebs are queuing up all eager to know whether they will win an Oscar for their latest performance.

First up is one of the over-excited children's presenters who bounces in and I half expect him to start singing 'I'm a Little Teapot'. This guy has so much enthusiasm it's unreal!

'Hi there!' he greets me excitedly, like a Red Coat entertainer – which I guess is probably what he was in a previous life.

'Hi,' I say with a smile. You can't help but like the guy, even if he is wearing a silky, purple and yellow polka-dot shirt and a pair of turquoise cord trousers. I can't help but notice that he also has a pair of lime green Crocs on his feet. Quick, someone call the fashion police!

'So, what can I do for you?' I ask as I shuffle my pack of cards. I hope I don't smell. It is awfully hot in this booth, you know.

'*He wants to know if he should marry Tristan,*' an effeminate voice informs me and it's not coming from the vibrant chap in front of me – unless of course he's also a very good ventriloquist in his spare time.

'Well, I really want to know if I should commit,' the presenter asks.

'*Of course he's totally wrong for him,*' the voice says. '*He doesn't love him like I did.*' And you are? I ask in my head. '*I'm Leonard, my dear.*'

'Um… can I just ask you if you knew someone called

Leonard?' I ask.

The TV presenter claps his hand to his mouth.

'Leonard? You mean Leo? He's here, in this room? Oh my God, I think I'm going to faint,' Mr TV presenter says as he looks around the booth in panic and I think he might just faint at any given moment.

'Well, he's not here, here, as in right here, but his spirit is here, if you get my meaning,' I say, even I'm getting confused now.

'So what does he say?' the TV presenter asks eagerly, like a child high on orange Smarties.

'He says that he doesn't think Tristan is the right one for you.' I pass on the message from the obviously gay spirit.

'Bitch! He would say that, wouldn't he? I mean it's not like he ever liked Tristan, did you, Leo?' The man in front of me shouts aggressively into the air, looking around him. 'He never did like him you know,' he says to me.

'He's too young for him. I mean come on, he's hardly got any experience has he?' Leonard snaps.

Oh help.

'Well, I'm going to marry Tristan whether you like it or not Leo! You're not here and he is! You left me remember, for that hussy Patrick and where did it get you? Huh? I'll tell you where, nowhere, that's where! Was he there at your funeral, Leonard? No, he wasn't and why was that? Because by then he was in France, canoodling with some Parisian producer, that's why, Leonard. I was there. I was at your funeral, crying for you.' The TV presenter snaps and breaks down in tears and then dramatically storms out of my booth, screaming something along the lines of, 'I can't do this!'

Err, hello? Did that chap not think it the slightest bit unusual that I could hear his dead friend, Leonard? Obviously not. Obviously children's TV presenters are used to having arguments with gay dead people all the time.

Next to enter my booth is a middle-aged woman I recognise as

Verity something or other from a recent Marks and Spencer advert. She breezes in to my 'booth', plonks herself dramatically in the chair in front of me and throws her fox fur shawl around her neck.

'So, Dharling, tell me what the future holds for me,' she drawls. The reason she drawls is thanks to the amount of botox the woman has in her poor face. Her original features would probably never recognise her now. Her lips are vibrant red and look like they've been inflated using a bicycle pump.

'You probably recognise me from *Once Upon a Time*. Fabulous director, Dharling!' the actress says. Err, nope, never heard of it, sorry.

'Yes of course,' I say as I shuffle my cards and pass them to her.

'*She had an affair with him, that's why she thinks he's bloody fabulous!*' a woman's voice comes into my head. She sounds like a Londoner and I stifle a giggle.

'So, what does my wonderful future hold then?' the actress asks.

'*She'll grow old, wrinkly and those stupid lips will drop off before long if she doesn't stop pumping them up – silly old trout,*' the other woman's voice adds. I can't tell her that! '*Oh, what a shame, because that's what's going to happen,*' the voice confirms. '*She's got a drink problem too.*' I have no idea who is talking to me, but she's obviously someone who knows this lady, and by the sounds of it someone who knows how to hold a grudge too.

'Well...' I study the cards in front of me, 'I don't think you will act forever more...'

'Not act? Me? Dharling, do you realise who you are talking to? I'm Verity Star!' The woman looks aghast.

'I feel that you will devote much of your time to animals and teaching other young actors and actresses your craft,' I add.

Verity waves her arms in the air, very Shirley Bassey style.

'We don't have actresses nowadays, dear, we are all actors. Of course I am a very giving person, it's my only fault,' Verity muses to herself.

'*Ha!*' The cockney woman in my head laughs loudly. '*Giving? She wouldn't piss on you if you were on fire!*'

'Excuse me, who are you?' I ask out loud – oh bum, I must stop doing that. The actress in front of me looks at me, her eyes popping out of her head.

'Excuse me?'

'Oh sorry, no not you. I know who you are,' I lie. 'I was talking to...'

'*I'm Rita. She knows who I am,*' the voice confirms.

'Right, um... Verity do you know, or should I say, did you know a Rita by any chance?' I ask Verity cautiously.

'Rita? What, Rita Monroe?' Verity asks.

'*The one and only, Darling!*' Rita cackles in my head.

I nod.

'What, is she here? With us now? Oh my God!' Verity places a hand over her heart and feigns gloom.

'Poor, poor Rita. Oh, we did get on well together. We were at the Palladium you know!' Verity confirms.

'*Lying bitch. I couldn't stand the old cow!*' Rita hisses.

'Poor, poor Rita. She liked the you-know-what,' Verity says in hushed whispers. I frown – I haven't a clue what the you-know-what is. 'You know, the old sauce,' Verity does a mime of a drunk drinking out of a bottle.

'Oh, right.' I get it now.

'*Why the fucking lying cow! It's her who can't say no to a Between the Sheets, and I'm not just talking about the drink either!*' Rita snaps in my ear.

I can see this double act have a few issues going on here.

'Well, Rita sends her love and is looking out for you,' I say with a most sincere smile.

'*Like fuck I do!*' Rita seethes, '*I'm just counting the days till she drops down dead then I'll really tell her what I think of the old trollop!*'

Call yerself a psychic? Ha!'

Well, I can hear you, can't I? I think to myself.

'Ah, bless her little heart,' Verity says with what could be a smile, although with those lips it's hard to tell, it could be a sneer for all I know.

'I'll leave Rita's love with you then,' I say, sounding not too unlike Colin Fry.

Verity sashays out of my booth, dramatically flicking her fox fur over her shoulder.

CHAPTER TWENTY-SEVEN

I wake bleary eyed and with a face that looks like I've been hit with the back of a shovel. Having taken readings for more than 200 celebrities I ended up collapsing into my hotel bed just as the sun was rising at four o'clock this morning. I couldn't even be arsed to undress and as a result, my beautiful burgundy dress looks more crushed than crushed silk and there's a bloody big stain of something, which smells faintly like coconut, slap bang in the middle of it – eww, goodness knows what that is. I don't remember drinking anything with coconut in it last night. Mind you, I was so busy that Larry's PA just kept popping in with refreshments for me all night. For all I know I could have been downing arsenic.

The evening was a great success – although I never did find out what happened to the children's TV presenter. The one time I managed to exit my booth on account that I was desperate for a pee, I noticed that Suze was standing on top of a table belting out Bruce Springsteen's, 'Born in the USA', at the top of her voice. The last time I saw Billy he was bitching to another perma-tan presenter from *Hooray, Hooray, It's Our Holiday*, about some actress on *Eastenders*. I don't know; the dizzy world that is celebrity, hey?

As I head for the shower I switch on my phone that rings into life signalling that I have twenty-odd messages. What did we do before mobiles? I wonder as I throw the phone onto the bed and step into the warm running water. There was a time when people would pop into their neighbours for a cup of sugar. Nowadays no one knows who their neighbours are. Instead of borrowing a cup of sugar they simply press a few keys and order a whole bag of it from Tesco.com. Apart from Ms Morris, I have no idea who lives in the other flats occupied by my neighbouring tenants. I occasionally glimpse people coming in or out of the house, but that's as far as our social contact goes.

As the water rushes over me I contemplate the previous evening's events. So that's what it's like to live in the world of celebrities then – lots of 'Mwah, Mwah, Dharling' and very little else from what I saw. And they are so insecure! If I'd been given a pound for every time I'd been asked if they would get any further in their careers, I would be a very rich woman indeed this morning. 'What about my next film role? Do you see me working with Harrison Ford?' Chill out, I wanted to shout! It's not the end of the world if you don't star alongside Indiana Jones you know!

I hear my phone bleep-bleep again as I wash the soap from my hair and the make-up from my tired eyes and tut to myself. Can't a girl have a shower in peace these days?

By the time I've towelled myself dry and slipped into the complementary fluffy white bath robe, there are more than 50 text messages on my phone. My voice mail box is constantly buzzing with more messages. It's either my birthday and I've forgotten, or everyone saw the TV awards last night and is texting to congratulate me.

I start to trawl through the messages…

Sam. Call me. Urgnt – Annette.

Y R U Nt answring ur phone? – Annette.

Call me ASAP – Larry.

Ugnt – call me – Larry.

Hv u seen yet? Not gd – call me – Matt.

Sam – can u ring me plz – Matt.

Shit Sam – wotz going on? Jack.

Need 2 tlk 2 u – urgent – Larry.

Call me as soon as u get this msg. We need 2 talk – Liam

What the? I do wish people would send grammatically correct messages. It's hard enough to work out what people are trying to say without abbreviating everything. And what the hell is going on? No sooner than I scroll through the numerous messages then another comes through, then another, then... well, you get the gist of it. Not content with saving stacks of messages, my Nokia now decides to go into overtime with its cat noise ring-tone – I thought it was cute to have a meowing phone ring, but now it just sounds as though a cat is being slowly and very painfully murdered. I don't have enough thumbs to read the messages and answer the phone at the same time, and no sooner do I hit the silent button than it meows again.

The only message that has stuck in my head is the one from Jack. If Jack has texted me then there must be something wrong, so I delete the other 49, ignore the meowing and ring Jack's mobile.

'It's me, what's up?' I say as light-heartedly as I can muster.

'Where are you?' Jack says, panic rising in his voice.

'I'm at a hotel in London, why?'

'Which one?'

'The Plaza, on West End Street. Jack, what's going on? My phone hasn't stopped ringing all morning. Did you see me on telly? Was I OK?' Now panic is in my voice.

'Just stay where you are, Sam. Do not answer the phone, do not talk to anyone, lock your hotel room door and just wait until I get there. I'll explain then. What room number are you?' Jack orders.

'121... but...'

The line goes dead.

Oh shit. This doesn't sound good. I feel hot and sick all at the same time. What is going on?

My mobile meows into life again and Larry's number flashes up on the screen. Don't answer the phone, Jack said. Shit. What should I do? Has the world gone mad? Have we been attacked by zombies? I hesitate, watching the screen light up while all the time the bloody meowing noise echo's around the room. Oh, oh, oh, I don't know what to do!

'Miss Ball?' a male voice outside says as a knock sounds on

the door.

Do not open the door, Jack said.

'Miss Ball? Are you in there?' the same voice asks.

Do not talk to anyone, Jack said.

I drop down to the floor and crawl underneath the bed to hide. The phone is meowing, the door is knock-knocking and I'm hiding under a bed in a top London hotel and I have no idea why. This really is not a good start to the day and I still haven't dried my bloody hair, which means it will look like a ball of tumbleweed any minute!

'Sam. Sam it's me!' a voice hisses through the door about an hour and a half later. It's Jack – or is it? I am so paranoid by now that I don't know who is who anymore. I've just spent the past two hours examining the shag-pile under the bed. My legs are as stiff as a corpse and every time I moved in a bid to get comfortable I managed to catch my hair in one of the bedsprings above me.

'Sam! It's Jack. Open the door,' he says.

'How do I know it's really you?' I ask as I attempt to crawl out from under the bed – ouch! Bloody bedsprings!

'What do you mean how do you know it's me? It's me, you wally! Now open the bloody door!'

This is all very MI5.

'Well, you say that, but I've been under the bed for two hours and I don't know what's going on,' I wail.

'Jesus Christ. Right, OK, um... right, your middle name is Abigail,' Jack says. He's correct, but then anyone could have found that out by looking at my birth certificate.

'Tell me something only Jack would know,' I say – God this is stupid. I know it's Jack. It's Jack's voice for goodness sake, but he did tell me to not answer the door to *anyone*.

'Oh, for fuck's sake, Sam. OK... um... oh yeah, you've got a birth mark in the shape of a strawberry on your right buttock,' he mutters.

'How do you know that?' I shriek.

'Because I've seen it on numerous occasions, when we've been swimming. Now open the fucking door, before I announce your bra size to the lift attendant. I look a right prick stood out here.'

I crawl over on my hands and knees and reach up and unlock the door. Jack, looking very sexy – oh my God, did I just think that? – dressed in biker leathers, a crash helmet on his head and carrying a large plastic bag, a spare helmet and a pile of newspapers in his hands, rushes in, shuts the door behind him and locks it. He takes his helmet off and looks at me for a moment.

'Man, you look like shit,' he says, reaching out to give me a hug. And I do look like shit. My hair, which I had every intention of drying has taken on a life of its own and I now resemble Medusa on a bad hair day. But I don't care. I hug Jack to me, inhaling the combined smell of leather and Jack and I want to hang on to him for as long as I can.

Finally Jack holds me at arm's length and looks at me with a very serious expression on his face.

'What's going on, Jack? One minute I'm getting up to all sorts in a dream about George Clooney and the next my mobile is bombarded with messages from people telling me to call them immediately.'

'You haven't spoken to anyone, have you?' Jack asks.

'No, well apart from you. Someone knocked on the door earlier, but I didn't answer it.'

'Good girl, now take a deep breath and look at these.' Jack unfolds the eight or so newspapers he's had clutched under his arm.

PSYCHIC TO THE STARS – FRAUD MORE LIKE!

MYSTIC CRYSTAL – WHAT A LOAD OF CRYSTAL BALLS!

'I MAKE IT ALL UP' – PSYCHIC TO THE STARS CONFESSES!

TV PSYCHIC, OR CON-ARTIST?

Every newspaper from the tabloids to the broadsheets

screams the same headlines, followed by a picture of me at the awards ceremony last night, smiling and waving to the photographer.

Oh, sweet Jesus!

My eyes scan the headlines. One after the other they all say more or less the same thing.

Samantha Ball, or Mystic Crystal, as she likes to call herself, claims she has no psychic ability whatsoever and makes the whole thing up...

Oh God, I feel as though I'm about to be sick. Tears cloud my eyes as I try to read the rest of the story that has gained national coverage, all the while my stomach feels as though it is about to throw up the entire contents of last night's buffet supper.

A source close to the psychic cheat, whose clients have included A-list celebrities and MPs, says, 'She told me herself she has no psychic skills and just makes it all up. The only thing she's qualified for is treating people with vegetable phobias. She thinks it's all a bit of a laugh.' Samantha Ball, 25, from Bath, who until recently was an unemployed graduate, began her extraordinary quest to deceive bereaved clients into believing she was contacting their loved ones. She freely admits that she has no knowledge of spiritualism and yet has managed to con her way into a very lucrative career, with her own radio show on Town FM, *daily appearances on BBC's* Morning Latte *show and numerous columns for women's magazines... Miss Ball was unavailable for comment...*

'Oh my God! Jack, have you seen this?' I stutter between tears. 'I'm in every fucking newspaper, on every fucking front page. I feel as if all the blood is draining out of me. I have to sit down. Jack kneels down beside me and places one leather-gloved hand on my knee. Unavailable for comment? I haven't even been asked to fucking comment!

'But who would do this to me? It's simply not true, Jack. I do have psychic abilities – admittedly I didn't think I did at first, but I do Jack, I really do!' I wail. 'Look at them all! They are all saying I'm a liar and fraud. What am I going to do, Jack?'

I start to cry into his shoulder, and then he pulls me closer into his chest. Once the tears start I can't stop them.

CHAPTER TWENTY-EIGHT

I feel like a fugitive on the run – or at least how I think a fugitive on the run would feel like right now. In the 30 minutes that Jack has been here, there have been four knocks on the door and numerous phone calls from reception informing us that people from the press wish to speak with me to get my side of the story – yeah, right.

I have appointed Jack as my spokesman – well, with all this going on, I need someone to help me. Funnily enough, I always thought of spokespeople as official-looking men dressed in suits, who read out statements to the press at the front of equally official-looking buildings, not a leather-clad biker in a vintage t-shirt and spiky hair.

As the phone by the bed rings into life again, Jack picks it up. 'Yes?'

'No, and can you please inform the press that Miss Ball is not available for comment. Miss Ball has left the building,' I hear Jack say. 'No, I imagine she is back home by now. Yes, her bill will be settled today – thanks.'

My eyes flash again over the headlines of the tabloids, which are spread out all over the bed. It feels as if I am in a very, very, bad dream and any moment now I will wake up, snuggled under my duvet with Missy sleeping on my head and think, thank goodness for that, it was only a dream.

But it's not a dream; someone – a source close to me apparently, according to the papers – has gone to a whole lot of trouble to ruin my reputation and it looks like they may well have succeeded. I have been vilified to the extreme. All I can think of is, who would hate me so much as to do this to me?

I look at the photograph on the front page of *The Sun*, taken last night: 'Con artist Samantha Ball at last night's TV award ceremony', screams the headline. As I slept, some sleazy photographer was busy emailing my picture to all the editorial offices of all the British press.

'Right,' Jack says in an authoritative manner, 'get yourself dressed in this, and we'll head off back to Bath. The longer we stay here the more calls we are going to get and the harder it will be to get out of here.'

'I can't go back to Bath, Jack!' I stutter. 'The press will be camped out on my doorstep.'

'Maybe, but you won't be there. You're coming back to my place,' Jack assures me.

'What about Missy?'

'I'll pick her up from your mum's later. For now we need to get out of London.'

'But I have to clear my name! I have to tell everyone that I am for real. Oh Jack. And what the hell is this?' I wail looking puzzled at the Scooby Doo costume Jack has handed to me.

'It's the best I could get at short notice,' Jack says.

Jack pulls me up from the bed and hugs me tightly.

'It's going to be all right, sweet cheeks. Honest, trust me, I'm a lawyer.'

'Strictly speaking you're not – a lawyer, that is. You never did your training contracts, remember,' I point out, and sniff loudly.

'Yeah, but they're not to know that, are they? And if we were in America I could legally practise law.'

'But we're not in America,' I add.

'And how many people with law degrees are there who can help you out right now, Scooby?' Jack asks as I pull myself into the life-size dog's costume. Surely he could have got me something different, like... oh, I don't know, but something other than Scooby bloody Doo!

'Good point; I'm sorry Jack, and thank you so much for coming. I don't know what I would have done without you.'

I'm tempted to ask where Jack's girlfriend is and what she makes of it all, but I don't.

Thankfully Jack had the foresight to work out where all the emergency exits are in the hotel and parked his friend Dillon's motorbike out the back by the kitchens. I feel more of a fugitive than ever, dressed up as Scooby Doo. All I need now is for the Mystery Machine to turn up and for Velma to announce 'I've got a plan!'

I put my black full-face crash helmet on my head as we tiptoe out of the hotel room and make our way down the fire-exit staircase. I am terrified that someone will see us and start taking photographs or try to stop us from making our getaway. I mean, we have a bloke clothed head to toe in black leather, with Scooby Doo tiptoeing behind him. Why is this happening to me? Don't cry, Sam, don't cry.

Within minutes, we're tearing down the motorway at 90 miles an hour. I'm hanging on to Jack's back for dear life as he manoeuvres the bike from the slow lane to the middle and back again, my tail swishing in the wind behind me. I desperately want to look behind me to make sure that no one is in hot pursuit of us, but I daren't move in case I lose my grip and go flying off the back of the bike – now that would be a nasty way to go. Knowing my luck today, I would hit the road and get run over by an on-coming truck.

'You OK?' Jack shouts into the microphone attached to his helmet, above the roar of the bike.

'Scoobyroobiedoo!' I squeal back, unsure if I am or not.

In just over two hours we are back at Jack's flat and I hurry inside as quickly as I possibly can for fear of being seen.

'You can take your helmet off now,' Jack laughs, 'I don't think the paparazzi are hiding in the cupboards.'

I gingerly take my protective hat off. I know I must look a sight – I never did get round to blow-drying my hair and I still have the body of a bloody Great Dane.

Having consumed a very large rum and coke to stop me shaking – not my usual tipple but that's all Jack had in, which I believe was left over from the Hawaiian party he had last year, I do hope it's still in date – I sit with my head in my hands. Meanwhile Jack puts on his lawyer walk and paces around the living room, swirling a glass of brandy in his hands – very Alfred Hitchcock, Jack.

Jack's flat is much as you would expect any other bachelor's flat would be like – in other words, a right mess, where nothing whatsoever matches. There are several empty cans of Fosters dotted around, the *pièce de résistance* being a collection of cans stacked – sorry, sculpted – into a miniature version of the Leaning Tower of Pisa.

The entire flat is furnished with second-hand items that have absolutely nothing in common. The Art Deco style sofa is not in any way in keeping with the 80s black-ash coffee table. Neither is the 60s hanging wicker chair, or the giant leather bean-bag styled like a Rubik's cube, sitting in the corner. Looking at Jack's flat you would think you had just walked into a second-hand furniture store.

'So,' Jack says, as he paces the wooden floorboards in his leather trousers. He has removed his jacket and underneath is a black t-shirt with the slogan, 'It's a great day until some bastard spoils it' – ain't that the truth. 'Who else knew you were going to the award ceremony last night?' he asks.

'Who didn't know more like! It was on *Town FM* and *Morning Latte*, that's a good few million for starters.'

'Right, so who would know and would hate you enough to do this to you?'

I know Jack is trying to help but these questions are not really helping me. I didn't even know I had a 'source close to me' and if I had, I would have been more careful what I said to them.

'You tell me. I haven't upset anyone or fallen out with… oh, hang on a minute. There was Clive-the-weirdo…'

'Clive the what? And just who is this Clive?' Jack looks at me as if he's interrogating a suspect.

'A client of mine, or at least he was a client of mine.'

'A client, eh? What sort of client would that be then?' Jack smiles.

'Not the sort you're thinking about for a start. He suffers from lachanophobia. He's Colin the Carrot man's cousin. I agreed to treat him, but he got a bit weird on me – waiting outside my flat, spying on me, phoning me up, the usual thing weirdos like to do on their days off. I told him to bugger off and leave me alone – he wasn't very happy about it.'

Jack grabs a notebook from his cluttered desk, which is actually an old cider barrel, and jots down 'Clive – lunatic' in big letters.

'Think he would want revenge for you dumping him?'

'I don't know. I suppose he might do. And I didn't dump him. I just gave him the brush off.'

Would Clive go to so much trouble to make me pay for not going out with him? Maybe he would. I didn't think he would turn out to be a stalking weirdo. Mind you, I'm not a very good judge of character at the best of times and it is little wonder I haven't attracted more weirdos into my life really.

'Clive,' Jack muses. 'OK, who else might you have pissed off recently?' Jack asks.

'God, you make it sound as though I do it all the time!'

'Think, Sam. Think of anyone who might want to ruin you.'

'I don't know, Jack. You? Why haven't *you* phoned me before this morning?' I suddenly say. Well, it is possible, I suppose. The last time we had contact I told Jack to f-off. No, Jack would never do that to me, I realise before he replies.

'Me? You are joking right? Who came and rescued you from the clutches of the world's media today? The only reason I haven't been in touch is because the last time you texted me you told me to fuck off, remember?'

'Well, you shouldn't have phoned in pretending to be someone called Stewart.'

'Who?' Jack says looking puzzled.

'Stewart, remember? You phoned *Town FM* claiming to be a caller?' I say, jogging his memory.

Jack shakes his head and looks at me as if I now have two heads.

'Haven't a bloody clue what you're going on about, Sammy,' he says.

'Yeah, course you don't,' I laugh.

'No, I really don't,' Jack says in all seriousness and by the way he is looking at me, he really doesn't have a clue what I am going on about. Oh bugger!

'We broke up. Me and Jasmine. Broke up,' Jack suddenly says as he continues to wear out the floorboards.

Yippee!

'Oh, I'm sorry to hear that,' I say. Secretly I am over the moon. She wasn't Jack's type anyway and I have to admit I felt a little left out in the cold. Before, whenever Jack got a 'girlfriend', she would fit into Jack's other plans of seeing his friends and band practice. With Jasmine, Jack kept her completely under wraps as if she were something special, and he dropped everyone and everything.

'Yeah, well, it would never have worked between us. Can you believe she asked me to marry her? I mean, seriously, can you see me as a married man?'

I look intently at Jack and actually, for a split second, yes I can. God, what am I thinking? Stop it, Samantha! I scold myself. Jack looks to his feet and quickly changes the subject.

'Anyway, can you think of anyone else?'

'What? Oh, I don't know, Jack. I do hundreds of readings a day, I don't know if I've told someone something they haven't liked or not. I suppose Liam could be a possible contender.'

'What, the chap from the radio station?'

'Mmm, we've been out a couple of times, but... well, you know how it is. I don't know whether it's going anywhere yet or not. Apart from knowing what he does for a living and what sort of films he likes, I don't know much else about him.' I don't think for a moment that Liam would be so nasty to do this, but then again…

'Liam…' Jack muses and writes his name down.

'He's a really nice guy… I don't think he would do something like this. And besides, he doesn't even know my real name.'

'OK, anyone else you can think of?'

'There was this woman called Beryl who wanted to know when she was going to be filthy rich – she wasn't very nice. Oh, and the other week there was that drug-addict girl, what was her name… Tina? Tanya, that was it. She was an odd one and I discovered that she had murdered her boyfriend. Maybe she knows that I know and is out to get me! Maybe I'm gong to be her next victim?' I say with panic in my voice.

'Look Sam, I've got to ask this…' Jack pauses…

'Have you been making it up as you go along?'

My stomach does a flip and I suddenly feel very sick, not to mention hurt that Jack might not believe me either.

'No, I haven't, Jack. I can honestly say that. Cross my heart and hope to die. OK, so I may have when I first started doing this, and originally I only took the stupid job so that I could pay off my uni debt, but for some reason I was spot on every time and…' How on earth do you tell someone that you hear voices in your head? They can still have you committed for that you know. Oh, sod it; I'll just have to come out with it. 'I know this is going to sound really weird, but I hear voices in my head, Jack,' I say. 'I'm like that kid in *The Sixth Sense*, I hear dead people. I really do Jack and yes, I know schizophrenics do too, but I'm not schizophrenic, Jack. I'm really not.' I look up, waiting for Jack's response and he doesn't disappoint – he looks shocked.

'For real?'

'For real,' I confirm. 'I know it sounds unbelievable but I really do hear real dead people. That woman you heard on the radio, the one you called an odd ball, that Tanya woman. She had killed her boyfriend and I only know that because *he* told me so, Jack! And only last night I had an old actress called Rita Monroe talking to me – err, she's dead by the way. She wanted me to pass on a message to Verity Star, the actress, you know, the one from the Marks and Spencer advert. And before that I had the dead friend of a young man who was involved in a car crash. He told me in great detail what had happened.' The more I think about the conversations I've had to date with dead people, the more incensed I am that I am being pulled to pieces by the press. This whole thing is going to ruin me, and I've helped a great many people.

'Right. Sorry, but I had to ask.' Jack comes and sits beside me. 'So what do I do now?' I ask.

'We need to get on to your agent, your bosses at the radio station, *Morning Latte* and the tarot lines and put them all straight. Oh, and we need to get hold of your brother, Paul, if anyone can track down who went to the press with this, he will. He's used to dealing with the gutter press and we also need to get hold of Matt to update the website and work on a campaign to clear your name,' Jack says.

Bloody hell, I feel like Dedrie on *Coronation Street*, when she was wrongly accused of something – I can't remember what, I was only young at the time. Only this time t-shirts will announce 'Save the Psychic One!' Banners will be hung outside public buildings announcing my innocence. I don't know whether I should just get my bucket and spade out of the cupboard and start digging a bloody big hole. I don't think my nerves can stand all this.

'And, we need to get someone like Max Clifford on board. You can't go burying your head in the sand this time, Sam…' Blimey, is Jack psychic now? 'We have to fight this and fight we will! We will clear your name!' Jack declares.

CHAPTER TWENTY-NINE

Larry is not best pleased with me at all. When I finally get hold of him he first of all swears like a Yorkshireman down the phone to me then promptly orders Jack to meet him in his office immediately. They both think it's for the best that I don't go out. Talk about feeling two inches tall! In fact right now I wish I was two inches tall, at least then I could slip into my jean pocket and just disappear from this horrible world. Larry has arranged to read out a statement to the press at lunchtime and has told me not to speak to anyone, call anyone or do anything with anyone. I am to remain incognito for the rest of the day.

Anya is another one who is also peeved that her efforts to make me a star have resulted in a major catastrophe for day-time television. The only one who seems to be on my side is Annette.

'Look, it will all blow over in a day or two,' Annette assures me, 'and besides, even bad publicity is good publicity. Just think of all the coverage you are going to get. I see it was on the local news this morning.'

'Oh God,' I groan. I can't think of anything else at the moment. I know Larry said don't talk to *anyone* but I can't sit here all day on my own. 'Annette, this is going to destroy me.'

'Well, I for one know you're genuine. You warned me about my car, didn't you?' Annette says.

'Yes, but…'

'Just keep your head down for a while. I'll have a word with our producers and put them straight. You'll be back at work in no time.'

'Thanks Annette. Oh, and don't tell anyone you spoke to me. Jack and Larry say I have to keep a low profile until we decide what to do.'

'Jack? Who's Jack then?' Annette says curiously.

'Oh, he's a friend I'm staying with at the moment.'

'A friend, hey?' Annette laughs.

'Yes, just a friend.'

I am sitting in Jack's un-matching living room with Missy on my lap, waiting to hear from him. I've tried and tried to get hold of Miracle, but she is away and her mobile is switched off. If anyone would know what to do it would be Miracle. I'm sure she's had her fair share of criticism in all her years of being a psychic. How on earth did I get into this mess? I should have stuck to treating (and dating) lachanophobia lunatics. I might not have got rich or fulfilled by it but at least I wouldn't be plastered across the tabloids and hailed as a fraud and a liar.

Missy snuggles up to me. She always knows when I'm down – down? I'm ten foot bloody under right now, Missy! I didn't sleep a bloody wink last night – I tell a lie, I must have slept at some point because I remember waking from a dream about being chased down the motorway by a torch-wielding mob on horseback shouting, 'Burn the witch! Burn the witch!', but apart from that incident, I didn't sleep a wink.

Jack kindly gave up his bed for me, having sniffed the sheets first and confirmed that they had indeed been changed – when is anyone's guess, mind you. He slept on the sofa and got up with the lark to a) inform the shop that he was taking a week off and b) to go and meet Larry for a 'crisis talks' meeting – Jesus, you'd think I'd just started the Iraqi war.

I have tried desperately to keep myself occupied while cooped up in this flat. I've even done Jack's laundry and tidied up his bedroom for him, which, on reflection, I realise wasn't such a good idea after all. I don't know about you, but I'm one of those people who just can't help myself from touching things in other people's homes. I'm sure it's an in-built curiosity gene that's to blame, you know. Or maybe it's just because my main life-partner is a cat. Whatever it is, I just can't help opening other people's drawers and rummaging about in them, or having a quick nosey under the bed.

Since the age of 16, I have known practically everything there is to know about Jack. What I didn't know, and what I do now, is that he keeps a 'special box' under his bed. Not one to simply push the black 'special box' back under the bed I felt I had no choice but to take a peek. Incidentally, it is cleverly disguised as a box of Black Magic chocolates, and the only give-away that it is a 'special box' with 'special' contents in it is due to the fact that it has a white sticker on it which reads, 'Jack's Special Box'. I mean if I had just pushed it back under the bed, I would spend every walking hour wondering what was so special in the 'special box', wouldn't I?

The reason I now wish I hadn't let curiosity get the better of me was because when I gingerly opened the lid of the 'special box' I discovered a lot more about Jack than I already knew. I discovered that he secretly loves Garfield the cat. I have acquired this secret knowledge because inside the 'special box' are several Garfield keyrings, a Garfield notebook and a miniature tube of Garfield toothpaste. I have also exposed the fact that Jack is also an avid autograph stalker – having felt the urge to look inside the Garfield notebook, I noticed that it is full of autographs of famous people such as footballers, high-profile pop stars and other bands he likes. I didn't have Jack down as a man who collects autographs.

As I continue to wade through the leaflets of places Jack wants to visit, beer mats with parts of song lyrics scrawled on them and a miniature James Bond Aston Martin, I lift out a piece of paper which is folded into four. The paper is yellow with age and as I carefully unfold it, a small photograph flutters to the floor. Picking it up, I look at it. The resemblance to Jack is amazing.

The woman in the black and white photograph has very big hair to match her equally big shoulder pads and is smiling. It looks as though it was taken in one of those photo booths that you find in every bus station in Great Britain, and at a guess I would say the woman was in her 20s when it was taken. There's no mistaking the resemblance to Jack. Turning over the photo, there are two simple words written in pencil – With Love.

I look down at the letter and read the elegant handwriting.

My darling baby,

I am so sorry. Please don't blame me. I did what I thought was for the best for you. I simply can't take you with me. I will be back for you soon.

Love, your Mummy

This is Jack's natural mother! Jack has never once mentioned her to me. Although I knew he had been in foster care for most of his childhood, not once has he spoken about his biological mother or father and I automatically assumed that she was… well, I wasn't really sure where she was, to be honest. It's not something that has ever come up in conversation between us.

Poor Jack. He's kept her letter for all this time, waiting for the day that she will come back for him.

I quickly put the photograph into the letter, fold it up again and place it back in the box in exactly the same place where I found it. I put everything back as I found it and push the box back under the bed. Tears sting my eyes. To think that Jack has been waiting all this time for his mum to return, not knowing where she has gone or when she will be back.

'Phone in and let us have your views? Are there any really genuine psychics out there, or are they all like Mystic Crystal Ball and out to rip you off? Get phoning and have your say, we'll be right back after this short break.'

My thoughts of Jack's mother are disturbed by the sound of a female presenter from the local *It's Morning Time* chat show, which is on the TV in the living room. The woman smiles through two tons of stage make-up, as a ticker tape with the show's phone number and email address scrolls by across the bottom of the screen. Why, the cheeky cow! I knew it was dangerous to leave the TV on.

Fresh tears sting my eyes as I try to blink them away and find something that resembles a pen in this mess that Jack so lovingly calls a home.

'Welcome back!' the presenter chirps four minutes later, as the studio audience of 35 or so applaud. I bet she needs the four-minute break to have her face re-plastered. 'The discussion today is about whether you think psychics are ripping you off,' the woman, who I already dislike intensely, twitters in her nasal voice.

'You have probably all seen the recent headlines about the local psychic, Samantha Ball, or Mystic Crystal, as she also likes to be known, who claimed that she was a real psychic and turned out to be a fraud...' she tut-tuts. 'I've got an email here from Alison from Reading,' Miss Make-up says as she looks down to the card in her hand. 'Alison says, "I think it's appalling, I really do. Praying on the bereaved like that. I don't think it's right. They should have a professional body to regulate these people. I think it's disgusting."'

'Well, Alison, I for one am in agreement with you there, love, as many of you are,' Make-Up-Woman says with a stern look on her face.

This is car-crash TV at its best. I'm watching as my name is being slated right before my eyes. I hope my mum isn't watching this. I know I should just switch it off and plug my iPod into my ears and escape from it all, but I just can't help myself.

'Oh, we have a caller on the phone. Hi, and you are?' the presenter asks.

'Oh hello, I'm Derek,' the caller says.

'Hi Derek, and welcome to It's Morning Time. What do you have to say on the subject?'

'Well, my wife died some years ago and I was always tempted to go to one of these mediums, but since hearing about this I don't think I'll bother. It's all a hullabaloo,' Derek says in a pompous fashion.

'*It's not and you know it,*' a woman's voice says into my ear and it's not Derek's or Make-Up-Woman's, I hasten to add.

'*I'm Gladys, his wife. Be strong, dear. Be strong and you'll prove them all wrong,*' the voice says and then fades away.

God damn it, I will be strong! I tap in the number that is flashing across the screen into the phone.

'Hello, and welcome to *It's Morning Time*,' the chirpy receptionist's voice chimes, 'and how may I help you this morning?'

'It's Samantha Ball here. I wish to be put through to the live phone-in... now!' I say.

'Oh, um... can you hang on a moment please?' the young woman at the end of the line stutters. She partly covers her mouthpiece, but I distinctly hear her say to someone, 'It's her! It's Samantha Ball on the line! The psychic woman. What should I do?'

'Um, I'm sorry to keep you waiting, Miss Ball. You are through to the studio,' the same girl says, after a moment's confusion.

'Thanks,' I say as I look at the screen to see Miss Make-Up hold her hand up to her earpiece, then her jaw drop.

'OK, can I just stop you there, Baby,' she says to some stupid caller named Baby, who thinks that they should bring back public hanging for people like me. She should talk! With a name like Baby, in any sane world she should be first in line for the gallows. I mean, she's a grown woman, for goodness sake! Surely she should have changed it by deed poll by now? Miss Make-Up holds her hand to her ear again and listens.

'Uh-huh, yes, thank you,' she mutters. 'Well viewers, we appear to have an exclusive call in from Miss Samantha Ball herself. Miss Ball, are you there?'

'Yes, I am, thank you very much,' I snap, 'and thanks to all of you for your support. Whatever happened to innocent until proven guilty?' I add.

'Well, perhaps you would like to give your side of the story exclusively to *It's Morning Time*?' the presenter suggests.

'Yes, I would like the opportunity, if only to shut you parasites up!' I snap. 'For your information I am not a fraud. All the thousands of readings I have done have been genuine and I have proof.'

'And what kind of proof would that be then?' snotty-TV-presenter-with-way-too-much-make-up-on says as she smiles into the camera as if maintaining direct eye contact with me.

'You can ask anyone I've given a reading to, whether it's been on my radio show, on the phone or in person. I have always been spot on. Ask anyone!' I say. I'm bloody fuming and have to go careful that I don't break out into a torrent of abuse.

'Well, that's as may be, but some would say that you are simply very good at speculating and reading body language?' the smarmy cow responds.

'What, on the phone? Or do you mean when I'm reading for someone on TV or the radio, when I can't actually see them? I know you're a bit thick but it would be impossible to read someone's body language if I couldn't actually see them, wouldn't it? Please!' I mock her – OK, so I know it sounds childish, but she started it. Silly cow!

'So, where do you think these rumours have come from?' the presenter asks. 'It says in the press that they have come from a source very close to you.'

'I have no idea, but what I do know is that these allegations are completely untrue and unfounded, and I will be damned if I am going to let some liar get away with trying to ruin my career. So whoever did this, if you are listening then look out because I will not sit back while some spiteful person has nothing better to do with their life, and tries to try to destroy me and my reputation!'

'*You're spot on,*' Gladys, the lady who I heard just earlier, says in my ear. '*You want to find out who did this to you? Then think about what you just said, my dear,*' the voice fades away again. I haven't got time to think this riddle through – I'm a little preoccupied saving the Psychic One here!

'So watch out because I *will* find out who you are!' I add.

Out of the blue, a member of the audience stands up and starts applauding me, followed by another person, then another, until there are 12 or 13 members of the audience putting their hands together for me. Wow! I feel like crying. OK, so the whole audience isn't with me, but a fair few are.

'Well,' the presenter chirps above the noise of the audience and presses her hand against her ear again, 'Samantha, perhaps you might like to join us on tomorrow's *It's Morning Time*?'

'Maybe later. I have to clear my name first.'

The members of the audience, who I have dubbed the first members of the 'Save the Psychic One Club', cheer again. A smile spreads across my face as I put the phone down.

'What the hell were you thinking?' Larry screams down the phone to me. 'Do you know how much damage you could have caused by phoning up that bloody TV station? I told you I was going to issue a statement, now you've made me look a right bloody fool!'

'When you've quite finished shouting at me,' I reply to Larry's outburst, 'I felt I had no choice. That bloody woman was winding them all up and trying to ruin my reputation even more than it already is.'

'Samantha, I am your agent and you should have consulted me first.'

'Yes, you are my agent, Larry, and you get a nice commission out of me for doing nothing more than making a few phone calls, so if you want to continue to take twelve percent of my income, then I suggest you stop shouting at me and let me do this my way. I will not let some jumped-up ass ruin me, and if it means going live on TV to tell my side then so be it. Now, do what you're being paid to do and organise a press conference. I want all the papers that have run this story to be there. Phone me when you've sorted it out,' I say and put the phone down.

I finally feel as though I am getting somewhere now and feel a fire burning in my stomach at the injustice of it all. Like hell am I going to hide away. I am going to find out who did this to me and I am going to make them pay for it.

CHAPTER THIRTY

Having had the courage to phone *It's Morning Time*, I now feel confident to take on the whole world and prove to them that I am not a liar and a fraud. And, with this in mind, I have recruited as many friends and family to help me clear my name and try to find out just who it was that went to the papers.

Jack, my brothers Matt and Paul and I are already making good progress. Paul has been poring over newspapers for clues as to who this 'close source' could be. He's already checked out Clive, who by all accounts has nothing more than a library fine to his name, despite being a first-class weirdo, but they can't hang you for that anymore apparently.

Paul has always had a fascination with underworld crime and consequently discovered that in Australia he could put this interest to good use and earn himself enough money to keep him in the surf-bum lifestyle that he had become accustomed to, by opening a small detective agency – by small we're actually talking beach hut small. Most of Paul's 'clients' come via word of mouth and are the sort of people you wouldn't really wish to meet in a dark alley – I wouldn't say his clientele were a dodgy bunch, but they usually hire Paul to pass messages from other small-time criminals, messages involving threats of missing fingers and the like. A far cry from your Miss Marple. I do hope that Paul's offer of helping me out doesn't mean that if he finds whoever went to the papers they will end up with some missing digits.

'This Clive, he's your typical weird bloke,' Paul echoes out of Jack's speaker phone with a slight Australian twang to his previously Bristolian accent.

'As opposed to what? Un-typically weird?' I ask as I leaf though today's tabloids.

'Very funny,' Paul says. 'He's typical in the fact that he's a loner, dresses like Mr Bean – in other words like a complete wally

– and he collects train time-tables from all over the country…'

'And you know this because…'

'Because he's also an eBay freak – he's got listings on there of time-tables for sale,' Paul says smugly. 'See, I told you, I'm a good detective.'

'So, you think we should eliminate him from our enquiries then, Miss Marple?' Jack says.

'I reckon. This is not his style. Stalking, yes, phoning up the tabloids, no. People like this Clive don't want to advertise the fact that they are odd. They don't like the attention,' Paul says. 'And enough already with the Miss Marple gags, smart arse.'

'OK, well keep up the good work, Tony Soprano,' Jack adds with a laugh. I bite my lip. Jack may be joking but it wouldn't surprise me one bit if Paul actually had a contact who was related to Mr Soprano. Paul's life is endlessly complicated.

No sooner do I finish speaking to Paul than the phone rings again – it's Matt.

'How's it going?' I ask with slight trepidation in my voice. Since my phone call Matt and his colleagues have been working all night on the website and making sure that word gets round that I am in fact genuine.

'Very well indeed. Thanks to the time you invested in the web readings we've had nothing but support and praise from people all over the world. Have you seen the site recently?'

'No, I haven't, I don't know whether you've noticed my lovely little brother, but I've been a little preoccupied lately.'

'Very funny. Well tell Jack to get that crappy laptop out and have a look.'

'Oi, I heard that and it's not crappy, it's just a little old, that's all. We can't all afford top-of-the-range computers, you know,' Jack laughs.

'Old? I think Noah used the model you've got, Jack!' Matt says.

Jack starts up his laptop, which seeing as it is so ancient takes an age to get going.

'Have you got it yet?' Matt says impatiently.

'Hang on, will you… yep… hang on… what's the web address again?'

'It's in your favourites under Crystal Ball,' Matt mocks a yawn. 'WWW dot Cr…'

'Jesus is he this slow at everything, Sammy?' Matt laughs.

'Give me a fucking chance. You'll be sorry when I'm rich and famous, I'll have the biggest and best laptop in the world,' Jack says. 'Right got it. Blimey, look at this, Sam!'

As Jack scrolls down the page – I wish he would just let me do it, I hate it when people insist on taking control of the scrolling business – there are pages upon pages of support messages.

'Mystic Crystal gave me a reading a few months ago and she was spot on about my whole life, she even knew the name of my grandfather and he's been dead like forever! Anyone who says she's a fraud needs a good kicking!'

OK, well, thanks for the support but let's not get too carried away here with encouraging violence towards non-believers, shall we?

Another message says: 'I can't thank Crystal enough for all the work she put into my reading. Mystic Crystal told me that I would soon meet someone who would love me for who I am and I would soon be able to stop pretending and within two weeks I met the most perfect partner. We are getting married next year and it's all thanks to Crystal.'

'Crystal is one well cool dude! Don't take no notice of those who say she isn't. She's ace. Crystal rocks!'

Ooh, not only am I a 'well cool dude', I also rock now! As Jack scrolls down there are even more messages. In fact there are hundreds, and not one says that I am a fraud or that I said the wrong thing, or that I made things up. For the first time in a week a smile spreads across my face.

'Click on the shop tab,' Matt instructs.

'Hang on. Click on the shop tab, Jack... Oh my God!' I say, laughing at what is before my eyes.

'I've ordered one for both of you, should be delivered tomorrow, along with a box in case there's anyone out there who wants to buy from you direct. We're having them imported from China so they're dirt-cheap. I figure we don't want to be seen to be making a profit out of this, so I'm putting a notice on the site to say that all profits from sales will go to the Macmillan charity,' Matt says.

I can't believe that Matt has designed t-shirts with 'Save Mystic Sam' emblazoned across them in our virtual shop and the fact that the money from them is all going to the Macmillan cancer charity is brilliant. I think of my dad for a moment. I'd like to think he'd be proud of us all right now.

'Who's the girl?' I ask, looking at the photo of a beautiful young woman, with very long legs and wearing nothing but a red Save Mystic Sam t-shirt, which just skims her bum.

'That's Stacey. She's Martin's girlfriend. Thought it might attract more buyers. Told you sex sells!' Matt says. I'm sure it will.

'I can't believe you've done all of this, Matt, and look at all the support I've got!'

'Well, just make sure you take as many opportunities to prove yourself. Like anything Sam, you have got to prove to people that you are genuine and you've got a lot of support, not only on here but on lots of other sites too.'

'I have? Oh, thanks Matt, for everything.'

I've been putting off this moment for days now and I know that I have to do it – phone my mother. Having binned my mobile because it seemed that the whole world and his wife had my number, my mum has been bombarding Jack with phone calls to a) find out where I am and b) well, find out where I am. Jack, bless him, has made up every excuse under the sun from 'I'm at the dentist having my mouth wired shut' to 'I'm in a police holding cell being held for questioning'. Mind you either of the above could easily happen right now.

'It's me, Mum,' I say cautiously when my mum answers.

'Samantha, whatever is going on?' My mother gasps, 'I've had journalists camped out on my doorstep for a week asking to speak to you. Jack told me to tell them that you were on holiday – mind you, I did take the opportunity to tell them that I had a book coming out and I told them about mine and Colin's book. I don't think they believed me when I told them you were away. Sammy, is anything wrong?' my mother asks.

Is anything wrong? What planet has my mother been living on the past week?

'Have you not read the newspapers or watched the news recently, Mum?' Sometimes I really wonder about my mother. I continue to torture myself by flicking through the previous week's newspapers.

'Oh no, love, I don't read newspapers anymore, much too miserable nowadays. It's all bad news anyway and I've been over at Colin's most of the time working on our book and he doesn't have a TV.'

'Right, well to cut a long story short, someone went to the newspapers with a story saying that I wasn't a proper psychic and that I just made it all up. *Town FM* have temporarily suspended me, as have *Morning Latte* and… '

'What do you mean someone went to the papers? Who?' my mum asks.

'Well, if I knew that I wouldn't be in hiding at Jack's place, would I?'

'Well, why are you in hiding? Why don't you just tell the papers it isn't true?' My mum obviously can't understand the enormity of all of this.

'Because Mum, the papers want to twist everything… hang on a cotton-picking minute…' I flick back to page four of *The Sun,* which shows the glamorous photo of me at the awards ceremony. '…You little shit!'

'Samantha!'

'I'm sorry, Mum, I have to go, I'll call you later,' I stutter and put the phone down.

'Jack! Jack! Look!' I shout.

Jack comes rushing out of the kitchen with a knife in his hand.

'Look at this,' I point to the photograph of me taken at the awards ceremony.

'Yeah, cute photo,' Jack says. 'And?'

'And this one,' I pass a copy of *The Mirror* to him, 'and *this* one,' I pass him a copy of *The News of the World*. 'Look at the bottom of the photograph.'

'Nope, I don't get it. Give me another clue,' Jack says looking puzzled and slightly weird wielding a kitchen knife around in the air.

'Look, who took *that* photograph?' I point to the name McIntyre. 'Now, look at *that* one, and *that* one. They were all taken by the same photographer Jack. Someone called McIntyre.'

Jack shakes his head, still looking bemused – for a law graduate he can sure be thick sometimes.

'And?'

'And, Jack, it's the same picture in every paper, taken by the same photographer. Look, they're all the same picture.'

'So, whoever sold the photograph could be the person who also sold the story on you, or else knows the person who did,' Jack summarises.

'Correct, Sherlock! I'll phone Paul and see if he can track down who took that photo.'

If anyone can track another person down it will be my brother. Being a surf-bum means he has that fine ability to mix with all sorts of people, including mobsters, fraudsters, sleazy paps and the like. If anyone can find out who took the photographs, Paul will.

CHAPTER THIRTY-ONE

'I have never been so scared in my life,' I whisper to Jack as we stand waiting in the wings of a conference room at the Marriott Hotel.

'You'll be just fine. Just be yourself, take a deep breath, then tell them what you want to say,' he says, squeezing my arm.

'Have you heard anything from Amy? I can't get hold of her. Her mobile is switched off all the time.' Since all this kicked off I haven't had time to speak to her. She must know what's been going on since it's been in every national newspaper and the topic of discussion of almost every day-time television programme on air.

'Nah, Dillon said he thinks she's gone to Spain to see her mother. I think all this business with her job has got her down.'

Her and me both.

'Mind you, maybe Amy's not the best one to turn to. You know what she can be like. She can't keep a secret to save her life,' I say recalling the last time I asked Amy to keep a secret. Before I knew it, she had told one person, who told another and the next thing I know, everyone on campus knew that I had a crush on a gay teacher!

'I think she's more cut up about losing her job than she likes to make out,' Jack says, 'but she'll bounce back. Amy always does,' he adds. 'Have you seen the number of people out there?' Jack pokes his head round the stage screen. I peep my head around the corner to see four dozen or so plastic chairs rapidly filling up with reporters and photographers.

Larry finally managed to organise a press conference with all the journalists and photographers who had decided it made interesting reading to plaster my name across their papers. Thankfully after four days of being headline news, I have been relegated to page four in the tabloids to make way for the new

Big Brother housemates, but it doesn't really make me feel any better to know that because of this I might never work again – anywhere. I'll have to change my name by deed poll and go to America and apply to have one of those complete plastic surgery makeovers.

I sigh as we wait for Larry to come back from wherever he's snuck off to. I decide to dress in a sensible, if somewhat sombre, trouser suit for the occasion and have pulled my naturally mis-behaving hair back into a sensible ponytail. I'm sure I don't know what I do in my sleep. Whatever it is I always wake up with hair that resembles a badly fitted wig. I know it shouldn't make any difference what I look like, but if they were determined to vilify me in their papers then I would prefer I look business-like rather than someone from *Prisoner Cell Block H.*

'Right, are you ready, lass?' Larry asks in his Yorkshire accent.

'No,' I say and I'm not. The notes in my hand are all crumpled and soggy from where my hands have sweated so much.

Larry puts his chubby arm around me.

'Look, it's all going to be OK. Just read out the statement that I've given you and stick to that. The press will glorify it anyway,' Larry laughs.

'Yeah, just like they did when they ran the story about me!' I snap. 'Larry, I am here to clear my name. I *have* to clear my name,' I say desperately.

Jack squeezes me on the other side.

'Come on. You'll be fine,' he says.

God, I hope they have water on the table. Or vodka would be good right now. I feel quite faint. I daren't look out to the audience until I finally reach one of the three chairs that have been put out for us on a mock stage.

When I do look ahead of me, I feel like fainting even more. The room is packed to bursting with photographers, reporters and some other people I don't recognise – probably the same people who attend court cases for the sheer hell of it and drive slowly past car-crashes as a hobby. Already flashes are going off in my face and shouts of 'Samantha! Over here!' can be heard from the back of the room. I can't see a bloody thing for flash eye and look down at my wrinkled notes on the desk in front of me.

Jack, Larry and I sit in a row, with me plonked right in the middle. Oh Christ, this certainly wasn't in my grand scheme of things. All that keeps going round in my head is the injustice that someone has deliberately gone out of their way to try to ruin me and that is the only reason I am able to sit here facing the nation's media.

'Ladies and gentlemen,' Larry begins, 'first of all, can I thank you for coming here today…' Thank them? Thank them? For what? For taking the word of some parasite, making headline columns about it and ruining my life, not to mention my career? Yeah, thanks a bunch, guys.

Larry places his hands flat on the desk in front of us. 'As you are already aware, as many of your newspapers have printed reports about Samantha, we feel it is only fair for Samantha to have her say.'

'So you reckon she's for real then?' a voice shouts from the back.

'So sue us!' another one shouts louder and the room erupts into laughter.

Larry looks at the throng of journalists and photographers from over his half-moon glasses.

'Maybe we will end up doing just that.' He smiles at the press pack. 'Now, I will hand this question and answer session over to Samantha. Please keep your questions short and to the point… oh, and just one thing, ladies and gentlemen, no funny business eh? Samantha.' Larry hands over to me and I stand up nervously.

'Thank you, Larry,' I croak. 'Before you all start firing questions at me, may I just say one thing…' I pause for effect. 'What has been reported in your newspapers is completely untrue. I don't know who informed you, but I can assure you that whoever it was – and I know that one of you lot knows – he is in for the shock of his life because I *will* find out, and God help him when I do.' Phew! I feel quite faint after that little speech. Hands shoot up with shouts of 'Samantha!'

'Yes.' I point to a youngish-looking man wearing a trendy pink tank-top who looks as though he might be at least a bit sympathetic towards me. I know they have a job to do and have to earn an income, but nevertheless shouldn't they have an ounce of truth before they report things to the whole world?

'Miss Ball, Martin Fry, *Bath News*. You are claiming that these reports are totally untrue, but we have information from a reliable source, so who's lying?' Fry asks. Hmm, and I thought he was going to be one of the nice ones – see, I told you I was a bad judge of character – and he looks ridiculous in that pink tank-top!

'So who is this reliable source then, Mr Fry? Would you like to share that with me?' I challenge.

'Can't tell you that, I'm afraid. Confidentiality and all that,' Fry smiles at me smugly.

'And what about *my* confidentiality? What about *my* reputation?' I say. Fry just shrugs and sits down again. Bastard!

'Miss Ball! Joanna Hammond from the *Evening Gazette*. How can you prove that you are a genuine psychic? Wasn't it true that you took a job with Mystic Answers only because you had a huge student debt to pay off and couldn't earn a living as a psychologist?' The petite woman journalist asks.

'You only have to ask the thousands of people I have given readings to for proof. Ask any of the people who have phoned into my radio show with *Town FM*. Ask anyone who called into *Morning Latte,* ask any number of callers on *Mystic Answers* or the people who log on to my website, ask anyone I've ever given a reading to. Ask Verity Star what I told her about Rita Malone, or anyone from the TV awards for that matter, Miss Hammond, and that will give you your answer,' I snap.

'Yes, but isn't it true that you don't actually have any training in the paranormal and until recently you didn't have *any* experience whatsoever of the paranormal? Some would say that the training that you do have in psychology could easily help you fake it when you claim to be contacting the dead?'

'Tell Pogo that she is being unreasonable and she should know better,' a voice comes into my head. Who are you? I ask silently. *'Oh, she will know,'* the voice says with a little chuckle.

'Miss Hammond, please may I ask you a question? Who used to call you Pogo?'

The reporter looks stunned for a moment and then shakes her head, violently.

'I've no idea what you're talking about,' she says and avoids my gaze by looking down at her notebook and then sitting down in her chair again.

'Oh right, no further questions from you then, Miss Hammond, I take it? Next please?'

Another hand shoots up.

'Martha James, Channel Five. Samantha, if you are so sure that you are genuine, would you be willing to take a live test for us?'

I look at Larry who looks like a nodding dog as his head nods up and down eagerly.

'Yes, certainly she will,' my agent says before I've even had a chance to consider this challenge.

Oh my good God! What I'm doing? Oh, bugger, shit and bollocks! What have I let myself in for now?

CHAPTER THIRTY-TWO

I feel like Hilary Swank in *Million Dollar Baby* – Jack and Miracle being my Clint Eastwood and Morgan Freeman. Since Larry kindly signed me up for national public humiliation, I have spent the past week being briefed by Jack, Larry and Miracle as to what I should, and more importantly what I shouldn't say, when I am being tested by a leading parapsychologist who goes by the name of Bobby Walters.

Despite praying and asking all the voices in my head to help me out here, I haven't heard one single voice. Not a bloody whisper! Where are these bloody voices when you most need them, hey?

'Now, he may well try to trick you into taking his lead,' Miracle advises me. Having been on some soul-searching holiday to the Himalayas with Max and consequently being completely oblivious to what's been going on here in the UK, Miracle arrived home to discover that I was in a deep pile of poo.

'Don't listen to him, or to anyone else for that matter. Go with your gut instinct. I'll warn you, Sam, this man is one of the top parapsychologists in the world. He's good and will do anything to prove that he is right.' Miracle says this with the sound of contempt, as though she has just eaten something unpleasant.

'I've managed to get tickets for Max and me so I'll be in the audience for moral support. Just trust in spirit and it won't let you down, kid. I'm so sorry you've had to go through all of this, Sammy,' Miracle says and hugs me to her huge bosom.

And she's not the only one. I wish I had never got myself into any of this now. Why couldn't I just be satisfied with doing a temping job or working in Tesco? I could have easily gone back to live with my mother – OK so it wouldn't have been easy but at least I wouldn't be headline news for stacking a tin of beans on the wrong shelf. Grrr to the whole world!

Larry informs me that Phil and Holly are eager to get me on their show – if I prove my worth, Channel Five will have me whether I'm a fraud or for real, they don't care either way really. Either way it makes good telly. Charming.

I've been trying to avoid anything associated with the media, including the newspapers, radio and the TV, but this proves somewhat difficult when Jack comes in with an armful of papers, turns the radio on in the kitchen and the TV on in the living room.

'You OK?' he asks as he dumps the pile of newspapers on the sofa.

'Hmm, I think so,' I say as I read through the notes that I've taken from Miracle about how to not look a complete idiot when I do this bloody test tomorrow. I wonder if they have one of those idiot's guides for this kind of thing – *The Idiot's Guide to Dealing with Parapsychologists*, perhaps?

'Coffee?' I ask as I make my way to the kitchen.

'Please. Have you spoken to Matt or Paul today?' Jack shouts from the living room.

'No, not today. I'm still waiting for Paul to track down who took that photograph.'

'Well, you're making headline news again, kid. Since Channel Five announced that they were going to prove you are genuine, you're back to page two again,' Jack laughs.

'Oh goody,' I say dryly as I watch the kettle boil.

'Sam!' Jack suddenly shouts out. 'Quick come here!'

'What's the matter?' I walk as quickly as I can back into the living room precariously carrying two mugs of coffee in my hands and a packet of Bourbons between my teeth.

'Look!' Jack says pointing at the TV.

It's the local *It's Morning Time* show again and standing in front of the audience is Miss Make-Up herself. The banner beneath her says, 'Is there really life after death?'

Oh not again. Can they not just drop it? When are these people going to think of something original to put on the TV?

'And don't for one minute think I am going to phone in again, Jack.'

'No, look! Up there!' Jack says, pointing to the far end of the screen where there are a group of five or six people all wearing white t-shirts emblazoned with 'Save Mystic Sam'.

'Ah, that's nice,' I smile. It is nice to see that there are some people out there supporting me.

'Err, look again Sam, who's that?' Jack is now off his seat and sticking his index finger into someone's face in the audience. I squint my eyes and bend down to get a better look. Jack only has a 15-inch portable TV, which is so old that it tends to lose half the programme you want to watch by intermittently turning itself off.

'Oh my goodness! Is that...' I turn the sound up.

Bizarrely, standing up in the audience is my landlady. What on earth is Ms Morris doing standing in the middle of the audience on a day-time television programme? She has her hands on her hips and her ample chest sticking out as if she means business. Oh no, she's not going to tell the whole world that I'm a lousy tenant as well as a fraud is she?

'Yes dear? Your name is?' Miss Make-Up asks.

'Valerie. Valerie Morris,' Ms Morris says.

'And, Valerie, what do you have to say about all this?'

'I have proof that there *is* life after death and I also have proof that Mystic Crystal or Samantha Ball *is* the real thing, because it was Mystic Crystal who contacted my late husband, Frank,' Ms Morris says.

I knew I'd heard that voice before! I knew it! But Ms Morris? Valerie? *The* Valerie. Oh my.

Valerie continues to inform the audience and Miss Make-Up of how, before she called Mystic Answers, she was beside herself at the loss of her husband Frank. They had always done every-thing together and when he had been taken from her, it felt as though her whole life had come to an end.

'Of course you get on with the day to day things and pretend that it's not hurting and that you're over it, but in truth you never do get over it and for someone like Mystic Crystal, Samantha, to give you a message, that only you would know, is worth all the gold in the world.'

Tears well up in my eyes. I hold my hand to my mouth. I can't believe that the woman I thought was the biggest battleaxe on the planet has actually taken the time to stand up and support me. And who would have thought that Valerie, the woman who called me regularly at three o'clock in the morning, would be the same woman who was living just above me? No wonder she wouldn't look me in the eye the other week when all this kicked off.

Jack and I stare at the TV. The small group of supporters chant 'Save Mystic Sam!' as the credits roll up. Miss Make-Up looks as though she is losing the plot as she tries to talk over the audience and inform the viewers of what she has in store for them tomorrow. She finally gives up and holds her hands in the air in submission.

'See, I told you she wasn't so bad,' Jack says, referring to Ms Morris. 'So she phoned you up then? You never said.'

'I didn't know it was her and she obviously didn't know Mystic Crystal was me either, otherwise I don't think she would have phoned me, do you? You know, I knew I recognised that voice from somewhere, I just couldn't figure out where and all the time it was Ms Morris, upstairs. Blimey, I won't be able to look her in the face again,' I blush.

'Well, she obviously thinks a lot of you to get up there and protest your innocence,' Jack says as he slurps his coffee.

'Oh no!' I suddenly think of something.

'What?'

'Well, what if someone reports that Ms Morris is also my landlady? I'll be in even more shit than I am right now. People will think I've paid her to go on TV for me.' It just gets worse the more I think of it.

'That is not going to happen, is it?' Jack says.

'Well, I didn't think I would be all over the papers and defending myself on national TV, but it's happened,' I say glumly.

Jack puts his arm around me.

'It will all be all right, Sam, trust me...'

'I know, you're a lawyer.'

As me and Jack go through my list of things I must remember to say and not say for the five hundredth time, Jack's phone rings. It's Amy.

'Amy?'

'Hi hun!' she trills down the phone.

'Amy,' Jack mouths and I roll my eyes to the ceiling and start doing a funny impression of Amy talking. For the first time in ages I stifle a laugh.

'Where have you been?' Jack asks. 'Oh, right, yeah Dillon said. Yeah, she's staying with me for a while. Hang on, I'll get her,' Jack holds the phone out to me.

'Hiya hun. How are you? Sorry I haven't been in touch for a while, I've been staying with my mum in Spain,' Amy says more brightly than I have heard her in ages.

'But you don't even like your mum,' I say – this is true. Amy and her mum Lorraine are very similar in that they are both very competitive and will do anything to get to the top. Sadly they compete with each other too, mostly for male attention. I remember numerous occasions when Amy and her mum had arguments because Amy's mum had taken a fancy to one of Amy's boyfriends. I wince as I think about it. Handbags at dawn is an understatement.

'I know, but what with losing my job and all that, I thought I needed a break to get my head round what I'm going to do next. We're getting on OK now. So how have you been? Had any more spooky experiences recently?' Amy says brightly. 'And why are you staying with Jack? I've been calling your flat all morning.'

'What, you haven't heard?' I say.

'Heard what?'

'About me being in the papers? Oh Amy, you must have seen the news?'

'No, I told you I've been in Spain. Why, what's happened?'

'Right, you know the night I went to the TV awards ceremony?'

'Yes.'

'Well, some bastard rang the newspapers up and said that I was a fraud,' I say, reliving the moment all over again in my head.

'No! You're kidding, right?'

'Nope. I've been in the press all week.'

'OMG, babes. Who did that and why?'

'God knows,' I sigh. 'I've spent the past week trying to gain back my reputation. I've got to go on live TV tomorrow and be tested by Bobby Walters.'

'Bobby who?' Amy asks.

'Walters. He's a top parapsychologist from the International Society for Paranormal Research.'

'What's that then?'

'He's the bloke who is going to try and prove that I'm a fake, Amy,' I add dryly.

'Oh, right. I am so sorry, hun. Do you want me to come with you?'

'No, you're all right. I tell you, Amy, if I ever get my hands on the person who did this to me I will not be responsible for my actions. The papers will have more to write than Samantha Ball is a fraud, they will be reporting that Samantha Ball is a murderer!'

'Blimey,' Amy says, 'you sound as though you mean that.'

'I do, Amy. This person has destroyed my career and my reputation with one phone call and I am having to work bloody hard to try and restore it and if tomorrow goes tits up, then I really am ruined.'

CHAPTER THIRTY-THREE

I have never been more scared in my life. The TV company have set up a studio / test centre specifically for today. You'd think that we were in the headquarters of The Secret Service the way people are running around with all sorts of technical equipment attached to them. I've been frisked and frisked again with a hand-held metal detector sort of thing to check that I don't have any hidden microphones or anything else hidden on me. I've been under close surveillance by a team of burly security guards who flatly refuse to let anyone into my dressing room – which incidentally has also been swept for any signs of bugs – and the minute anyone approaches my little room one of them steps in front of the door and looks menacingly at them. Crikey. They won't even allow Jack in the room, so I am sitting here on my own worrying if I am making the biggest mistake of my life.

Maybe I should have told Larry that I wasn't interested in performing for the media by having to prove myself. At the end of the day I have enough money to coast for a while. I could just leave the country and join Paul in Australia. No one would know me there and I could get a sensible job as a caretaker of Koala bears or something and not have to endure being pointed at by passers by. What if I fail the test? I won't be able to go out again. Children, encouraged by their parents, will throw things at me in the street and I'll have to live in hiding in Jack's flat for the rest of my life, asking him to pop to the shops every time I need a Kit-Kat.

The dressing room is pleasant enough in a tangerine and cream décor sort of way, with brown vases full of gold twigs dotted around the place, and I'm sure if I were some celebrity promoting my new book, instead of a psychic proving that she is indeed psychic, that I would feel a lot more comfortable in here. As it is, I don't. I don't feel comfortable one bit, and I wish I could fast forward time so that this would all be over. I'm not even allowed a phone just in case someone tries to send me messages down it. God, talk about being a prisoner.

Please, is there anybody there? I ask in my head. Bloody typical. When I was doing readings the voices just didn't stop talking. Now, when I need them most, there's just silence in my head. Where is everyone? I don't understand this and I have to say, the prospect of joining my brother on the other side of the world is looking more appealing by the minute.

Anyone? Look, you got me into this bloody situation, so now it's time for you to help me out here. Rita? Darren? Dad? Anyone?

Silence. Maybe this has all been in my head after all? Maybe I am going mad. Maybe I am schizophrenic?

'You're on,' one of the security guards unlocks the door and instructs me. He holds the door open and then leads me by the arm down a long corridor. The noise from my high-heel boots echoes in the narrow space and I feel like someone on death row, walking to meet their maker.

Here we go then. Larry pats me on the back as I pass him in the corridor and the security guard assigned to me glares menacingly at him. Larry holds his hands up as if to say, hey man I wasn't doing anything! I smile hesitantly at Larry, take a deep breath and try to look confident as I walk quickly behind the security guard.

I am so glad I put my Impulse on this morning. Why am I putting myself up for this? I'm sure someone once said even bad publicity is good publicity – oh yes, it was Annette, wasn't it? Maybe if I just run now and go into hiding for a few months, this will all blow over. I can't believe the injustice of it all. I mean, I wouldn't mind so much if it was true and I did make it all up, but I've spent months now getting used to all these voices that keep randomly popping up in my head and I'm not going to let one person go and ruin it all for me now.

'This way, Miss Ball.' An official looking woman with a

clipboard and a microphone placed on her head guides me to a small room and quickly shuts the door behind us.

The white room is sparsely furnished with just a black moulded plastic table and chair placed in the middle of it. A large TV screen is set into the far wall opposite me. In every corner there are cameras that whir to signal they are watching my every movement. I can't blink without the motion detector whirring into life.

The stern looking woman clips a small microphone onto my black shirt.

'We're almost set up here,' she says into her headset. 'Right, I'll tell her. You are not to leave this room. Do you understand? Would you like some water?'

'Yes miss, mam… um, yes please,' I say, looking and feeling more frightened than Bambi. There isn't even a bloody clock in here. Is this what prison feels like?

'Yes, the subject would like water.' Subject? Subject? Who does she think she is? The woman instructs to whoever she's talking to that I would like a drink of water. I wouldn't know. Evidently I'm not allowed to talk to anyone in case they tell me some secret information. I'm just the bloody 'subject'.

The woman walks out of the door, passes me a bottle of water and then goes again, locking the door behind her. Let's hope there isn't a fire; I'll never get out of here alive.

'Miss Ball, I am parapsychologist Bobby Walters. I will be conducting the paranormal tests which you are to perform today for Channel Five. Are you comfortable, Miss Ball?' a voice echoes inside the room. Eh? I look around the room.

'Um… yes… I think so,' I mutter.

'Good. We will begin in exactly five minutes. For this experiment, you will be given a series of tests via the monitor in front of you. If you feel that you cannot answer a particular question, please indicate this by saying 'pass'. Is that clear?'

'Yes. Thank you, Sir,' I say.

My hands and legs are shaking so much. I put my head in my hands.

'Miss Ball. Are you ready?' the voice asks.

'Yes. Yes, I am.'

'Then we will begin. Test one. Miss Ball, please look at the TV monitor in front of you and please tell us who this item belongs to,' the voice instructs.

I look to the opposite wall and see that the TV on the wall has a picture of a copper bangle on the screen. OK, now I've heard of this before. Miracle told me about this. Now, what was it called? Bugger, I can't remember. Tele-something-or-other. Anyway, this is not the time or the place to wonder what the correct terminology is. Right, come on then, spirits, tell me something about this object, I will them in my head.

Nothing. What? Nothing? My mind is a complete blank. There is literally nothing coming through. I keep looking at the image of the copper bangle on the screen in front of me and still I get nothing. Oh no! Please! I need someone to tell me who this bangle belongs to!

'Miss Ball?' Bobby Walters says.

'Yes, just a minute, please,' I say nervously as I place my head in my hands again. The cameras in my small room whir in motion to detect my movement. I feel so hot and dizzy. I take a sip of water – it doesn't help matters one little bit. Oh come on for goodness sake! You've spent months shouting at me in my head and when the chips are down you don't say a bloody word!

'Would you like to pass, Miss Ball?' Mr Walters asks.

Oh no. I'm going to fall at the first bloody hurdle.

'Yes. Pass,' I say out loud. For all I know the bangle could have come from Claire's Accessories. I haven't a clue and at this moment in time, it's apparent that the entire spirit world has gone on bloody strike!

'You are passing on the first test, Miss Ball. Is that correct?' Bobby Walters says condescendingly

'Sorry, yes. Yes I am. Just give me a moment please,' I say, nervously.

Still nothing. Oh great. Just bloody great! I'm going to have to go on my gut instincts here.

'Thank you, Miss Ball,' Bobby Walters says, and I'm sure he is shaking his head as he does so.

'Test two, Miss Ball...'

'In the envelope which is shown on the screen in front of you, there is a piece of paper with a shape drawn on it. Can you please tell me what the shape is, Miss Ball?' Mr Walters says.

I look up to the screen and see a red envelope. OK, come on, Sam, think, I urge myself. What shape is it? A star? A circle? A sausage? I haven't the faintest idea.

'Miss Ball?' Bobby Walters asks.

'Um... a star. It's a star shape in the envelope,' I say out loud. In fact I haven't got a clue what shape it is. It could be the shape of the bloody Eiffel Tower for all I know right now. I really do not have a clue what shape is in the envelope.

The following tests range from trying to predict the name of Bobby Walter's great grandmother, to telling him how many people in the audience are holding keys in their hands. Still I have no inner voices to tell me, so I am passing or guessing on each and every test he gives me. I just know that I've messed this up big time.

Eventually, after what seems like days, but in reality is probably half an hour later, Bobby Walters' serious face appears on the TV screen in front of me.

'Thank you, Miss Ball. Your parapsychology tests are complete. As you can see, members of the audience, the tests we set Miss Ball prove that there is no such thing as the ability to contact, what many claim, is the afterlife. Miss Ball passed on 23 answers out of a possible 25, proving that there is no possible way that Miss Ball can be clairvoyant or have any extraordinary or paranormal skills. Of the answers Miss Ball got correct, in my opinion, it was purely by chance or guess work...' Bobby Walters says. And yes, the two tests, the shape one and the one asking what Bobby Walters' wife's favourite colour was, I did get right, but that was purely by guess work, I'll give him that.

From the screen in front of me I notice the camera pan round to show the whole audience nodding solemnly in agreement. A multitude of faces appear of people of all ages in the audience looking intently at Mr Bobby Walters on the stage.

All of a sudden, as the camera pans around the audience, my head is full of voices. Oh, great, better late than never, eh, guys?

'Tell him I still love him and always will,' a woman's voice tells me.

'Tell her that it's amazing here in heaven. It's paradise,' another voice talks over the first one.

'I want my mum to know I'm OK,' a young boy's voice tells me.

'Tell my family I'm all better now and my legs are just fine,' an elderly woman says.

'Please tell him not to smoke. He saw what it did to me,' a man warns.

'Hang on a minute, please!' I say.

'Miss Ball, do you wish to say something?' Bobby Walters says smugly.

'Yes, I have some messages for people in the audience,' I say quickly.

'Oh really?' the smug bastard actually laughs.

The camera looks around the audience.

'Stop the camera there please!' I say as it rests on a middle-aged man in the third row up. Suddenly my head is spinning with voices again.

'Sir, the man in the green sweater? Yes, you, Sir,' I say. I'm up and out of my chair and staring intently at the TV screen in front of me.

The middle-aged man points to himself.

'Yes, you. Your wife Sheila has just asked me to tell you that she still loves you and always will,' I say breathlessly.

'Sheila!' the man says with a look of surprise on his face.

'Err, just a minute. The tests are over Miss Ball,' Bobby Walters butts in.

'Is Sheila your wife, Sir?' I ask, ignoring Mr Walters.

'Yes, yes, she is… was,' the man answers.

'Now just one minute…' Mr Walters says.

'Does she say anything else?' The man in the audience, who now looks as though I've just told him he's won the lottery, talks over Bobby Walters.

'Tell him I like the green carpet in the hallway.'

'Oh yes, she says to tell you she likes the green carpet you put down in the hallway,' I say with a smile.

The middle-aged man claps his hands together as if in prayer and smiles to the false studio ceiling.

The audience gasp.

'Miss Ball, it's a bit too late to try and convince people now,' Bobby Walters says.

'Oh shut up, you stupid buffoon! Cameraman, could you please zoom into the lady in the red dress, forth row up on the right? Yep, that's her,' I say breathlessly. The lady in the red dress blushes. 'Excuse me, madam, I have Marcus here. He says he's your son.'

Tears well up in the lady's eyes and she claps her hand to her mouth.

'He says you don't have to keep his room as it was. He's happy for you to use it as a study for James if you want to,' I say, relaying the words that are coming through to me from a young man.

'Oh my goodness!' the woman in the red dress says. 'That's my son, Marcus, and she's right, we've always kept his room just as he left it… that was eight years ago. We wondered whether we should allow our other son James to use it as a study, but we didn't know whether we should or not.'

The audience gasp again and I can see Bobby Walters looking as though he is about to pop with rage. Suddenly voices start to come fast and furious and I have a job to keep up and repeat everything that is coming through. I scan the audience and catch sight of Miracle sitting there with her new chap Max. Both of them are wearing 'Save Mystic Sam' t-shirts and both have huge smiles on their faces. Gerry the security guard from the BBC studios is sitting next to them, also wearing a supporting t-shirt, only if I'm not mistaken, I'm sure it's a size or two smaller than what he would have usually worn.

'Please tell Jamie that I'll be cross if he gets that motorbike,' a woman's voice says.

As quick as I'm instructing the cameraman to zoom in and pass a message on to someone, another voice comes into my head.

The audience are sitting looking aghast and cheering every time I pass on a message to someone else. Bobby Walters is looking absolutely furious with me. Ha-ha Bobby Walters, stick that up your parapsychological bum!

All of a sudden I spot my mum and Colin in the audience. They are sitting next to Jack and the three of them are also wearing my 'Save Mystic Sam' t-shirts. My mum is desperately trying not to smile, but I can tell she really wants to.

'Sammy Puddleduck...'

Suddenly my dad's voice comes into my head. I know it's my dad because he's the only one who has ever called me Sammy Puddleduck, on the account that as a child I had an obsession with Beatrix Potter's little duck, Jemima.

'I am so proud of you, kid. Tell your mum that I'm OK and I'm happy that she has found someone else to love and look after her. I've met up with Uncle Harry and Grandma Jess. I'm watching over you all. Keep on going, kid, you're going to be just fine.'

'Miss Ball...' Bobby Walters says.

'Just a minute, Mr Walters. Can you ask the cameraman to

zoom in to the lady with curly hair, sitting next to the man with ginger hair... top row, fifth along?'

The cameraman does as he is told and my mum looks at Colin.

'Mum, Dad says to tell you that he's OK and that's he's happy that you have found someone else. Oh, and that he's up there with Uncle Harry and Grandma Jess.'

My mum looks stunned for a moment and then looks at Colin and smiles. He takes her hand in his and kisses it.

'Well done, Sammy Puddleduck, I knew you could do it,' my dad whispers.

I want to ask him so many questions, such as, why it's taken him until now to come through to me and why he didn't help me earlier on with the tests, but perhaps I needed to prove to myself that this was all real and that when it comes down to it, you can do all the tests in the world, but it's real people that count in this game, not stupid bloody tests, conducted by stupid bloody parapsychologists.

CHAPTER THIRTY-FOUR

Oh, how the worm turns, as they say. No sooner have I finished passing messages to all and sundry in the audience than I have reporters queuing up wanting to interview me – ha, they weren't so keen to get my side of the story when they were happily typing up that I was a fraud and a charlatan, were they?

With this in mind, I have told Larry that I am not willing to give interviews to anyone at the moment and I expect to read a full apology in every newspaper who vilified me before I will even consider talking to anyone.

'But we could... I mean *you* could make a mint out of doing these interviews, Samantha,' a panic-stricken Larry says. 'I've got *Hello* magazine lined up. They want to do a full photo shoot with you at The Dorchester,' he says. 'What am I going to tell them?' Larry is in full panic mode now. A photo shoot and a four-page spread with one of the top magazines in the UK is worth a large amount of commission for him. 'And I've had *Morning Latte* on the phone wanting to renew your contract. I've also had *It's Morning Time* on the phone saying that they want you on next week as a special guest to advocate their new lifestyle programme, *Life Beyond the Grave*, for them...'

'Oh yes, the woman with too much make-up – no thanks Larry,' I say, thinking of the silly cow presenter who did her best to make me look like a complete moron.

'And Phil and Holly want you on their show next week... you know what a huge fan you are of Phil and Holly,' Larry coaxes. And I am a *huge, huge,* fan of the fabulous day-time duo, but I am also fuming with anything and everything associated with the media at this moment. The only person I have agreed to talk to is *Town FM*.

Annette has been the only person who has spent hours on the radio protesting my innocence and getting people to log on to my website and support me. She has been the only person in the media to have the balls to say what she thinks, instead of jumping on the 'burn-the-witch' bandwagon.

'Look Larry, this has been a pretty shitty time for me of late and at the moment all I want to do is go back to my flat and live a normal existence,' I say, losing patience with my agent. I know he means well and I also know that if I do all these interviews that have suddenly been requested of me I can turn this whole mad thing round to my advantage, but to be honest, I am hurt. I am hurt that someone has gone to so much trouble to hurt me and I would much rather curl up on the sofa with Missy and a box of chocolates.

'Well, take a few days to think about it,' Larry says in my dressing room – funny that now I've proved myself the little room originally entitled the 'wait here' room has now become known as 'Miss Ball's dressing room'. 'I'll tell all of them that you need to take a few days to recover from all the media attention and that we will be in touch,' he says hopefully, 'Oh, and I've also got a publisher lined up for your autobiography,' he adds excitedly.

'Autobiography! I'm only 26 years old, for God's sake, Larry!'

'Well, you've had quite an experience here. Mind you, you could be right, we might need to hold that idea for a few years, but we can always do an inside-the-mind-of-a-psychic kind of book, I mean look at that psychic barber bloke, Gordon Smith and *Most Haunted*... very popular,' Larry rubs his little chubby hands together and I'm sure I can see pound signs kerching-ing in his eyes.

'Right, that's enough now, Larry, sod off and leave me alone, I'll call you tomorrow when I've had a decent night's sleep,' I smile at him and thankfully he takes the hint and goes on his way to think up new ways of promoting me.

I look at my reflection in the mirror opposite me. I look as though I've aged by 10 years. My hair looks more like dreadlocks than pretty corkscrew curls and as hard as I try I can't manage to straighten the frown lines out of my forehead. I was lucky to be blessed with good skin but it's obvious that media attention overload is bad for your health. In fact, it is so bad that they should have a government health warning issued to anyone who is considering becoming an overnight success.

I put my head on the desk in front of me with a thump. I am so tired I could easily cry myself to sleep.

Knock, knock.

'OK if I come in?' Jack's voice whispers by the door. I raise my tired head from its resting position.

'Come in.'

Jack closes the door behind him and leans against it. He looks as tired as I feel. His normally spiked-up hair is flat and he looks as though he hasn't slept in weeks.

'How you doing?' he asks.

'Oh, you know,' I shrug. 'How are you doing?'

'I'm cool. You did well out there, kid. There's loads of people out there want to meet you and say thank you. You can't hide in here forever, you know.'

'I know.'

'You did it, kid. You showed them all and left that Bobby wanker bloke speechless. You should have seen the look on his face.' I know Jack is desperately trying to make me feel better, but I don't. Yes, I made my point. I gave people messages from their loved ones and proved that I was genuine all along, and I did hear voices from people, and yet I feel completely and utterly deflated.

Jack squats down beside me and grabs my hand. For a moment we look at each other and then look away again at the same time.

'It's all over now, Sam. You can get on with your job. You've proved to the world that you are genuine,' Jack says quietly. Right now I so want to hug him to me.

And then Jack's mobile signals that he has a text. He stands up and reads it, frowning as he does so.

'What's the matter?'

'It's from Paul...' Jack says, still in frowning mode.

'What's he say?' I ask as I wipe eyeliner from under my eyes in a bid to make me look less like the living dead.

Jack frowns again.

'Nothing much, just wondered how you're getting on,' Jack says, and snaps his phone shut. 'Come on, you've got fans to meet and greet.'

The last thing I want to do is meet and greet people but Jack is right; a lot of them have come to support me and the least I can do is talk to them. The TV production company kindly rustled up some caterers from the canteen who put on a kind of sponta-neous 'after-the-show' buffet. I do wonder if I hadn't heard those voices just in the nick of time, whether we would have been booted out to the fish and chip shop down the road.

'Thank you so much.' The man whose wife Sheila passed on a message for him hugs me to him. 'You don't know how much that message meant to me,' he says, but I think I do.

'You're very welcome. Excuse me a moment, will you?' I ask as I spot my mother talking to Gerry. She is asking him if he knows Trevor McDonald because she would like to ask Sir Trevor to front one of his *Tonight* programmes on the effect carrots can have on the male libido.

Gerry looks completely terrified in my mother's company and backs himself into a wall.

'Um... I don't know him... sorry...' he says.

'But you must do! You work for the BBC!' my mother says, 'Colin, Colin, come here, dear. Let me introduce Gerald to you. Colin, meet Gerald. Gerald this is my... very dear friend and co-author, Colin. Colin, Gerald knows Sir Trevor McDonald,' my mum says as Colin joins them with a plate of prawn vol-au-vents in his hands. Despite his size, Gerry, or Gerald as my mother insists on calling him, looks absolutely terrified.

My mum can be terrifying at times, especially if it comes to fighting a good cause – in this case it being carrots and how they can affect a man's sexual performance. How she came to this conclusion, I really do not want to know. Give my mum a challenge and she's like a dog with a bone, she will not let go of it until she has got a result. I step in to save Gerry.

'No, Mum, Gerry doesn't know Trevor McDonald. Gerry is a security guard,' I add, ushering Gerry away from the clutches of my mother.

'But he works at the BBC,' my mother squeals after me.

'Yes, Mum, but Sir Trevor McDonald works for the other side,' I add.

'Oh, that's a shame,' she muses. 'Oh, Sammy, I want to speak to you in a moment...'

'OK, Mum,' I say as I move Gerry away from my mother and towards a bowl of fruit salad.

'Thanks for coming to support me. Please excuse my mother,' I say with a smile.

'I've seen worse,' Gerry says. 'You were very good out there you know and thanks... you know, for the advice...' Gerry says, '...about the jogging...' Gerry wobbles his tummy, 'See, I'm already losing weight,' he laughs. 'My wife thinks it's amazing.'

'You're very welcome, but I still don't understand why you're here.'

'Me and my missus are big fans of yours ever since she phoned in to that *Morning Latte* one morning and you gave her a message from her grandmother. You made her day. I told her, I said, Lynne, there's this psychic bird just joined that new morning programme, she's pretty good from what I hear. Didn't take much convincing, did my Lynne – she's into all that weird psychic stuff. Watches all those Very Haunted programmes or whatever they're called. She was straight on the blower to you,' Gerry laughs. 'I expect you remember her... grandmother's name was Doreen?' Gerry says.

I nod, but I have to admit in my time as a professional psychic – which is all of about six months now – there have been so many messages that I couldn't tell you who I've spoken to and who I haven't, dead or alive.

I give Gerry a hug and make my excuses for the loo where I discover my mum re-applying her lipstick. It's been a long time since my mum wore lipstick and I smile to myself. She really is a beautiful woman and I feel so lucky to have her, even if she can be a bit flaky at times. I'm sure she isn't really as daft as she makes out sometimes, but I'm her daughter, and like all daughters, sometimes I think my mother has totally lost the plot.

'Are you OK, Mum?'

My mum smacks her lips together and then reaches for a slither of tissue paper to pat her mouth.

'Yes, love and very well done tonight. I really thought you were going to make a right show of yourself up there and you very nearly did...' Gee thanks, Mum, '...but you came good in the end and fancy you getting all those names right. I was quite amazed. You really do have The Gift don't you?' my mum muses. 'I still don't know how you do it, I really don't, but I'm very proud of you, Sammy.'

'I know you and many other people don't know what to believe about whether there is life after death and I'm not doing this to prove a point, Mum. I'm doing it to help people who are so overcome with grief that they can't think straight. As you know, it wasn't my first choice of career, but it helps people, Mum.' I smile at the thought of all the people I have passed messages on to in the past months.

'I really did hear Dad, you know,' I say, knowing full well that up until now she has successfully evaded the subject of me talking to dead people, 'and he really is happy for you and... Colin... I'm happy for you too, Mum.' You have to be careful with my mum on subjects of a sensitive nature. She will put on this 'I'm fine' exterior but before long the bottom lip will wobble and the last thing I want to do is to make her cry.

I remember quite clearly at my dad's funeral she played the part of hostess to exemplary standards – making sure that everyone was in the right car and that the funeral directors had remembered to take Dad's favourite CD to the crematorium.

Mum made sure that there was enough room for everyone to sit down in the church by enlisting the help of the local Boy Scouts to bring additional chairs, and yet underneath the façade of the coping widow stood a woman who was heartbroken to the extent that she couldn't see past the next day.

A week after my dad's funeral, my mum broke down and cried and cried and cried until she could cry no more. Our roles were suddenly reversed with Me, Matt and Paul caring for her, making her dinner and trying to persuade her to get out of bed so that we could at least change the sheets.

'Are you OK, Mum?' I say, watching her lip start to wobble in the mirror. Mum bites her lip and takes a deep breath.

'He's nothing like your dad, Sammy, and I'm not trying to replace him. I could never try to replace your dad. He was the most wonderful man in the world,' she says.

'And he still is, Mum,' I whisper. 'He's still around us all the time and he still loves you. He just wants to see you happy.' I wrap my arms around her and as I do so her shoulders heave upwards and the floodgates open. And there we stay for the next 30 minutes.

CHAPTER THIRTY-FIVE

It feels as though I've been away for ages. In reality it's actually only been two weeks. Thankfully things have died down in the newspapers and I received three apologies in writing and requests to tell my side of the story in all three newspapers, which I've declined. I've had enough of the media to last me a lifetime and they only sensationalise everything anyway, so why bother.

I gingerly walk up the staircase to Ms Morris's flat and tap gently on her door. I don't know why she always makes me feel so nervous, but she does.

'Ah... hello Samantha, come in,' Ms Morris gives me a nervous smile as she opens the door to let me in. I hand her a huge bouquet of flowers and a box of Roses – despite being covered with pretty wrapping paper you can always tell that it's either going to be a box of Roses or Quality Street, by the give-away shape. You would have thought one of them would have thought of a different shape by now, wouldn't you?

'These are for you... to say thank you... you know, for supporting me...' I stutter.

She smiles and for the first time I notice it's a genuine smile.

'It should be me thanking you, dear,' she says as she walks me into her small kitchen and searches for a vase big enough for the flowers. 'I had no idea you and Mystic Crystal were the same person. It was only when I saw that picture of you in the paper that it clicked. How silly am I?' she chuckles.

Her flat is pristine and sparkles like a new pin. Beneath the blue anorak that I usually see Ms Morris in is a very tidy lady. Her long silver hair is pulled back into a neat bun and held in place with a multitude of brown hairpins. Her pink twin-set and knee-length pleated skirt complete her neat appearance.

'I didn't realise you were Valerie either. We've been talking for all these months and I had no idea. I knew I recognised the voice, but I didn't think for a moment it was you,' I laugh. Ms Morris laughs too as she fills the vase with water and arranges the flowers in it.

'Is that Frank?' I ask, noticing a small silver frame with a black and white photograph inside it of a young man in uniform on the windowsill.

Ms Morris smiles.

'Yes, that's Frank. Handsome chap in his uniform, wasn't he?' I nod.

'Well...' I hesitate, not quite sure what to say to her now. I had imagined that now we knew so much about each other we would get on famously, but find I am at a complete loss for words. I want to ask her about her son in America and how she met Frank, but I still feel as though Ms Morris my landlady and Valerie my caller are two different people.

'Do you think you will continue working for Mystic Answers?' Ms Morris asks suddenly.

'I think so,' I smile. 'And you are more than welcome to call me any time Ms... Valerie.'

She continues to arrange her flowers and although her back is to me, I'm sure there is a little smile on her face.

Being back in my own flat feels really strange – it's so tidy. For the past two weeks I've been holed up at Jack's place where the floor also acts as a waste-paper bin, a laundry basket and a wardrobe. Washing up only gets done if and when there are no clean plates from which to eat from and sheets are only washed if they don't pass Jack's sniff test. For someone who is so particular about his personal hygiene – Jack will not go out of the house without matching deodorant, aftershave and talc on – he sure is a slob when it comes to his home.

Missy jumps on the bed and snuggles down into my pillow as if to say 'home sweet home, at long last, it's like living with a pig at what's-his-name's – the bloke who throws cats in the air.'

Before I can say, 'Honey I'm home!' the phone starts ringing. It's Jack.

'You got back OK?'

'Yeah, just got in. You all right?' I say, flinging myself on to the sofa.

'Yeah, just off to rehearsals with Dillon. You want to come along?'

'Nah, you're all right. I think I'd better log on to the website and see what's been happening while I've been away.'

'Cool, OK, see ya tonight?'

'Yeah, that will be nice. Use my key to let yourself in. I may well have retired to my bed for ever more,' I say, thinking of the prospect of snuggling up under the duvet and never, ever coming out again. It's a dangerous world out there and I'm surprised more people don't take to their beds on a regular basis given how bad it is in the big wide world sometimes.

'OK, loves ya!' Jack says. He doesn't realise quite how nice it is to hear him say that again.

'Loves me too,' I say and put the phone down.

Right, now to work. I log on to find the forum busier than ever with so many messages of support for me it's amazing. People from all over the world, people who have never met me have written all sorts of wonderful things about me, including a few names I recognise from the radio show. There's Steve who was in the car crash with his friend; Michelle, the girl who wanted to know if she and her chap would ever get married. And, oh my goodness, there's even a message from Verity Star herself to say how accurate I was about her 'dear old friend' Rita. Ha, I bet Rita is spinning in her grave at being described as dear and old in one sentence! I feel very humble indeed and a lump comes into my throat.

I ought to write a personal message of thanks to these people. As I begin typing, my brother Paul pops up on my live talk messenger service. He's up late. It must be around two o'clock in the morning over there.

'Hi baby sis. How yer doing?'

'Good and you?'

'Good, got a new board today – real cool!' he types. Lord knows how many surfboards he's got now. I mean how many boards does one man need to go surfing? Does one surfboard even differ from another surfboard, I wonder? Is one really good at catching little waves but not so hot on the bigger buggers? I have no idea.

'Did you get my message the other day about the photographer?' he adds.

'No, what message?' I type.

'About who took the photograph of you. I told Jack to tell you.'

'No, he didn't say anything. Did you find out who it was?'

'Yes, it was a Scottish photographer by the name of… hang on, I've got it here… he goes under McIntyre, but his official name is Lord Kenzie McIntyre. His father's the famous Lord McIntyre – the chap who does all the Royal photographs. Apparently the son, Kenzie McIntyre, occasionally works with him as a freelancer for the glossies and tabloids. Not that he needs the money, mind you, he's loaded.'

My heart misses a beat for a moment as I re-read what Paul has typed.

'Are you sure?' I type back.

'Yeah, do you know him?'

'You could say that… he's Amy's boyfriend.'

CHAPTER THIRTY-SIX

You cannot believe how livid I am. I am bloody fuming. I have been sitting in the same spot staring at a blank screen for nearly 45 minutes, going over and over the news Paul has told me, and I can only come up with one conclusion: that it was Amy who told her boyfriend to get a photo of me, and then either she or Kenzie went to the papers with the story that I was a fraud.

I've only met Kenzie once and he doesn't know me well enough for me to confide anything in him, so logic dictates that it has to be Amy. And I did say to her at the beginning of all of this that I didn't have a clue what I was doing and that I made most of it up, didn't I? How could I have been so bloody stupid? And why didn't I think of her before? Why, because she has been my best friend for the past 20 years. Amy and I have shared everything together – problems, shoes, clothes, beauty tips, even boyfriends on occasions – well, OK, it was only the once and that was because she didn't want to hurt Mark by dumping him, so she told him that I wanted to go out with him instead – and we were only 13 years old.

I simply can't bring myself to believe that Amy did this. I mean, I know she was a bit sulky with me for going to the awards ceremony when she was having a career crisis, but would she really do that to me?

Picking up the phone I tap in Amy's mobile number, clenching my fists to prevent me from screaming down the phone at her.

'Hello flower!' she trills.

'Hiya!' I say as happily as I can muster. Deep down I just feel sick at the thought that someone I could trust with my life has deliberately tried to destroy my entire career.

'You're back home then. How are things going?' she coos in her sympathetic voice.

'Yeah, they're going well. Now all that mess has been sorted out,' I say, sounding relieved. 'I just wondered, if you're not doing anything, whether you'd like to come over? It's been ages since we had a good chat and I bet we've got loads of things to tell each other. With all this media business I haven't had much time for my best friend,' I add.

'Um... yeah, ok, that will be great. I'll be round in about half an hour.'

'Cool, I'll see you then,' I say and calmly put the phone down.

I take a deep breath and mentally count to ten. I can't believe that Amy could ever contemplate doing something like this to me. We've been friends for years. The only thing I don't have is hard evidence that it was actually Amy who went to the newspapers. I mean, it's not like I can phone the tabloids up and say, 'Oh, by the way, who was it that sold the story to you again?'

Ah-ha, but maybe I do. I pick up my address book and go through all the numbers until I come to the K's. Karen from college... Kevin... Kevin? Who the hell is Kevin? Oh well, ah, Kenzie. I remember Amy giving me his mobile number when my mum asked if I knew of anyone who could do the photography for her and Colin's book. Amy told me that Kenzie used to be a professional photographer. I tap the number into the phone and wait patiently for someone to answer.

'Yep,' a voice answers.

'Oh, hello, is that Kenzie?'

'Yep,' he answers – a man of many words, eh?

'Oh, hi Kenzie, it's Samantha here... Sam, Amy's friend,' I say, trying to sound cheerful and light-hearted.

'Oh, um... yeah... all right?' Kenzie says in his Scottish drawl which, despite initially thinking it sounded very sexy, now just irritates the hell out of me.

'Yes, fine thanks. Look, I'm sorry to bother you. I know that it was Amy who went to the papers with that story, but we've sorted things out now and are friends again,' I say like an excited schoolgirl. 'I just wanted to ask you if you still have a copy of that photograph of me? You know the one from the award ceremony? My mum loved it and I thought I would get a copy done for her birthday.'

'Oh… um… yeah, about that Sam. I'm sorry and all that, but you know, a good news story is a good news story and Amy said that you wouldn't be too upset by it…' Kenzie says.

'Upset? Me? God no. In fact you should see the publicity I got out of it,' I say with gritted teeth. 'No such thing as bad publicity!' I trill.

'Oh cool. Anyway, yeah I'll get a copy made up for you and give it to Amy. No charge,' Kenzie says.

No sodding charge? No sodding charge? The pair of you try to screw up my career, my reputation and my whole life between you and you're giving me a free sodding photo? I want to scream, but I don't. Instead I say, 'OK, that's great. Thanks Kenzie. See you again soon,' and put the phone down. Let the games begin!

I feel like the villain in a James Bond movie and if Missy wasn't currently reclining on my bed for her morning nap I might be tempted to force her to sit on me and let me stroke her, with a menacing look on my face… Ah, Mr Bond… I suddenly feel like saying in a broken English Accent. Now I have some concrete evidence that it was Amy who went to the papers I can really go to town on her.

Amy takes no time in taking up my offer of coffee and a chat and is soon on the doorstep ringing the bell to my flat. My mind races with all the evil things I could do to her like put arsenic in her coffee; slash the tyres on her BMW coupé; gouge her eyes out with a nail file…

'Hi,' I say as brightly as I can as I open the door. As usual Amy is looking tall, blonde and gorgeous and breezes in with her Balenciaga handbag swinging off her tanned arm. The thing is with Amy is that she will never, ever, be seen in last season's fashions. In fact she is so up on the fashion industry, she is often two steps ahead of them. Amy won't let the mere fact that a new design doesn't suit her get in the way of being the first to have the very latest in the fashion stakes. Me, I'm more of a *New Look* girl – if it's cheap and practical, I'll buy it.

'Hi you!' Amy gushes with a 'Mwah, Mwah,' air kiss aimed at each cheek. I used to think this behaviour was quite endearing, but since her endeavour to ruin my life, I now find it nothing more than bloody annoying. In fact, I now find everything about Amy bloody annoying. From the way she flings herself down and puts her feet up on *my* sofa to the way she constantly flicks her long hair extensions over her shoulder when she is talking to me.

'So, what's been happening since I've been away?' she says all wide-eyed and eager as if she doesn't know.

Humm, well, where shall I start… I manage to find a job I am really good at, I get my own radio slot and then I'm asked to appear live on day-time TV, where I'm a huge success, until I attend an awards ceremony where my best friend's shit of a boyfriend takes a photo of me and my best friend decides to make a few quid by ringing up the newspapers and telling the whole world that I'm a fake and then uses that money to go to Spain… Is what I desperately want to say.

'Oh, you know,' I shrug, 'nothing much really. Been busy with work and things. How about you? Did you have a nice time at your mum's?' I enquire as I pass an arsenic-free cup of coffee to her.

'Yes, it was nice to catch up with her again.'

'I thought you couldn't stand your mum?'

'Well, I needed a break, you know, after the shock of losing my job…' Amy says, giving me one of those feel-sorry-for-me looks.

'So how is your mum?' I ask.

Amy's mum, Lorraine, is a slighter older and a more surgically enhanced version of Amy. In human years she's probably about 50, but she's had so many nips and tucks that she could easily pass for Amy's little sister. Lorraine has always put Lorraine first, ever since Amy was a small child. She would willingly dump her on anyone who would have her so that she could grab another session on the sunbed or go off on 18-30 holidays on her own.

'Oh, you know, much the same,' Amy says looking down at her perfectly manicured nails. 'I have a new father though! He's a surgeon.'

'I thought Derek was a surgeon?' Derek was Lorraine's fifth husband and Amy's fifth father/uncle or whatever Amy calls them. 'What happened to him?'

'Oh, you know my mother! Why have one surgeon when you can have two? She got caught with her knickers down with this new one. Derek divorced her and now she's with William, the new one, but she's also seeing Martin, a cosmetic surgeon from Spain,' Amy explains.

Blimey! No wonder Lorraine looks like a Barbie doll. Once she's had one job done she goes and finds herself a new surgeon/husband and gets an even better deal.

'How's yours?' Amy says.

'Oh, you know, much the same,' I say. If my mum knew that it was Amy who had started all of this I don't think she would ever forgive her. My mum was one of Lorraine's dumpees for many years and has always treated Amy as if she were her own.

'Obviously this business with the papers has upset her,' I add and take a sip of my coffee.

Amy reaches out a hand to me and pats my leg.

'Yes, it must have been awful!' she coos dramatically. 'I don't know how you managed to keep going. Some of the things that had been said in the papers about you… I mean, God, I was livid when I read them.'

'I thought you said you hadn't heard about it until I told you the other day?'

'Ah… well yes, but when you told me I went straight out and bought all the papers,' she says, slightly flustered, and starts to fidget uncomfortably in her chair.

'What, in Spain?' I say, taking another sip of my coffee.

'No, I mean, I got back issues sent to me... well, I got my mum to get them for me. She knows a nice little Asian who runs a shop out there and... well, he...' Amy stutters. Before she has chance to make herself look even more stupid I stop her.

'Look Amy, quit the acting. I know it was you who went to the papers,' I say quietly but firmly.

'What? I don't know what you're talking about,' Amy flushes a shade of red as if she has just come out in a nasty rash.

'I think you do. You see, Amy, when I was beside myself at what the press were writing, I just happened to notice that all the newspapers were carrying the same photograph of me. All the papers were carrying a photograph that was taken at the awards ceremony and all were taken by the same photographer, McIntyre. All I had to do was find out who had supplied the photograph to them and contact them to find out who it was that sold the story on me,' I pause for effect – wow, I feel like Hercule Poirot summing up his murder theory to Hastings. 'Paul – you know, my brother, the one with the detective agency in Australia – well, he tracked the photographer down and it just happened to turn out to be one Lord Kenzie McIntyre. *Your* gorgeous Lord Kenzie McIntyre was the one that took that photograph, Amy.'

'What? *My* Kenzie? Sam, you've got to believe me, I don't know anything about it. I don't know what he works on. He helps his dad out occasionally on magazine shoots and...'

'Award ceremonies,' I spit.

'I swear on my life, Sam, all I know is what you told me and what I read in the papers.'

'The copies your mum ordered?' I confirm.

'Yes, the copies I back-ordered... from my mum... from the little Asian...'

'Newsagent.'

'Yes. From the newsagent.'

'Look, Amy, I don't know why you can't just admit that it was you who went to the press. For what ever reason, jealousy maybe because you couldn't come to the awards ceremony, or because you knew your own job was on the line...'

Amy stands up and puts her hands on her hips, which means she's about to get all shouty and defensive.

'Now just you hang on a minute!' as if on cue her voice goes up an octave. 'I don't know what the bloody hell you are going on about, and I find it quite offensive that you could even think of suggesting that I had anything to do with this.'

'Amy, I know it was you – Kenzie told me,' I say wearily – I do wish people would just own up to things they did, it would make life so much simpler if they did.

'What? Don't be so stupid! My Kenzie wouldn't do that!'

'Me, stupid? Was I the one who got my boyfriend to take a photo and then make up a whole bunch of lies about my best friend? Was I the one who almost ruined my best friend's life because of it? Err, no that was you Amy!' I try very hard to stay calm, but I think it's about time Amy had a taste of her own medicine.

'It wasn't me who was so jealous that she had to go and make up a whole load of lies about her best friend!' I shout. 'I can't believe you would do that to me, Amy. I thought we were best friends.'

Amy looks furious and I'm not altogether sure if it's because she's been found out or whether it's because her boyfriend has dobbed her in.

'Well, it serves you right!' Amy snaps. 'You said yourself that you made the whole thing up and that you didn't know what you were doing. You said you were only doing it for the money...'

'That was at the start, Amy, and besides I confided in you. That's what best friends do, they confide in each other and *keep* each other's secrets!' I shout at the top of my voice.

'Ah, so you admit it now! Well, it still serves you right then!'

Amy shouts back and pushes me back against the sofa. 'You thought you were so clever getting that job at the BBC, you couldn't shut up about it! You knew I might lose my job and you still harped on and on about how clever you were and how many new deals you were going to get! And even when I asked you if I could help you, you told me you didn't need any help!' Amy shouts in my face. I'm certainly not having that! As I stand back up Amy pushes me down again.

'Why, you little...' I jump up and push her back. She totters unsteadily in her four-inch heels and falls backwards to the floor. Call me a mad woman but I just can't help myself. Amy has been asking for this. I launch myself Spiderman-style off the sofa and straight on to my former best friend who yelps like a puppy as I land on her.

'You bitch!' she screams in my face and grabs a long curl of my hair and tugs on it until I let go of her throat.

'Ow! You cow!' I counter attack as she pulls a clump of my hair out and digs her long fake nails into my cheek.

Amy rolls over with me clinging on to her. Her leather trouser clad legs fly in the air as I cling to her blouse in order to keep my balance.

We're so busy rolling around on the carpet taking chunks out of each other that neither of us hears the door open. As I am in mid roll I look up to see the lounge door open.

'Oh shit,' Jack says as he looks down upon the two of us scratching, biting and generally beating a pulp out of each other.

As I look up I hear Amy's hundred-and-sixty-pound blouse rip. Good!

CHAPTER THIRTY-SEVEN

'Time out, girls!' Jack shouts as he tries to separate the pair of us. I am not giving up without a fight and no amount of Jack shouting 'time out' like a teacher in the playground, is going to stop me from thrashing Amy.

'Samantha! Amy!' Jack shouts louder as if he is telling a pair of seven-year-olds off for unruly behaviour.

'Oh fuck off, Jack! Look what she's done to my shirt!' Amy shouts back as she grabs my leg and pulls it toward her in the attempt of preventing me from escaping her clutches. As she pulls I kick back like a reluctant donkey at a donkey derby. Amy flies back in the air, giving me a breather to compose myself.

'Girls! This is not solving anything!' Jack shouts, panic rising in his voice – you'd think he'd be quite pleased, isn't this every man's fantasy, two girls fighting with each other?

'Fuck off, Jack! Do you know what she did to me?' This time it is me who screams, 'It was that cow that went to the papers! It was that cow who tried to ruin my reputation.'

'Reputation? What reputation is that then? A reputation as a lying bitch?' Amy screams in my face as she grabs for my hair again. Ow, I have such a headache now.

'Ha, you're a fine one to talk! At least I have a career, loser!' I shout back into her face – I know, childish, isn't it? But she did start it.

'Please girls!' Jack begs. 'Sam, get off her now!' he adds as I launch myself onto Amy's back and sink my teeth into her shoulder.

'Ow! That hurt!' Amy yells, reaching behind her to try and claw my eyes out with her inch-long talons

'Good! You deserve it, you little cow!' I yell back – I have to say, as a rule I don't generally promote violence, but given the circumstances I don't feel that I have a great deal of choice, it's fight or be smashed to a pulp with Amy.

'I give up,' Jack sighs and raises his arms in the air in an I-give-up kind of a way. He walks out of the room.

Phewwwwwww! A loud whistle blows at high pitch making us freeze on the spot.

'That is enough!' Valerie shouts at the top of her voice. 'You! Yes *you* madam!' she points at Amy who looks up, terrified. 'Get off *my* tenant this instant and get yourself out of *my* flat.'

'But… she…' Amy stutters.

'But nothing. I know all about you, you little traitor. Go on with you. Get out!' Valerie says sternly. It reminds me of our school days when Amy was often the instigator of the daily school fight. She would start a rumour about someone – usually one of the younger girls in the third form – and before you knew it a fight had broken out on the school playing field and Amy would be right in the middle of it.

Amy stands up and hobbles to the door. One of her four-inch heels has been snapped off in the brawl and is wedged in the cushion of my sofa. Amy bobs up and down as she tries her best to strut out of the flat. She flicks her now straggly hair behind her and manages to catch one of her red talons in it.

'Ow! Ow! Ow!' she wails as she struggles to remove the nail from her matted mane. Valerie folds her arms and taps her foot impatiently on the floor as Amy bobs pass her and Jack and out of the door.

'Just look at the state of you,' Valerie says as she and Jack try to help me up to the sofa. My lip has doubled in size and my nose is numb – and it bloody well hurts. I do hope it's not broken. I think Amy may well have broken it when her stupid fat arse landed on it. My head, which is now minus many locks of hair, hurts like hell. I didn't know women could be so bloody vicious. My knees look like two great big blood oranges from all the rolling around on the floor and I have carpet burns and that many punctures in my arm and neck from Amy's stupid nails that if I have a bath I'll bet I will be like a bloody shower-head.

'I don't think we'll be seeing much of that young lady for a while,' Valerie says, dusting her hands off as if she had just dealt with something very unpleasant – which isn't too far from the truth, actually.

'Now, Jack, you help to get Samantha up and I'll get us all a cup of tea, dear,' she instructs. Blimey, my landlady is full of surprises, isn't she? One minute I know her as the cantankerous, anorak-wearing old biddy from upstairs and the next she is a fully-paid-up member of the Save Mystic Sam Society. Jack pulls me up and suddenly, without warning I burst into tears.

'Oh God… Um… Valerie!' Jack yells back to the kitchen. 'She's crying now, what should I do?' he asks anxiously and drops me back to the floor again.

Jack, bless him, has had to mop my tears up on many occasions – weddings, christenings, the many times I've been dumped by ungrateful boyfriends – but on this occasion I feel he's entitled to ask for help because I'm not just crying this time, I am positively howling, and not too unlike a werewolf. The fear in Jack's face tells me that this is way outside of his comfort zone.

Valerie rushes in with three mugs of tea on a tray and places my mug on the floor beside me – which is where I am lying, curled up in a ball and howling to my heart's content.

'Just leave her to it,' Valerie advises Jack in a whisper. Jack looks at me with worry as though I might suddenly jump up from my foetal position and attack him with the TV remote that is clutched in my hand – I have no idea why I have the TV remote in my hand as I'm not planning to watch anything right now.

And there they leave me for what must be over an hour. As I howl in to the carpet, Jack and Valerie retreat to the kitchen in a bid for a bit of peace and quiet.

'Don't worry, dear,' I hear her say. 'She will be back to normal in a while. With everything that has gone on it's little wonder she hasn't had a breakdown before this.'

'Hummm,' I hear Jack agree. 'I didn't really know what to do with her,' he says. 'How did you know what to do?'

'I used to be a psychiatric nurse. I've experienced much worse than that,' Valerie says, calmly.

Oh bollocks, now she thinks I'm mentally insane.

CHAPTER THIRTY-EIGHT

'Are you OK now?' Jack asks tentatively.

'Mmmm,' I mumble into the phone from under the duvet. It's eight o'clock on a Sunday morning. Jack and Valerie stayed for a while, but when they failed after three hours to coax me up from the carpet, they threw a duvet over me and made their excuses – Valerie claiming that she had to go because there was a *Morse* on telly that she hadn't seen. Jack mumbled something about popping out to the shop to get some crisps and I didn't see him again. I just lay there on the living-room carpet beneath a 12-tog for the next 15 hours.

'So... um... are you... um... going to work today?' he ventures.

'Huh?' I murmur. 'What day is it?'

'Sunday. You're supposed to be in the studio at lunchtime,' he reminds me.

Oh, bugger, what with the wrestling match with Amy, I completely forgot all about that.

Annette had left a message on the phone the day before to say that I had my old job back and that the producers were all mightily impressed with my stint on TV. The only problem being that I'd completely forgotten all about it and all I want to do is stay under this duvet forever.

'I'll come with you, if you like?' Jack offers.

'Huh?' I am still a bit incoherent.

'I'll come to the studio with you. Give you a bit of moral support.'

I suddenly sit up and shake the duvet from me – ouch, my lip hurts rather a lot.

'Hang on a minute,' I say as I replay the events from the previous day in my head. 'You knew that it was Amy who went to the papers,' I say, remembering what my brother told me.

'Ah, yeah...' Jack stumbles, 'I was going to say something but...'

'But what?' I snap. I'm a bit annoyed that Jack knew about Amy and yet didn't pass the message on to me. Had he done so I might not be nursing a lip the size of Wales or dousing my puncture marks in TCP antiseptic.

'I... I was going to tell you, honest Sam, it's just you were having such a blast after the show and everyone wanted to congratulate you and... well, I just didn't want to upset you,' Jack says quietly and I'm slightly touched – but I'm still angry with him.

'So?' Jack says.

'So, what?'

'So do you want me to come to the studio with you or not? I just thought you might want a bit of support, being your first day back and all that.'

'Yeah, sure. Thanks Jack. Speaking of which, I'd better get a bath before I go out – I stink.'

'Well, I didn't like to say anything...'

'You cheeky git. Right, pick me up at ten.'

'Yes, boss,' Jack laughs. 'Love ya!'

'Loves me too.'

I'm still a bit nervous as we drive towards the studio. This is the first time since Amy decided to announce to the world that I was a fraud that I will have been live on air. Apart from that stupid psychic test with the studio audience, this is the first time that I have had to face the public and to be honest I'm dreading it.

'You OK?' Jack asks as we turn off the motorway and head towards the signs directing us to Weston-super-Mare.

'I guess,' I say with a shrug, 'a bit nervous about going back on air.'

Jack squeezes my knee.

'Don't be nervous. You've got loads of adoring fans out there.

Just look at the website, more and more people are logging on to it than ever before.'

'Ah, but for what reason?'

'To support you, of course. Why else would they log on? You are daft sometimes, you know. Look, you know what you're doing, you obviously do a good job and you wouldn't be feeling like this if it wasn't for Amy being so stupid and going to the papers. Are you going to name and shame her?'

'What would be the point? It won't alter what she's done to me. I still can't understand why she would do that. She was supposed to be one of my best friends, Jack.' I shake my head at the mentality of it all. Jack shrugs too as if he can't understand the mentality of it all either.

'I don't know why she did it, Sam. Jealousy perhaps? You've got to remember, you practically had overnight success when Amy was faced with losing her job. Amy's always been the ambitious one and I guess it was a bit of a kick in the...'

'Shhh, shhh a minute!' I say as I turn up the radio. 'Listen.'

'Make Time for Time' resonates out of the car's speakers. Jack looks first at the radio and then at me.

'But that's...' Jack stutters.

'You! Jack, that's your band!' I scream, turning the volume up on the radio as Jack's dulcet vocals fill my car with Otherwise's ballad, 'Make Time for Time'.

'But... but how?' Jack stutters as he listens.

'I have no idea,' I say. I am in fact as gobsmacked as Jack is right now. And it sounds fantastic. Although he would never admit it, Jack is not only young and good looking, he also has a brilliant singing voice.

'And that my little darlings was a fantastic song by an up and coming band called Otherwise and you can take it from me, these guys are going to be big!' Annette says as the song comes to a soothing end.

'But...' Jack stutters.

'And I would like to thank whoever left their demo tape on my desk and all of you out there, just remember where you heard them first. This DJ is telling you that Otherwise is going to be big and I should know, I've listened to a fair few demos in my time,' Annette says with a familiar laugh in her voice. Oh, how I've missed Annette.

'Ah!' I gasp. 'It was me! You know that tape you gave me? The demo? I put it in my bag and forgot all about it. It must have dropped out of my handbag.'

'Ah man! Did you hear us? Our first radio airing! I've got to ring Dillon and tell him,' Jack laughs. I haven't seen Jack smile so much in ages.

'Hey, you might be doing your first live interview any minute, if I know what Annette is like,' I say as we pull in to the studio car park.

It's good to see Annette again and it's good too to be back in the studio with familiar faces. I get the standard thumbs up from Jeff and surprisingly from Liam too – considering I used every excuse in the Girls-Guide-of-Handy-Excuses-For-Not-Going-On-a-Date book, Liam and I are still good friends. I think he probably thinks he had a lucky escape anyway since I was suddenly spread across every tabloid in the country.

Annette spots me and Jack and waves. I see she has Colin the Carrot Man in the booth with her and what's that? Oh no. My mother is sitting next to Colin. I drag Jack into the reception area and we listen to Colin's tales about white carrots – I didn't know you could get such a thing, but apparently you can.

'And that's not all...' I hear my mother's posh voice – this is the one reserved for talking with the vicar, estate agents and apparently now radio show hosts. This is similar and yet quite different from my mother's telephone voice. My mother's telephone voice is more clipped than her posh I'm-a-radio-presenter voice and she uses it on the likes of unsuspecting sales people who dare to call her after 7pm.

'Did you know, Annette, that just half a cup of cooked carrots contains four times the recommended daily intake of vitamin A and they are an excellent antioxidant for combating diseases such as lung cancer, protection against strokes and heart disease? Research also shows, Annette, that the beta-carotene in vegetables supplies this protection, and this is not found in vitamin supplements, so it doesn't matter how many vitamin tablets you take, you can't beat the carrot for the real thing!' my mother enthuses.

Annette nods and when she can get a word in edgeways says things like 'really?' and 'wow!'

'And they are an excellent source of fibre, vitamin C, vitamin K, folate and iron,' Colin adds. Blimey, you'd think they were a double act for the Save the Carrot Campaign.

'Well, Cathy, Colin, I would like to thank you both for coming in this week and telling us all about the wonderful health benefits of the humble carrot and if you wish to buy a copy of Cathy and Colin's book, *The Truth About Carrots*, it will be available in all good bookstores in time for Christmas. If you can't wait until then, Cathy and Colin have very kindly given us a signed copy to give away, if you can answer this question…' I can see that Annette is desperately trying to take all this very seriously, despite wanting to wet herself laughing.

'OK,' Annette coughs, 'please tell us one disease that carrots can prevent. Answers on a postcard to *Town FM*, Windsor Street, Weston-super-Mare, BS49 5TT, to arrive before next Saturday where Colin will draw out the correct answer.' Annette flicks a few switches on her dashboard and heaves a sigh of relief.

'Was that OK?' my mother asks. 'They seemed very responsive, don't you think?' She looks at Colin who pats her hand with his own freckled mitt.

'I think you did marvellously, Cathy,' Colin smiles.

'Really?' my mother blushes.

Annette takes a sip of bottled water and suggests the pair of lovebirds go to the canteen to get some refreshments.

'Oh, thank you so much for this wonderful experience,' my mother says as she is practically pushed out of the door by Annette who has well and truly had a gut-full of carrot talk for one day.

'You're very welcome,' Annette says and flumps down in her seat. 'Is your mother always this enthusiastic?' she asks as Jack and me sit down in the reception.

'Um… yes,' we both chorus.

'Oh, Sammy, Jack, did you hear me?' my mum says as she spots us.

'You were brilliant, Mrs B,' Jack says and throws his arms around her and kisses her on the cheek.

'Yes, you really were, Mum.' And she was. I sometimes forget that my mother is a person too and it's been a bit of a struggle for her the past two years. She is finally coming out of herself and gaining that much needed confidence.

As I enter the studio, Annette throws her arms around me and hugs me to her while Annie Lennox warbles away in the background.

'It is so good to see you again, young lady,' she says kissing me on the cheek. 'And this gorgeous young man is?' she says looking at Jack and smiling flirtatiously.

'This gorgeous young man is the lead vocalist on the record you just played, 'Make Time for Time' by Otherwise,' I say proudly, smiling up at Jack who has gone a lovely shade of scarlet and is busy studying his feet.

'No! No way!' Annette says. 'So it was you who left the demo on my desk?'

'No. Yes. Well, not intentionally. When I got the job here Jack asked me if I would give you his demo and I completely forgot…'

'And she calls herself a friend,' Jack says. 'Ouch!'

'Anyway, I'd put it in my bag and it must have dropped out

the last time I was in here,' I explain.

'Well, I'm glad it did,' Annette says. 'I hope you don't mind Jack, but I've given a copy to my brother, Kevin, who works for Music Management. He wanted me to track down where you were but with only a demo to go on and no name I was beginning to think that we would never find you. Do you think you'd like to meet with him?' Annette asks Jack.

'Hell, yeah,' Jack says. 'I mean yes please.'

CHAPTER THIRTY-NINE

Don't you just love Christmas Eve? It doesn't seem to matter where you are in the world, it's always the same: husbands rushing around for the last-minute suitable gift, which looks nothing like a just-remembered-at-the-last-minute-bottle-of-perfume for their wives; mothers rushing around for the packet of chestnut and cranberry stuffing that they had forgotten; children rushing around with that pre-Santa excitement look upon their faces.

For me, Jack, Mum and Colin, Miracle and Max, and Paul and Matt, this Christmas Eve is being spent in the land of sea and sun – Australia. After the past four weeks of having to prove myself to the world that I am not a fraud, Paul suggested we all fly out there for a holiday and I have to say, the offer of sunning myself on a lounger on a paradise beach couldn't come at a better time.

Since the prove-you're-a-psychic-or-we'll-hang-you-out-to-dry incident with Bobby Walters, Larry has been inundated with offers of work for me: everything from endorsing a collection of wailing dolphin meditation CDs to writing a book called *How You Can Become Psychic*. How you can become psychic? I haven't the bloody foggiest idea, so that's going to be a short book isn't it? I mean, one minute I am desperately ringing up for guidance so that I can pay Ms Morris her rent and the next I'm hearing voices in my head. I don't profess to know how all this psychic stuff happens. I try not to read for friends and family because I think it would feel a little uncomfortable if I were to see something bad happening, but I have found that suddenly people who wouldn't normally give me the time of day are asking me to tell them what is going to happen to them – and, thankfully, I'm always spot on.

The bit in the middle is still a complete mystery to me and what I want to know is, why, if all these dead people insist on talking to me, they can't tell me something useful such as next week's lottery numbers or how much is too much luggage to take on an aeroplane to the other side of the world?

'I'm telling you, you've got too much luggage,' Jack said prior to leaving for the airport.

'Have not.'

'Have so.'

'Not.'

'So.'

'Not, infinity.'

'So, infinity and one.'

Well, you get the idea and as it happened, Jack was right. I did have too much luggage. Quite a bit too much in fact which meant I had to pay a surcharge or face leaving it at Heathrow airport.

'So, have you decided if you are going to go for this qualification thingy? I've never heard of it before,' Jack asks as we lie on the beach, basking in the hot sunshine. Being of dark complexion anyway, Jack has already got a beautiful bronzed body and we've only been here for three days. I, on the other hand, being fair-skinned, have bright red feet with white marks on them – a telling sign to everyone that I've been wearing flip-flops, and my shoulders look like two big fat tomatoes and sting quite a lot too.

'I guess I might as well,' I say. Having gotten over my hissy fit with the world and taken a few weeks off to recover from the press attention, I think I might as well follow up on Miracle's suggestion and study the paranormal to get accredited by the British Association of Clairvoyants and Mediums. It will mean taking more tests, but this time I won't feel under any pressure to prove myself to some jumped-up tosser on the telly. Now I have discovered that I can hear dead people, I would quite like to explore the possibility of being able to see them. As things stand I have a feeling of who I am talking to, or rather, who is talking to me, but it would be quite nice to be able to see them once in a while.

The idea of providing therapy to veg phobics seems less

appealing to me than it originally did. My original visions of being the answer to every lachanophobic's prayer was that I would have a lovely little clinic, overlooking the city of Bath, where every day I would calmly get to the root of my clients' problems and happily sit back at the end of an evening, feeling content that there was one less lachanophobic in the world. I was going to be the Paul McKenna of veg-fearing folk.

In reality, I discovered that people who have a problem looking a carrot in the eye have more to worry about than vegetables attacking them – they are stark raving bonkers, and also dress really badly.

'And what about you? Are you going to go ahead with the contract with Annette's brother, Kevin?'

'Hell, yeah!' Jack says at the prospect of signing the band with Music Management. 'Though Dillon and Steve reckon we should just carry on as we are. Dillon reckons we have more control over our music…'

'What? Playing the odd gig in the Pig and Whistle? Jack, you've wanted this chance for ages. Don't let it go now just because Dillon and Steve don't like it.'

'I know. He's always complaining that he hates his job and this is his big chance to get out of insurance and into the music industry. Did I tell you they want us to play at The Brits?'

'Only about a million times, Jack. Humm… playing to millions of people at The Brits, or playing to a handful of piss-heads at the Pig and Whistle… tough one,' I laugh.

'Oh, you know Dillon, he's not big on change, is he?'

'Well, tell him Mystic Crystal told him that if he doesn't take up this opportunity he is doomed to a life of assessing other people's insurance claims and his ears will shrivel up and drop off.'

'I'll tell him then,' Jack says, not taking his gaze from mine.

'What?' I ask, feeling a little self-conscious.

'Nothing, I was just thinking how good it is to see you smile again,' he says.

Oh thank God for that.

'Well, I've got you to thank for that, haven't I? If it wasn't for you picking me up from the hotel and sorting things out for me, I would probably still be hiding underneath that bloody hotel bed.'

'That's what friends are for – helping each other out of tricky spots like being accused of being a fraud, that sort of thing,' Jack laughs.

For some reason unknown to me I have an urge to jump on Jack and kiss him and if I had the courage do it, I would, but I don't. I have no idea why I have this sudden urge. It's like one of those times when you see your work colleagues out of work for the first time and they look so different, more relaxed. Maybe it's the location or the fact that we have spent three days more or less sprawled out on the beach watching the world go by, but Jack just looks different here on the beach in Australia. No, stop it, Samantha!

'I still can't believe that it was Amy. Mum was livid about it.' I recall my mum's reaction when I finally told her who had gone to the newspapers and sold a false story on me.

'After all I've done for that girl,' my mum said, and I could see she was bitterly disappointed in Amy.

I go quiet for a moment as I look up to see a bright red kite flying against the backdrop of the cloudless, blue sky. Two little boys are desperately trying to keep it suspended in the air, despite there being a serious lack of wind.

'What are you two up to?' My thoughts of how perfect it is here are disrupted by Miracle and Max walking up the beach toward us. They are holding hands and look like a couple advertising a sun-drenched Saga holiday.

'Just discussing what we are going to do after Christmas,' I say smiling up to the pair of them. They look so happy together – they even step in time with each other!

'And? Have you decided to take up all these offers from Larry?' Miracle asks as she plonks herself down at the bottom of my lounger.

'I think I just might, and I also think I will take you up on that offer of training.'

'That's good because I'm getting too old for this game and at some point in the near future we will want to retire. I will need someone I can trust to take over the business for me,' Miracle says with a smile.

'Hang on... we?' I ask, a bit surprised to hear Miracle suddenly using the plural.

She smiles as she looks up at Max.

'Are you going to tell them or am I?' he says.

'We're getting married!' Miracle screams.

'Married?' Jack and I chorus in unison.

'Uh-huh,' Miracle says smugly as she looks adoringly at Max, who looks equally adoringly at his new fiancée.

'Well, this is cause for celebration, don't you think?' Jack says as he launches himself up from his lounger and heads for the surf-bar to get the drinks in.

Jack and I are still sprawled out on the beach as the sun begins to settle on the horizon. In a few hours it will be Christmas morning and the beach will be choc-a-bloc with dads all firing up their portable barbecues in preparation for the traditional Christmas dinner on the beach. As nice as it is to be able to eat your Christmas lunch on the silky sand in 94 degrees, it's not quite the same as cosily snuggling up to a warm fire, is it? But then I guess the Aussies would say the same if they were to do Christmas in the UK: 'Crikey mate, it's not quite the same as sitting on the beach in 94 degrees is it?'

CHAPTER FORTY

My mother is the first one up out of our group on Christmas morning, and is eager to let everyone know that Santa has paid a visit to them. My mum's favourite time of the year is Christmas and it shows. Seeing as Jack and I didn't get to bed until four o'clock this morning, my mum's six o'clock wake-up call is a bit like one of those Christmas presents that you really wish they hadn't bothered getting – in other words, very much unwanted.

Ever since we were kids, my mum has made Christmas a very special time of the year. Every Christmas Eve she would allow us to stay up very late and attend Midnight Mass at the local church and then we would be allowed to open what she would call our 'Christmas Eve Present', which would usually be an item of jewellery for me and something grown-up like a pair of cuff-links for the boys. This would be followed by being allowed to sleep in our parents' bed, while they slept downstairs to let Santa in – because we didn't have a chimney.

Christmases at our house were always huge family occasions with uncles, aunts, distant cousins and basically anyone and everyone my mother had come into contact with, being invited for a traditional Christmas dinner, whether they had prior arrangements or not.

My mum would be up at five o'clock shoving home-made chestnut stuffing into a mammoth-sized turkey. She would have already made the Christmas pudding and brandy-laced Christmas cake back in May and would spend the entire Christmas morning stuffing, mixing, chopping and sautéing.

The first Christmas without my dad was a tough one for all of us, especially my mum, who insisted that we should have the same traditional Christmas that we had always had. Paul, Matt and I spent Christmas Eve doing what was always Dad's job – decorating the tree – and we all joined Mum at Midnight Mass.

At our mum's insistence that we stick with tradition, we retired to our rooms – me in my mum's bed and the boys in the spare room. I could hear my mum sobbing on her own downstairs as she waited to let Santa in.

But this year is different. Having come to terms with my dad's death in her own way, my mum is adamant about living life to the full and is determined to make sure everyone does the same. The fact that we are on the other side of the world and in the middle of a heat-wave has not deterred her in the least in giving us the traditional Christmas that we all know and love. The pudding and cake, which she made in May have flown halfway round the world and she spent her first day in Australia tracking down a suitable turkey – despite the fact that the hotel we are staying in is providing all the usual food (including a turkey) at a lunchtime barbecue on the beach.

'Come on, Sammy, up you get dear, it's a beautiful day!' I hear my mum sing from below the duvet. Before I have a chance to clamp the duvet shut over my head, my mum has pulled it from my paws and is grinning inanely at me from above.

'Ho-ho-ho!' I hear as I blink my eyes to make sure that I am not dreaming. There is a small green elf with huge pointy ears and a very red and very sunburnt Father Christmas peering down on me.

'Mum? Colin?' I mumble. In some ways I hope it is my mum and Colin, otherwise this could turn out to be a very disturbing dream indeed.

'Merry Christmas, Sammy!' Mum and Colin chime in unison.

Oh, God give me strength!

'Come on, come on, up you get, lazy bones, it's Christmas morning! Jingle bells, jingle bells…' my mum, or Chief Elf as she will now be known, yells.

'OK, OK, I'm up!' I yell back as I roll over onto my side in a bid to avoid another rendition of 'Jingle Bells' from Santa and his bloody big-eared elf.

'Come on, Colin, let's see if Paul's up yet,' I hear my mum say as the pair of them leave my room, bells jingling on their hats as they go. Grrr, to my mother and Colin the bloody Carrot Man.

Ah, peace at last.

Before I can continue with my dream about being interviewed by a huge carrot – bloody carrots – Jack bounds in like a Jack Russell on speed and jumps enthusiastically on me. Oomph!

'Merry Christmas!' he sings. 'Come on, it's already getting warm out there.'

'I only got to bed two bloody hours ago,' I moan.

'Stop moaning and get up, I've got you a present,' Jack beams.

Ooh, a pressie, now he's got my attention.

'OK, OK, I'm getting up,' I say as I roll out of my comfy hammock. Having never slept in a hammock before, I always imagined that it would be a very difficult thing to get the hang of. In fact, it's quite the opposite. OK, so actually getting into the thing is a bit of a challenge, but once in there and as long as you don't wriggle about too much, you are guaranteed a wonderful night (or two hours in my case) of slumber.

'Good, but I'm afraid I lied... about the present... I haven't really got you one. Santa said you haven't really been a good girl this year,' Jack laughs as he runs out of the room with me in hot pursuit in my new pink polka-dot pyjamas – a present from Valerie.

As I chase Jack down the beach, fellow tourists who are already setting up their barbecues and getting their surfboards out, shout out various yuletide greetings. We both yell a few greetings back as I chase Jack into the foaming sea.

'Why you...!' I shout as he swims further out into the sea.

How surreal is this? Here I am, the other side of the world, 6.30am on Christmas morning chasing my best friend into the ocean. It's still Christmas Eve in the UK – how mad is that?

'Yeah, that's it, you run!' I yell as Jack swims further out.

In the distance a speedboat with Santa sitting in the back

races past. Santa waves a cheery wave and heads off to a small island just off the coast where, as I understand it, he visits the kids before he returns to greet the tourists on the beach. Santa, or the Swag-Man as he's known to the kids in Australia, hands out small gifts to the children who are visiting Australia as part of the Australian Tourist Board's initiative to attract more visitors during the festive season.

Jack waves first to Santa, and then to me, about fifty feet out from the shore. I wave back. Jack waves again and then bobs under the water. I stand on tiptoes and shield my eyes from the sun and see Jack bob up again between the waves. He waves and then goes down again.

'Just you wait until I get you!' I shout into the sea. 'You can't hide out there forever you know! I hope the evil jellyfish sting you!'

I wave again and beckon for him to come back to the beach. My pyjama bottoms are soaked with salt water and I now have a lovely white tide-mark just below my knees.

'Come on, Jack! Santa won't bring you any presents you know!' I shout as I see him bob down again. 'I'm starving, let's get some breakfast!'

Still standing on tiptoes I look to see where he might pop up again. Despite being so early in the morning, the waves are quite big. No wonder everyone is preparing their surfboards back up at the top of the beach. It looks as though it's going to be an ideal day for surfing the waves.

'Jack?'

My expression turns to concern when I don't see Jack bob back up again. I cup my hands around my mouth.

'Jack?' I shout again as I try to see him above the waves. I can't see him. Where has he gone? Maybe he's swum under the water. I crouch down to see if I can see him in the waves. Oh shit. Shit, shit, shit! I can't see him anywhere.

'Jack!' I shout as I start wading through the waves. Despite the morning sun already warming the earth, the water is so cold and the early morning tide drives hard against my skin. I try to dive into the waves, which just keep pushing me back again.

After several butterfly strokes – thank God for those swimming lessons that involved wearing my pyjamas – and after much swallowing of salty water, I see Jack's arm waving just above the water. Oh thank God.

Jack's arm disappears again.

'Help him, Samantha! Samantha, Jack's drowning!'

My dad's voice yells into my head. Oh my God! No! Jack really is in trouble.

I swim as hard as I can against the waves until I reach Jack, or at least I reach Jack's limp t-shirt sleeve. Jack is lying facedown in the water and I clamp my fingers around his neck as I desperately try to remember how to tread water – I was never good at it in swimming lessons. I frantically try to roll Jack over on to his back, but he is so heavy, I just can't manage to do it.

'Oh Christ, come on Jack!' I shout above the waves as the salt water washes into my mouth and out again. Despite the glorious morning, the water is freezing and is quickly making my legs go numb. With all the strength I have left in me, I heave Jack over and notice that his pale face looks almost serene against the cobalt blue sea.

I wrap my arm around Jack and start to swim back to the shore, dragging him with me. Tears start to sting my eyes. Please don't die, Jack, please don't die.

As we reach the beach I collapse on top of him on the shoreline. Scraping my hair off my face, I look down at Jack's crumpled body. What am I supposed to do now? I've forgotten all that I learnt for my bronze lifesavers' certificate. Think, Sam, think!

'Help! Someone help me!' I scream into the air. It's as though the whole world has stopped still. I feel as though we are the only two people here.

'Just pummel his chest and give him mouth to mouth, Sammy,' my dad's voice comes into my head. *'Do it now or you will be too late. You will lose him if you don't act now.'*

I do as I am told and pull Jack's t-shirt up to his neck and clasp one hand over the other one to form a fist and then push down into Jack's chest. One, two, three, four, five. One, two, three, four, five. One, two, three, four, five.

As I continue to push down, there is still no sign of life from him.

'Give him mouth to mouth, Sammy,' the voice instructs me again.

Clasping shut Jack's nose, I tilt his chin backwards, open his lips and force a deep breath into his mouth. His lips are soft and unresponsive and taste faintly of the sea. Jack's long dark eyelashes have tiny salt crystals forming on them and it looks as though he has been frozen in time.

One, two, three, four, five…

'Oh, come on Jack. You are too young to die now!' I shout at him. I try to repeat the CPR procedure again but the tears in my eyes are clouding my ability to see to the extent that I have double vision and I can't concentrate. I shake my head in an attempt to pull myself together – and it is then that I hear his voice – in my head.

'Sam? What's happening to me? Help me, Sam! I don't want to leave you.'

It's Jack's voice inside my head and yet his lips are not moving. Jack is not talking to me, he's still lying next to me, lifeless on the white, grainy sand. Which means if Jack is lying next to me and yet I can only hear his voice in my head, this can only mean that… oh, no. No, no, no!

'No Jack! You can't die on me now!' I start shaking his lifeless body. I don't know what I will do if he dies now. I simply cannot imagine my life without Jack in it. I cannot imagine getting up in the morning without knowing that he will be ringing or texting me, or knowing that he will pop round in some outrageous outfit in a bid to make me laugh. I cannot imagine never hearing Jack sing again, or listening to him telling Valerie a rude joke. I just cannot imagine Jack not being in my life.

'Come on, Jack. You can't leave me now, not after all we've been through. I love you, God damn it, so wake up...'

With one last effort I shakily heave his limp body onto my lap, tilt his chin back again and blow into his mouth with every last ounce of breath I have left inside me. Jack's chest heaves up and down. As I blow into his mouth again his head turns slightly. He splutters and projects a stream of water from his mouth and down his stubbly chin.

'Jack?'

'Oh man!' he croaks faintly.

'Jack! You're alive!' I scream, 'Oh my God! You're alive! You're alive!'

Pulling him up so that he is able to sit up straight, I wrap my goose-bumped arms around his waist and hold him close to me. The tears I've been desperately trying to hold back flow out of me like rain.

'Shit. What just happened there?' he whispers.

CHAPTER FORTY-ONE

By the time the paramedics arrive on the beach my body has decided to go into shock and I am shaking so much that I feel like a jellyfish. Despite his protests that he's fine, they insist on taking Jack to hospital, just to make sure that he hasn't suffered any brain damage. Sometime between me screaming for help and giving Jack CPR, Santa came to shore, ran past us up the beach and alerted the life-guards who brought all manner of life-saving equipment, including several foil blankets to wrap us in. Ironically with my chicken-like legs, I look like one of my mum's turkeys all ready to go on the barbecue.

As we travel in the ambulance to the hospital I am suddenly overwhelmed with the events of the past hour and try as I might, I just can't stop the tears flowing. I look at Jack, strapped to a stretcher, and he smiles weakly back at me, and winks.

Inside the hospital the foyer is decked out with the biggest artificial Christmas tree I have ever seen. Fake snow adorns the front windows and everywhere I look I can see decorations hanging from the walls and ceilings. Despite having to work on Christmas Day, the doctors and nursing staff have all made an effort to get into the spirit of things, and are decked out in shorts, t-shirts and festive Santa hats, or at the very least have reindeer antlers plonked on top of their heads and tinsel tied around their stethoscopes.

'Thanks,' Jack says to me as we wait for yet another doctor to confirm that we are both fit and healthy to return to the beach.

I shrug.

'That's what friends are for – saving you from drowning, that sort of thing,' I smile.

'You know what was really weird?' Jack says as he looks up to a foil star twinkling on the ceiling above us.

'What?'

'Well, when I was out of it, I... oh, it doesn't matter...' Jack blushes.

'No, tell me, what?'

'Well, it was really weird. It was like, well, I don't know what it was like really. I've never felt so peaceful in all my life. Everything was still. It was really odd. It was like, you know, in the movie when someone dies and it looks like they go through this white light?'

I nod.

'Well, it was just like that and then suddenly I realised you weren't with me and I was frightened. Something, or someone, told me to come back. I saw your dad, Sam. The next thing I knew I was spewing up salt water.'

'You died, Jack.' I know it sounds blunt, but I think he needs to know what really happened.

'Shit, no?'

'You died and came back again. You were calling me – in my head. My dad told me how to help you. You came back because it just wasn't your time to go,' I add.

Jack looks shocked for a moment and then smiles at me.

'Oh yeah, you know I said I hadn't got you a Christmas present?'

I nod.

Jack reaches over to his wet clothes and fumbles about in the back pocket of his shorts.

'I lied,' he smiles and hands me a small blue velvet box.

As I open the lid, tears well up again – I really must stop all this crying – as I look at the tiny silver ring with a single crystal placed in the centre.

'I got a crystal because... well... because that's your name. Happy Christmas, Sam – oh, and thanks again for saving my life.'

'You're very welcome. All in a day's work, and thank you for the ring, it's beautiful.' I look down at the crystal sparkling back at me underneath the fluorescent lighting.

Jack swings his legs off the stretcher and stands up, still a bit wobbly, in his hospital gown. He bends down and kneels on the floor beside me.

'Look, I know it's not the most romantic setting, but...'

Oh My God!

'Sam, you know, when that wave took me by surprise, I really thought I was going to die back there...'

'Err, you did die, Jack.'

'Yeah, and you brought me back. I don't want to waste another moment of my time here on earth, Sam, so here goes...' Jack takes a deep breath. 'I love you, I always have loved you, and I never, ever want to lose you. I kind of lied about Jasmine... I mean, I know we weren't really suited and all that, but the real reason we split up was that I was constantly comparing her to you... Will you marry me, Samantha Ball?'

I feel quite faint. No wonder I haven't been able to settle down with anyone. No one has ever quite measured up to Jack and I don't think they ever will. I look down and despite him looking a bit daft on the floor, dressed in a hospital gown that has a huge gap down it, revealing his pure white bum, I can't help but feel giddy with love for him.

'Yes! Yes! Yes!' I shriek. 'Of course I will marry you!'

EPILOGUE

Just over a year ago I was £22,000 in debt, jobless, single and quite possibly about to be made homeless. Today I am engaged to my best friend, Jack, I have a job I love, and we are about to move into the most idyllic cottage in a little village on the outskirts of Bath.

Annette's brother, Kevin, has signed Jack and his band Otherwise to Music Management and they are fast on their way to becoming one of the most popular Indie bands in the UK. They are planning to embark on their first ever UK arena tour, which incidentally includes supporting the Manics at Wembley, and of course, I will be going with Jack – I mean you never know when you might need a psychic, do you?

Miracle – and yes, it was her real name – is set to marry Max and settle down in semi-retirement in Brighton, although she still keeps her hand in running Mystic Answers with me.

Valerie has decided to sell the flats she owned and move into residential flats where she has officially become the bossiest tenant they have ever had. She is also a frequent visitor to our home and if she's not spending the weekend with us, she's spending it with my mum and Colin at Mum's house in Bath.

Speaking of which, my mum and Colin have published their book, *The Truth About Carrots,* and now spend much of their time touring the country with the Cathy and Colin Roadshow – they are not appearing at Wembley, however.

Snake-in-the-grass Amy has moved to Spain to follow in her mother's footsteps and find an eligible cosmetic surgeon who is willing to marry her – that or a footballer so that she can fulfil her dream of becoming an official WAG.

Missy, well, she has finally forgiven Jack for using her as a missile, but only because it's him who feeds her and she's met a very handsome tomcat by the name of Spencer, so she's in love and as we all know, love can do strange things to a girl, so watch this space, babies could soon be on the way!

And me? I have finally accepted that I can talk to real dead people – always handy when you're feeling lonely and need someone to talk to. I help run Mystic Answers with Miracle and we are about to launch our very own psychic academy for other people who suddenly discover they too can hear dead people and are wondering if they are insane.

I'm still working with Annette at *Town FM* and Larry, my agent, makes sure I get the best possible deals with newspapers, magazines and personal appearances. Now, I must go – I have a wedding to organise…

Coming soon

Oh Great, Now I Can *See* Dead People

Samantha is back, and this time she is busy not only planning her wedding to Jack, but also trying to get their new house in order in time for their honeymoon and, as ever, things don't go quite according to plan.

When Sam is asked to demonstrate her psychic skills at her mother's WI meeting on Halloween night, her mind is so pre-occupied with organising her wedding that she inadvertently forgets to close the circle, resulting in a whole host of unwanted spirits causing mayhem and mischief all round, including possessing half the village.

If rounding up unwanted visitors isn't enough, Sam discovers that her new house, Crystal Cottage, is haunted with a spirit that is constantly demanding her attention and her newly appointed spirit guide, Ange, is only interested in what's going on in *Heat* magazine.

Sam struggles to cope with the demands of her new career, which include working as a paranormal detective for a TV show and continuing her work with Annette on *Town FM*. Sam is now able to not only hear spirits, but can see them too.

Can Sam juggle life between this world and the spirit world, sort out her spirit guide's problems and get to the church on time?

Visit Deborah's websites at
www.deborahdurbin.com
www.deborah-durbin.webstarts.com

Soul Rocks is a fresh list that takes the search for soul and spirit mainstream. Chick-lit, young adult, cult, fashionable fiction & non-fiction with a fierce twist.